PRAISE FOR *ALL SYS*

"A scary and action-packed thrill ride. You'll • after you've raced to its heart-pounding conclusion

"A tightly plotted tale."

"Boush's novel reads like something the gut...with civilization itself hang... ... ... into a movie. In the meantime, wake up and read the novel."

—*Paul Levinson, author of* Cyber War and Peace

"An exciting and riveting tale that at many times seems just all too real."

—*Journaling on Paper*

"With his debut novel, Sam Boush proves that he deserves to be listed with the likes of Tom Clancy, David Baldacci and Dan Brown...a must read."

—*SA Examiner*

"Sam Boush is an author I'll be following. Fine, concise writing, a fascinating plot, and likable characters that grow on you. That's always a treat."

—*Mystery Suspense Reviews*

"A tightly written and tense cyber-thriller that will have you on the edge of your seat. Boush imagines a nightmare scenario that's so plausible, it's downright terrifying. A gripping page-turner from start to finish."

—*Dylan H. Jones, Amazon best-selling author of* Anglesey Blue

"A thrilling and action-packed novel that will make you question just how much we all depend on technology and how vulnerable without it we can be."

—*Lovely Loveday*

"This exciting book grabbed my attention early and never let go... Cyber war is not just fiction, it's the future. For that reason alone, All Systems Down is a must-read."

—*R.P. Eddy, best-selling author of* Warnings

ALL SYSTEMS DOWN

THE CYBER WAR – BOOK 1

SAM BOUSH

For Tehra

Sirens blared across all twenty-five decks of the USS *Gerald R. Ford*. Lieutenant Kelly Seong grabbed her flight suit and slipped inside, practiced hands buckling the straps of her Aramid coveralls. "A goddamned drill at 4 A.M.," she mumbled as she attached her flotation vest and checked her oxygen mask and survival gear. Not that she really needed to. The equipment hadn't changed since her last flight five hours earlier. But protocol kept her alive.

Red lights flashed, and the *boing, boing, boing* of the alarm ricocheted along the corridors of the ship. Sailors ran to stations. A petty officer shouted orders to passing swabbies. Despite the cacophony, men and women hurried through the upper decks with purpose. General Quarters drills occurred frequently. Every Jack and Jill on the Ford supercarrier had an assigned station and knew where to be.

Well, *nearly* everyone. Kelly exhaled sharply. Where the fuck *was* Orion?

"You seen Beetlejuice?" she asked a cadre of her squadron mates. The men shrugged and raced on, a playing-card spade peeking out from the back of the flight helmets they carried under their arms. They were Black Aces. First to fight, first to strike.

Orion, as far as she was concerned, hadn't yet earned the ace on his helmet. He was what they called a "nugget," a first-tour aviator fresh from naval flight training. Technically, he was her weapons systems officer. The wizzo. In the cockpit of their Super Hornet, he engaged air-to-air or ground targets and operated the laser- and satellite-guided ordnance. In a "turn and burn," Kelly would make the turn while he dropped the burn. She would if he were any good. Unfortunately, he was as green as a grasshopper's right nut. And here she was, expected to mentor the bastard.

She checked his bunk then the hangar deck. Alarms blasted too loudly to call for him, and the rush of hundreds of sailors made it hard to spot his little cornbread head. The other airmen of the Black Aces beat feet to the ready room. GQ brought the supercarrier alive, even in the dead of night.

Not that the ship ever really slept; 24 hours a day, the "Jerry" hummed with activity. At any given time, two-thirds of the four thousand souls aboard would be awake, working on the floating fortress currently cruising two hundred miles east of Honolulu.

Kelly beelined past the flight lockers toward the ready room where the rest of the squadron would already be waiting. If her wizzo couldn't get his ass in the saddle he'd suffer the consequence. Over her career, she'd seen better pilots than him wash out.

She peered in the ready room. Not there. Then back to the lockers.

"Jesus, what time is it?" Orion Bether shouted above the din, in that whiny voice that set Kelly's fist to balling up all on its own.

He slinked over to his locker and was now making a hash of getting into his flight suit. Just like a fucking nugget.

She punched him in the shoulder. "Beetlejuice!" she shouted. "Where the fuck you been? You look like shit, by the way."

"Ouch!" He groaned, massaging his shoulder.

Like Kelly, Orion had been pulling twelve-hour shifts, though that was no excuse for the bags under his eyes and his generally un-shipshape appearance. His sandy blonde hair, short and squared, still managed to stand up like a sailor's happy sock after a six-month deployment. He dropped one of his Nomex flight gloves, revealing, most glaringly, that his flight suit hadn't been fastened at the crotch.

"It's balls thirty. And for fuck's sake, if you're going to button salute a boat goat, at least get her to buckle you up at the end."

Orion reached down and cursed, fumbling to pull the strap closed while juggling his helmet and flotation vest. Kelly didn't wait for him, leading the way to the ready room. He hopped after her.

"She's no boat goat, Moonshot. She's a 2-10-2 if I've ever seen one." Then he laughed that obnoxious cackle of his. A girl who was just a two on a scale of ten when on land could easily be a ten out on deployment, where the ratio of men to women was forty-to-one. When they got back to land she'd be a two again. Few Navy men were below fucking an ugly girl at sea.

"Listen up!" The call spun them around in salute. Mike Montez stepped into the room right behind Kelly and Orion. The squadron commander was a short guy, black hair, usually calm as a pickle in a salt bath. But in the light of the hangar deck, his dark cheeks were flushed, eyes excited. "Black Aces," he said, "this is not a drill. I'm going to repeat myself. This is not a drill."

"Sir," Kelly said. "The call on-speakers sounds a lot like a training exercise." During a true GQ, loudspeakers would call all hands to man their battle stations. Tonight, there'd been nothing but sirens.

"Chrissakes, Lieutenant Seong. I know what I know, and we're buns to our guns. Maybe they're having some technical difficulties up on the island."

That drew some laughter. The Admiral sat up in the island—the control tower rising above the flight deck—and wherever he went, clusterfucks seemed to follow.

"I don't know much, but here's what I got," Montez continued, sweeping his gaze across the eighteen pilots in front of him. He bit his lip and smiled, like he was about to give them some good news. "Ten minutes ago, at zero-four-hundred hours, our radar sweeps caught more blips than your collective wives have boyfriends. And they're moving in on our position. It might be nothing. Might be seagulls or flying peckers. But, sonafabitch, it looks a lot like bogies. I don't have more details than that. So get in your birds and beat wings west. Stand by for orders when you're airborne." He clapped his hands. "To stations!"

Halle-fuckin'-lujah. It wasn't a drill. Maybe she'd actually get to see some real action, for the first time in years.

"Lieutenant Seong. Lieutenant Bether." Commander Montez stopped Kelly as she advanced on the exit. "Hold up." While the other pilots, flight engineers, and wizzos ran out of the ready room, Kelly and Orion pressed in close to their commander. "Brush and Wildfire are coming off a training run. Their bird is hitting the trap in two minutes. She's got live ordnance and half a tank of fuel, at most. I want you two to take her up the minute she lands."

"A hot switch?" Orion asked.

"Yes, Lieutenant. Now get your asses up and aft." He tore out of the ready room, leaving them alone.

"I've never done a hot switch," Orion confessed.

"Then this is on-the-job training." Kelly helped Orion into his flotation vest, then handed him his helmet. "How fast can you run, sailor?" The question was rhetorical, and she didn't wait for him to answer before dashing up to the hangar deck. Orion fell in, close behind.

Kelly had performed hot switches many times and didn't feel any nerves. It meant that she and Orion would have just three minutes to switch out with the landing flight team. They'd forgo the normal preflight checks and would have less fuel. The bonus was they'd be lead jet in this foray—and Kelly loved to lead.

Sprinting through a narrow corridor on the hangar deck, she located the ladder to the flight deck. A sailor, running the opposite direction, clipped her with his shoulder. Dozens more men pushed past. The siren wobbled and shifted. A grinding noise now.

Why had the general quarters alarm changed? It didn't matter. With both hands she grabbed the rails and ascended to the surface of the supercarrier, into the October night.

The flight deck of the Jerry shone through the darkness, illuminated with a thousand bulbs. A vibrant city. A red-light district at night. Officers and mates hopped over the lighted pathways. Adrenaline seeped through her, pulsing in her veins. She hoped, as she slowed to a safer speed, that the fight would last long enough for her to get in a few good hits.

Starboard, the six-story island dominated the landscape, the most prominent structure on an otherwise flat surface. From there, the air boss and mini boss would direct the dozens of F-35C Lightning II and F/A-18E/F Super Hornet aircraft that shuttled across the deck, ready to catapult into the sky. She scooted past the island, around munitions in large, white bins and over cables, following markings to where she'd rendezvous with her own multirole fighter jet.

Sweat dripped down her face, though whether from the heat or anticipation she couldn't tell. Even two days before Halloween, the North Pacific sizzled. In a lot of ways, it felt like her hometown, only hotter. And muggier.

What time is it back in Duluth, anyway? It had to be early afternoon. Mom would be working the phones to sell combines and tillage equipment to small-acreage Georgia farmers. Pop would be out buying sweet plum candy for the trick-or-treaters.

Kelly forced away thoughts of home. She needed to focus.

More sailors swarmed the deck of the supercarrier, like a thousand bees in a shook-up Coke can, zipping to stations. Every man had a purpose, his role indicated by his shirt. Maintenance guys, hook runners, and catapult crews wore a forest green vest over a somewhat lighter green shirt. Chock and chains wore blue. Purples supplied fuel. Red shirts loaded bombs. But to Kelly, they were all faceless nobodies that existed for the sole purpose of getting her bird ready to fly.

There was only one thing Kelly liked about the Navy. Flying.

Everything else about this service branch sucked. Two weeks out of port and the food started to taste like preservatives and powder. The racks stunk. The showers were so small the crew called them "rain lockers." And then there were the shower bunnies—clusters of hair, grime, and semen that stopped up the drains.

But flight was life.

Nothing on earth compared to soaring at eleven-thousand feet and watching the target approach in an instant. Flights were long, and the payoff was short. But nothing made her feel alive like rolling in over the bad guys at Mach One, pushing that button, and watching ordnance erupt below.

Of course, it had been years since her last active duty combat. The world was quiet. Too quiet. No wars or even military conflicts. Maybe America had just fucking won. Maybe there would never be another world war. Her gut yawed at the thought.

Up ahead she saw her carrier-capable Super Hornet on approach to land, fourteen feet above the deck, tailhook out to snag the arresting wire—the trap.

The Super Hornet landed flawlessly, catching the trap and accelerating. The pilot brought it to full power at the end, just in case the wire broke and he had to pull up to get off the carrier. It had been known to happen, and this kind of accident killed men on the flight deck as well as in the plane.

Fortunately, the wire held and the jet jolted to a stop.

Kelly didn't have time to celebrate the other pilot's safe night landing. The flight crew ran to the plane and hauled out the boarding ladder from a jigsaw-shaped door on the side of the fuselage. As soon as the pilot and his weapons systems officer climbed down, Orion scampered up the ladder. Kelly followed.

Buckling into her seat, calmness filled her. Everything was routine. She punched in her coordinates and performed a quick inspection of her flight controls. "Beetlejuice, systems check?"

His reply came in through her helmet. "Systems a-go."

"LSO, this is Bravo-60 on a hot switch. Gimme a CAT. Over."

The landing signal officer, a white shirt, waved a pair of traffic wands, incandescent red, signaling her toward the bow. "Bravo-60, you're on CAT Two. First in line. Over."

There were four "CATs"—short for catapult—on the Jerry, like the starting blocks at a track meet. Once fired, they could launch a thirty-three-ton aircraft off the deck in seconds. And when the Jerry really got going, she'd be launching birds off all four CATs at once, sending a death-dealing warhawk into the sky every twenty seconds.

Kelly obeyed the white shirt's signals across the deck until she rolled to a stop at CAT Two. The magnet clicked below. The white shirt indicated the go-ahead with his traffic wands. The air boss shouted a confirmation. Her catapult was cleared for takeoff.

"Bravo-60 is ready," she said through her radio.

"Full *shhhszzshhsshhshszzzshzz*," a reply came from the tower.

"Tower, I'm getting a lot of static on your end. Repeat the command."

"They acknowledged 'full tension,'" Orion said over her shoulder.

It went against protocol not to have heard the command herself, but she could see the white shirt flagging her forward. And hadn't her squadron commander required haste? *Fucking Navy. Pay a billion dollars for a plane, can't maintain a working radio.*

"Whatever," she said. "Full tension is go. Military power is go."

A yellow shirt, the plane director, touched his helmet, nodding to the shooter. And with that, the shooter fired the CAT, launching Kelly's Super Hornet forward.

The G-forces of the catapult slammed her back in her seat, head and neck straining to stay upright. The combat fighter broke free down the stroke, accelerating to more than 160 mph in mere seconds. The CAT threw her jet off the flight deck and over the open sea, in starlit darkness, ascending, and the punch of acceleration knocked into Kelly like a body blow, as it did every time. Violent. Loud. The catapult could launch her a thousand times over the ocean and she'd never get used to it.

She pulled the aircraft away from the water and brought the wheels up into the fuselage. They soared, airborne.

"Beetlejuice, I'm going to take this bird west. Radio the carrier to see if you can get us specifics on these radar blips."

"10-4."

The darkness outside stretched into eternity, ocean and horizon melding together, both black and indistinct. At night, she always tried to take it slow and let her flight tools do their job. They called it "flying the instruments." She called it common sense.

Down in the void of the Pacific, her strike group would be at battle stations. The guided missile cruiser and two destroyers would be circling the Jerry, protecting her. A nuclear sub patrolled the waters a quarter-mile below the surface. Even the combat support ship provided a defensive flank for the supercarrier, their flagship.

Kelly swiveled back toward the vertical red and horizontal blue lights of the optical landing system that pilots called "the ball." Beyond, white lights dotted the deck, illuminating the runway. Otherwise the carrier sat in obscurity. Quiet.

"Beetlejuice, do you have a copy from the island?"

"Negative, Moonshot. They're radio silent over there."

"Try the emergency channel."

She could hear him clicking through stations. "Nah-nothing." His voice caught like a deer mouse in a snap trap. "Our, uh, our radio must be out. With the fucking hot switch, we didn't catch it."

"That's crazy. It was working a minute ago. I'm gonna give it a try."

Kelly moved her dial to the emergency channel. "Bravo-Bravo, this is Bravo-60. Come in." On the other end, the shush of static. "Come in, Bravo-Bravo." Nothing.

"Try one of the other birds," Orion suggested.

"Who's in the air?"

Orion craned his head around. "I don't have a visual on any others. Do you see any on radar?"

Kelly tapped her cockpit radar display. "I'm not picking up any birds. We're on lead. They should be right behind us."

That pissed her off. It was just like the fucking Navy to send her out in the darkness against an unknown threat without anyone on her six for backup. "I'm circling back. We're no good to anyone with a tits-up radio." A hard turn of the stick brought the plane windward and back to the east.

"Jesus, Moonshot. We need orders to head back, right?"

"You wanna radio in for new orders?"

"Radio's busted."

She rolled her eyes and continued to follow the protocol that prioritized the safety of the plane and its pilots. They flew back toward the supercarrier.

As they neared, Kelly fixed her gaze on the flight deck, a half-mile away but still clearly visible. Bathed in moonlight. Beautiful.

One by one, the lights on the USS *Gerald R. Ford* blinked out. First the red lights of the landing strip. Then the white deck lights. Then the optical landing system, the ball. All out. Gone in less than a second.

Kelly gasped. Sweat collected on her palms and between her fingers.

This was impossible. In the eight years she'd flown for the goddamned US Navy she'd been in some hairy situations, seen some real crazy things. But no one she'd ever flown with had ever seen the lights of their carrier turn off. Wasn't supposed to fucking happen.

"Beetlejuice, are you seeing what I'm seeing?"

"Motherfuuhh … we're gonna crash." His voice held an edge of panic.

"Anything from the island?" Blood beat at the back of her eyes. "Anything from the Jerry at all?"

He didn't reply at first. Then a prolonged exhale of "Craaaap."

The only light on deck came from a lone F-35 shooting forward on the catapult, down the stroke. She could tell even from here it wouldn't be fast enough. The CAT hadn't been correctly calibrated. Or it had lost power.

In slow motion, the catapult propelled the jet until it flipped lifelessly off the bow and toward the sea. At the final second, the pilot ejected—an explosion from the cockpit that sent him vertically into the sky. Then the last light winked out as the jet disappeared into the Pacific.

With her world now illuminated only by moonlight, Kelly never saw the pilot land. Never even saw the splash of the F-35 hitting the water.

But it didn't matter. A fellow pilot losing a plane into the ocean didn't matter. The blackout on the Jerry didn't matter. At least not compared to what was happening inside her plane.

"Was that Tater's bird?" Orion said over her shoulder.

Kelly didn't reply. Instead, she stared at her cockpit controls. The systems on the Super Hornet were failing. The Navigation Forward Looking Infrared—the advanced sensors that let her see—dropped offline. The Doppler ground mapping radar followed. Then the target designator that delivered laser-guided bombs.

Even those system failures paled in comparison to the reading from the fuel gauge. *Where the hell are we going to land?* Her hand shook on the stick.

And the dial moved steadily toward empty.

2

Brendan stuffed his hands into the pockets of his only suit jacket. The lining was torn, and it hardly kept out the cold. It didn't fit well, either. Too tight along the shoulders. It was a lousy interview suit, but he didn't have much of a choice. He wasn't going to spring for a new one. Not with funds running low and a family to support.

He took a breath and nudged open the door.

The lobby seemed typical for a robotics company in the trendiest pocket of Portland, Oregon. High-definition screens lined one of the walls, broadcasting sports, an out-of-town technology convention, home shopping, and news. The Sparx logo sat above an empty security guard desk. In the center of the lobby stood the giant statue of a vacuum-cleaning robot, shaped like a disk. It filled most of the space, polished and gleaming in contrast to the fashionably rusted overhead beams.

"Hello?" Brendan said. "Anyone here?"

His cautious footfalls echoed on the stone tiles. A whisper of music hummed in the background, intended, perhaps, to calm visitors, though for Brendan it pronounced the solitude and the emptiness. He edged farther inside, toward the desk, and knocked on the mahogany. This was probably where he'd spend his days if he got the job. And he needed this job. It was a step down, but his pride would just have to take the hit. Pride wouldn't pay the mortgage.

From across the lobby, the elevator door whooshed opened and a man gamboled out, waifish and young, an air of authority despite his build. "You must be our three o'clock. Brendan, is it?"

"Brendan Chogan." He moved to close the vast distance between them.

"Well, I'll say. You certainly look the part of a security guard." His manicured eyebrows arched while piercing gray eyes travelled up and down Brendan, lingering uncomfortably on his shoulders. Only then did the man offer his hand. "I'm Milo Jones, General Manager."

Brendan took it with care. It seemed like the kind of hand that might break easily, smooth and white.

"Come on upstairs. I've got a room where we can get started." Milo led the way to the elevator. "So, you were a police officer?"

"No, sir. Parking code enforcement."

With a ping the elevator door slid open, and Milo skipped inside. "Like a meter maid?"

Brendan ran his hand over the back of his neck where the hair had started to bristle. "Something like that. Foot patrol and dispatch. Mostly wrote code citations."

The elevator started up with a gentle lurch, the innuendo of music crooning, too soft to hear but impossible to ignore. Brendan shifted, aware of the space of his body in the compartment. Mirrors on both sides revealed him as he towered over Milo. Ungainly. Hulking. He wished one of them would say something to drive back the silence.

Finally, a bell rang. The door yawned open on the sixth floor exposing a bullpen of workers. Men and women sat at desks, beanbag chairs, and barstools. No one glanced up as he passed. They seemed deep in thought, headphones on, typing away on keyboards too small for Brendan's fingers.

"This is one of our coding floors," Milo said, leading him forward. "Primarily engineers."

"What are they working on?"

"Machine learning models, perceptual awareness, that sort of thing. I can't really tell you more than that."

Brendan nodded as if he understood, though his eyes had drifted to the walls. Giant framed posters of fictional robots dominated the room. Rosie from the Jetsons, R2-D2, RoboCop. The Terminator.

Milo directed Brendan toward an all-glass conference room where twenty chairs surrounded a long, oval table. "So, what has you making the switch from parking code enforcement to security?" With the push of a button, the white board behind the desk rose and disappeared into the ceiling.

"City laid me off," Brendan said, trying to sound casual. "Moved to an automated ticketing system."

"Ahh. Well, that makes sense," Milo said, flashing a perfect set of poodle-white teeth. "Lose some jobs to make more and better ones."

Brendan knew enough to keep his mouth shut.

Milo motioned him into a chair but didn't sit himself. "When we run your background check, are we going to find anything?"

Brendan took a seat, rubbing a thumb over the bent cartilage of his nose, like he sometimes did when he was nervous. "When I was twenty I got into a little scrape. Might be in there."

"Tell me about it." Milo leaned forward, platinum pinkie rings tapping against the wooden tabletop.

"Broke a guy's hand when he put it on my wife. She was just my girlfriend back then. Charges went down to a misdemeanor, but I lost my boxing scholarship. Coulda been worse."

Milo twisted his mouth, but then nodded. "Anything in the last ten years?"

"No, sir. Just the one brush up. Way behind me."

A moment of silence. Milo's eyes bored into him, fingers drumming an out-of-time rhythm. "Well," he said after far too long, "your credentials meet our minimum requirements. What we're going to do now is have you take a little online test." He pulled a glass and steel tablet from a drawer in the conference table. It was a new model, one that Brendan hadn't seen before. Sleek and modern, he couldn't help comparing it unfavorably to the ancient one the girls had at home.

"Sounds good." Brendan folded his arms and tried to keep his foot from bobbing and weaving on the carpet. The chair was small, and his knees knocked against the underside of the table.

"After you're done here, I'll show you out."

Brendan raised an eyebrow. "Out? What about the interview?"

"Oh. I must not have explained clearly. The online test *is* the interview."

He flitted around the room and patted Brendan on the shoulder. "Mostly, we're checking for cultural fit. Just answer as best as you can. I'll be back when you're through." The glass door shut behind him.

Brendan set his jaw and fought against the urge to get up and leave. This town didn't have many open jobs for a guy like him, and he needed this one. He wouldn't run.

Before he even touched the thing, the tablet switched on. A picture displayed—him, in the upper right corner, wearing the too-tight suit, the angle of the shot telling him it had been taken by a security camera on the way in.

```
Name: Brendan Andrew Chogan
Age: 35
Previous Employer: City of Portland


        Press Screen to Begin
```

The multiple choice questions started out straightforward enough. *How easy is it for you to stay relaxed and focused under pressure? How tidy do you keep your home and work environments? What kinds of problems do you like to solve?*

After twenty minutes, the questions grew stranger. *Could a computer think for itself? What is the objective nature of morality? Are human beings just machines?*

And after thirty minutes, the questions became truly unconventional. *What is the death of anything, truly? Why is there something rather than nothing? Is the universe a three-dimensional hyper-spherical surface in four dimensions?*

Brendan's eyes glazed over. He stood to stretch and, twisting his back, he chanced a glance out into the bullpen. On the other side of the glass, engineers milled about. Agitated. Some had removed their headphones. Most were pointing to their screens.

Brendan's own screen flashed from the table top. A message appeared on the tablet that didn't match up with the questions he'd been answering for the past thirty minutes.

No force in the world can check the advance of our army and people. We rush forward like the blizzards of Mount Paektu. Final victory undoubtedly belongs to us.

That was all, just a few sentences. It was so odd. A joke, maybe. He wasn't familiar with human resources humor.

A knock on the glass, and the door breezed open. Milo capered into the conference room wearing a half-smile that oozed forced sympathy. "Mr. Chogan," he said. "I'm afraid I have some bad news for you."

3

The sun rising over the Yalu River was the best part of Pak Han-yong's day.

It began with darkness. In the distance, on the far side of the river, his homeland lay swaddled in unbreaking night. The fields and the factories, the port and the mills all slept. Then the horizon would lighten, from black to blue to gold, and the three faraway smokestacks appeared from the port city of Sinŭiju; first as silhouettes, then as gray fists, casting long shadows.

Next, the sun. Crimson light burned at the edges of red pine forests and reflected off the rice paddies. River, land, and air awoke to the glory of the Supreme Leader and the world's chosen people. Tears sprung, as they always did, as light brought his beloved North Korea to life.

He observed it all from his desk on the tenth floor of the Shanghai Hotel in Dandong, China, across the border from the land of his ancestors.

China. After two years, Han-yong still had trouble internalizing the wealth of this nation. The Chinese lived in skyscrapers, profligate buildings of steel and glass. So different from his home city of Chongjin, where families lived modestly in single-story "harmonica homes," so named because of their resemblance to the tiny boxes that make up the chambers of a harmonica.

On Fuchun Street, ten stories below, cars bustled. Unnecessary, extravagant. In Chongjin, nearly everyone was content to ride a bicycle or take public transit. And when they did drive, his people didn't smoke like the Chinese. If you smoked, you wouldn't catch the constant engine problems of your soviet-made Volga or ZIL.

Even from thirty meters above, it was apparent how the well-fed Chinese had been made soft by water that flowed reliably and electricity that ran all day. Food here wasn't rationed by the gram. No one in China grew strong and clever from struggle and strain. There were no hardships here. And for that, he despised the Chinese, military allies or not.

"Long live the Shining Sun of North Korea," he said. *These people aren't better than us. We have nothing to envy in the world.* He lowered himself into the seat of his desk, rearranged his mouse so it squared perfectly with his keyboard, took a final sip of tea, and continued to monitor the attack that had started hours earlier.

Today, Han-yong fell into his routine, despite the enormity of the day's events. Routine was the scaffolding that held his life together. He had woken in the earliest hours, barely speaking to his five roommates in the converted hotel room, had slipped into his pressed uniform, and spit-polished the single silver star on his shoulder. Then, after quickly wiping dust from the portrait of the Supreme Leader that hung alone on the wall, he'd moved to the common area to drink his tea and work until sunrise.

Two years of waiting, and today it has finally begun. He rubbed his hands together. Every day Han-yong worked here, visited the canteen, and bunked in his room. He rarely slept more than five hours. And never, in those two years, had he left the tenth floor of the Shanghai Hotel.

For all the differences between China and North Korea, there was only one that mattered, and it was why Han-yong was here at all. The Internet. On the North Korean side of the river, the global Internet, for all practical purposes, did not exist. There was a limited internal network that pointed to a handful of websites. But North Korea had fewer Internet protocol addresses in the whole country than could be found on a block in some Imperialist cities.

Here in China, though, the Internet reached nearly every corner of the globe. And because of that, Han-yong and the other elite hackers of Unit 101 could touch a banking system in London, a hospital network in New York City, or a data center in Tokyo.

"Junior Lieutenant Pak!" The gruff voice of the senior lieutenant shattered Han-yong's reverie and brought him spinning from the window, springing to his feet, fingertips raised to eyebrow in salute. "You are to come with me."

The senior lieutenant was very different from Han-yong. He was loud and assertive, tall by North Korean standards, and good-looking enough that he probably did well with women when he took leave—an amenity provided only to senior officers. But, most grating, he was a traditional military officer, untrained in online warfare, and knew just enough to stick his fingers where they didn't belong.

Still, there was nothing to do but obey.

They waded the corridors in silence, past the desks where scores of other hackers from his unit sat immersed in a war that had begun with an attack on an Imperialist supercarrier only hours earlier. As Han-yong sauntered through the ranks of Unit 101, his pulse quickened with pride. They were the elite, plucked from grade school from across the country and enrolled in Command Automation University in Pyongyang. They had trained with the singular focus of learning to hack into secure enemy networks. They had become warriors. Instead of tanks or drones, their weapons were in code. They had mastered digital viruses, worms, the dedicated denial of service attack, trapdoors, and botnets. They had simulated cyber war amongst themselves and infiltrated foreign targets. At every stage, they had been tested and evaluated, and only the most gifted had come to wear the uniform.

The senior lieutenant stopped the door that led to the stairwell. "The colonel has ordered a meeting with you," he said, one hand placed haughtily on his hip, not bothering to meet Han-yong's eyes. He'd assumed the pose of a Manchurian guerrilla fighter from the war movies. "You will speak when spoken to and answer all inquiries in full."

Han-yong couldn't help himself. "Sir, what inquiries?"

"About the interconnect logic bombs," the senior lieutenant snapped, unlocking the door. The stairwell beyond was devoid of decoration, except for a creamy swirl on the vinyl tile, like the pattern on the lid of a paint can. "Hurry now." And he started up the stairs, feet tapping a marching rhythm.

The Imperialists of North America had many weaknesses, but Han-yong had been ordered to focus on the power grid. The system was a relic of the 1960s, set up with no thoughts for security, but instead as a way to balance the supply and demand for electrical power across vast swaths of territory. In their arrogance, the Americans had organized just five power-grid interconnections across the entire country, electrically tied together and operating at the same frequency.

While it may have so far proven a sufficient way to balance loads—power companies with little demand could transfer electricity to areas with greater demand—the reality was that a single significant disturbance could collapse all of the systems tied to the interconnection. And Han-yong did not have the means to cause just a single disturbance.

He had the means to cause thousands.

The project was code-named *Sonnimne*, after the smallpox gods of Korean mythology that long ago crossed the Yalu River. It was both a nod to the new pestilence they would unleash and a reference to how the plague had already spread in secret, machine to machine, substation to substation.

Han-yong had planted logic bombs—malware that could be triggered in response to an event—in substations across the United States. It had taken months of steadfast work. The difficulty was writing the combustible code within a Trojan application in a way that was at once difficult to detect, easy to spread, and powerful once deployed. While the wait and the work had been excruciating, the payoff would be enormous. And imminent.

They reached the top of the stairs, and the senior lieutenant produced a key to open the gray-painted industrial steel door. The eleventh floor was reserved for high-ranking officers, their quarters, and computer servers that required additional security.

Sweat beaded on Han-yong's brow. The colonel ranked just three steps below a general, and was likely the most senior military official Han-yong would ever speak to in his career. A slipup here might find him dishonored and discharged, or eating rats in a reeducation camp.

They rounded the first corner through the carpeted corridor, where

Han-yong noticed, with more than a little satisfaction, that the smell of mildew pervaded every bit as strongly as in the floor where the junior officers worked. The senior lieutenant pulled up short in front of a door with a brass room number in the Western style. Before they could knock, a man inside bellowed, "Junior Lieutenant Pak Han-yong. Come in. Come in."

The voice was not what he'd expected. Friendly. Jovial, even. Han-yong poked his chin through the doorway.

Nothing about the scene that greeted them was as he had imagined. The hotel suite was gaudy by North Korean standards. The walls, which should have been bare except for the requisite photograph of the Supreme Leader, were decorated with paintings of mountains and birds in a style that Han-yong vaguely recognized as Japanese.

The room was not sleeping quarters, but an office far larger than the room Han-yong shared with the other soldiers. At the center of the space, a heavy-grain oak desk displayed unrecognizable artifacts: three swords on a wooden rack, an unfolded fan with red tassels and a painted orange sun, a clay jar in the shape of a boar, and a half-dozen other oddities that Han-yong had never seen. They were beautiful, and he felt guilty for admiring the work of foreigners.

The colonel himself was also a surprise. A crisp military uniform did nothing to hide his bulk. No one Han-yong had ever met carried more than a few pounds of extra weight. How could they, when even prison guards and soldiers, who received the best rations in the country, still lived off just enough to fill their bellies?

"Junior Lieutenant," the colonel began, leaning back in his chair, "your commanding officer tells me we are ready to move forward with project *Sonnimne*. And I understand that you have implanted code throughout the US system of interconnects?"

"Not exactly, sir." Han-yong hesitated, unsure of how much technical detail to provide. "I created a zero-day exploit. A new kind of virus, sir. It uses entirely original code." The colonel raised an eyebrow. "That means it can't be detected by malware filters," Han-yong continued. "The virus triggered a patch update in the operating systems of the high-voltage distribution facilities and spread throughout."

The colonel inclined forward, his chair squealing under the weight. "What do you mean by 'spread throughout?' How many facilities have the virus?"

Han-yong paused, careful to give the correct information. "All of them, sir. All of the distribution facilities in the United States now have the virus."

The senior lieutenant let out a dry cough. Otherwise, for several seconds no one moved or spoke. Han-yong shifted his weight between feet.

"But … that must be thousands," the colonel said.

A trickle of sweat trickled down Han-yong's brow toward his eye, but he ignored it. "Yes, sir. There are over nine thousand electric-generating facilities and over three-hundred thousand kilometers of high-voltage lines spread between them. These substations alone carry seventy percent of the most-hated nation's electricity. They all have the virus." The sweat droplet fell into his eye. He blinked it away.

"Do you mean to say that we have a virus that can wipe out seventy percent of the American electrical grid?"

"No, sir. When the majority of the US power grid goes down, the lower-voltage lines won't be able to sustain the added load volume. They will topple under the stress. This virus will wipe out one-hundred percent of the American electrical grid."

The colonel's mouth hung open as if he were about to speak, but couldn't, while the senior lieutenant wore a self-satisfied smirk that reminded Han-yong of a least weasel with a bellyful of stolen eggs.

The colonel's jaw tightened below a layer of fat. "If the virus is dispersed so completely, then why has nothing happened? The lights are still on in the West."

Now it was the senior lieutenant's turn to explain. "The virus has two stages. The first is the spreading stage, which is only recently complete. The second stage is activation, when the logic bombs that have been hidden in the code will deploy. We are ready to deploy that on your order, sir. Today, if desired. Along with the hundreds of other attacks Unit 101 has prepared."

Han-yong nodded, proud that his efforts fit so well with the whole. Each team member had his own projects designed to attack global enemies; separate and equally deadly projects to take out Imperialist infrastructure. Some cyber soldiers had built malware to disable railways. Some had built code to choke airline traffic. Still others had built viruses to cripple the Imperialist military communications.

"At your command, we can activate the logic bombs with a keystroke," the senior lieutenant continued. "The virus will cause the power grid to overheat and self-immolate. I have no way of knowing how long it would take to repair, but every time the Americans try to rebuild the lines, we can bring them down again."

At that, the colonel laughed heartily, the fat of his jowls jiggling with mirth. "You both are too young to appreciate the irony in what we are about to do. You see, when the Soviet Union collapsed decades ago, our system also faltered. The subsidies that had sustained us fell away, and our power plants rusted into disuse. Our streets went dark. And many of our cities are still without power, as you know. The fatherland is still in the dark."

Han-yong nodded. All too well, he knew of the humiliations his countrymen had suffered under the sanctions of their enemies.

"But our time has come," the colonel continued. "Like the thousand-*li* horse, we are too swift to be mounted, too elegant to be cowed. At last, it has all come together. The fight has only begun, and already the enemy falters. So now we will strike at the heart. Today we will lash out with this and everything we have. This is our chance to repay, blindness for blindness, a world that sent us into blackness."

4

"That didn't take long," Brendan said, doing his best to keep composed, though he hadn't been able to keep his brow from knitting together. It stung, having a computer tell him he wasn't fit for a job even before finishing the online test. But it was just the latest uppercut in a week that had already landed a few solid hits on him. "Thanks for your time."

Milo gave a half bow. "We were happy to have you. Here, let me show you out."

They walked together toward the elevators in silence. All around, engineers had abandoned their desks. No one seemed to be working anymore. Several of them stepped on his feet, just another humiliation to stack with the rest.

"Hey, boss!" shouted a tangle-haired man with more teeth than mouth. "Think you could get IT up here? We've all been getting some pretty weird messages on our computers. Looks like spam or a virus or something."

Milo flicked his fingers, dismissive, ambling steadily on. "Of course. Let me walk this gentleman out first."

"Seriously, boss. I don't think this can—"

"Guys," interrupted one of the other engineers, a young woman with a pierced cheek and a cell phone raised over her head. "I just got a call from my boyfriend in Texas. He says they got it there, too."

Milo skidded in the middle of the bullpen, a trail of ruffled carpet. "They got what in Texas? That 'final-victory' message?"

The young woman nodded. "That's the one. That's what we're trying to tell you. It's some kind of virus. It's everywhere."

Milo frowned at Brendan. "Mr. Chogan, would you mind waiting right here? I'll be back for you in a minute." Without waiting for an answer, Milo took his arm and gently guided him to a seat. The hand that touched his sleeve did so daintily, like he imagined a dancer might. It sent goosebumps crawling over every inch of him.

Brendan sank into the beanbag sofa, more like a giant pet bed for humans. A virus wasn't too unusual. These tech guys were getting their briefs in a bunch over nothing.

"How'd you break your nose?"

Brendan looked up at the young guy sitting in a chair beside him, acned, a mop of brown hair. "Can't remember," he said. It was an honest answer. His nose had been broken enough times that no single occasion really stuck out.

"So you're interviewing for a job here?"

"Security guard."

"I wouldn't mess with you," the young man said, picking at his teeth with a fingernail. "Anyway, my uncle says I should practice my small talk. And since our computers are down ..." He paused, hopeful, holding out a box of candy. "Want a Red Vine?"

Brendan took one but didn't eat it. "Thanks."

"Crazy, right?" The guy smacked loudly, chewing the Red Vine with his mouth open. "I mean, first that stupid Mount Pikachu message. Then our computers get lit up. And now they're saying the Internet is savaged."

Brendan raked his hand through a mess of brown hair. Some of it came free in his fingers. "Internet's broken?"

"Yep. All over Portland, so our manager is saying."

"No Internet at all?" He shook the hair onto the carpet. Vailea said if he kept pulling it out he'd be bald by forty.

"I know, right? Whole city without a connection." The young man took another bite of candy, smiling between chews. "Never heard of it before."

Brendan studied his shoes, the creases in the black leather, the slight parting between the sole and the toe cap. How many more interviews before he had to buy a new pair? Perhaps he could glue it again. Maybe it would hold this time.

Mostly, though, he thought about the email he'd seen on the tablet, and the news that the Internet had stopped working across town. People sometimes misjudged him as unintelligent because he often stopped to think. He liked to push ideas around in his head until he could really get a hold on them. But he wasn't stupid, far from it.

He was still mulling over the Internet situation when the engineer with a boyfriend in Texas raised her phone over her head again. "Guys. *Guys!*" she shouted over the commotion. "It's getting worse. Now they're saying the Internet is out everywhere."

"What do you mean, 'everywhere?'" someone said.

"Everywhere. Like across the entire country."

He'd heard enough. "Gonna grab some air," Brendan said, pushing himself out of the bean bag sofa. It didn't offer enough resistance, and he sunk back in.

"Want another one for the road?" the man said, holding out his Red Vines, unclipped fingernails digging into the blue box.

Brendan flopped over, ungracefully, and wiggled free. "No. Thanks, though." The young man's face dropped in slight disappointment, shifting quickly to indifference. Another Red Vine went into his mouth.

On the way through the bullpen a floating sensation took hold of Brendan, all too aware of the commotion from the engineers. They crowded the space. Some angry, some just excited. Cell phones rang, their owners hollering into them, sharp, urgent cries. The woman with the boyfriend in Texas bit her lip and waved the freehand that didn't hold the phone.

Brendan's chest tightened, stomach folding in on itself like it sometimes did in crowds. The news about the Internet going down wasn't exciting, it was unsettling. He pictured his German Shepherd, Lykos. When something was wrong, the dog's hair bristled on the back of his neck. That's how Brendan felt. Something was very, very wrong. The Internet didn't just go down. Not everywhere.

"Hey team, gather around." Milo stood at the center of the bullpen, feet spread. "I've got Gaston from IT here. He has something he wants to share."

Brendan kept moving toward the elevators, watching the turmoil over his shoulder.

"Okay, so, the Internet is down," Gaston said, tall and thin, voice squeaking like a teenager's. "Um, I can't tell you when we'll be back online, but, um, obviously, I can tell you this is a major disruption. I got a text from our Internet service provider. They say it's not just us. It's New York, LA, Chicago ... every major city. Maybe the whole country. They don't really know. And they don't have a clue when it will be back online."

The room erupted.

Brendan hit the elevator button. The bell rang, and he stepped inside, directing the lift to take him down while fishing out his cell phone. The Internet may be out, but as far as Brendan knew, his phone should still work. He needed to warn Vailea. Something strange was happening.

His phone had the same cryptic "Mount Paektu" message that he'd seen on the tablet, but he swiped it away and typed out a quick note to his wife.

```
Babe the Internet's down. Can you bring
the girls home? Got a bad feeling.
```

The girls would be out of school by now, probably running errands with Vailea. It made him feel better to think they'd be heading home. People would take any excuse to go a little crazy. And even something as insignificant as being unable to write emails was sure to bring weirdos out of the woodwork.

He sped through the lobby, intending to leave as quickly as he could. But a flash on the screens along the far wall brought him to a halt. The row of televisions no longer showed sports, weather, or tech conventions. Now, all of the TVs were on the same station, a bright red breaking news banner across the bottom of the screen. Brendan stepped cautiously closer and fumbled along the side of the monitor for the volume control.

"...the situation is growing more and more disturbing. No word yet from the

President or the National Security Agency, but this outage appears to be a major hack. Our experts here in the newsroom are calling it potentially the most serious breach in the history of the country. If you're just tuning in, it seems that computers from coast to coast have lost connectivity to the Internet altogether. Now we turn to our correspondents in Manhattan to tell us about effects on ATMs in the city…"

Brendan needed to get home. Pretty soon, people would be panicking. Pretty soon there could be riots. He should be with his wife and daughters—now.

He gave the television a last glance.

"…not just ATMs, now hospitals are being forced to cancel operations…"

He pushed open the lobby door and burst out into the cold October air. But before putting his phone away, he sent another text to Vailea.

Also, I didn't get the job.

5

For the better part of two hours, Xandra Strandlien had sat in on what was probably the most important meeting in the history of United States Cyber Command. Over that time, she'd heard arguments, opinions, and outright hostility. She'd listened to what some of the most powerful men in the country had to say about the critical infrastructure attacks.

And so far, what she'd learned was that no one knew anything.

"It's the Russians, goddammit," Major General Nelson said, seated across the table, pounding his fist on the thick oak for emphasis. The major general looked Hollywood-typecast for his current role as Commander of Air Force Cyber, from his masculine jawline right down to his desire to bomb Moscow into a pile of smoldering bricks.

"The Russians did the same thing to Ukraine and the Republic of Georgia," he continued. "It's typical of the *Rossiyskoy Federatsii*. The denial of service attack has their fingerprints all over it. It's gotta be the Ruski FSB."

The only civilian present, Xandra was surrounded by twenty armed service members in the Pentagon war room. It was an imposing situation, to say the least. But once she overcame the stern glowers from the officers, it wasn't really too different from teaching graduate students at MIT. Except grad students asked harder questions.

She'd gotten the call early that morning from the Department of Defense, pulling her out of a hackers conference in Las Vegas and onto a last-minute flight for DC. The DoD summons had come, initially, because of incursions into Navy mainframes. But in the hours since she'd arrived, the scope of the assault had grown. The situation had gone from bad to dire.

"This attack came from the Chinese, not the Russians," a sergeant major from Army Intelligence said. He rotated a laptop toward them so they could see the map on his screen. "Our analysts tracked the IP addresses of the hacks to Liaoning Province. The trail ends there, and we can be fairly certain that's our origin point—"

"It's not the Chinese. How many damn times do I have to tell you?" The nostrils of a lieutenant general from Marine Corps Cyberspace Command flared, his cheeks burning as he spoke. "It came from inside the country. Domestic terrorism. I've got a guy over at the FBI who tells me it's right-wing radicals."

"Come on, this screams 'state actor.'" A captain from Naval Network Warfare Command held up a stack of paper and let the reports fall loudly on the table. "Terrorists couldn't wet dream this kind of attack."

As they bickered, Xandra refocused her attention on her boss. Admiral Mehmet Kalb looked angry—which was how his face usually looked. But now, in addition to his perpetual frown, his skin had colored to an unnatural shade of red.

Admiral Kalb wasn't just Xandra's boss. As head of US Cyber Command, he was all of their bosses, as well as the senior officer in the room. And though Xandra wasn't usually gifted in recognizing facial expressions—or social situations, for that matter—it was pretty obvious Admiral Kalb was not happy with the progress they'd made that afternoon.

Finally, and predictably, he erupted. It happened while a vice admiral from the Tenth Fleet prattled about a foreign submarine in American territorial waters. As if there weren't bigger issues on the table.

"Enough!" The admiral slammed down an open palm. His glare swept across the strategic commanders from Fleet Cyber, Air Force Cyber, Marine Forces Cyber, and Army Cyber. "Enough," he said again, this time with a dangerous calm. "Gentlemen, no two of you has the same answer. Russia. North Korea. Iran. China. Domestic terrorists. Islamic terrorists. If you point your fingers at the Canadians, you'll have implicated every goddamned population on the globe."

Was that a joke? No one was laughing, so Xandra didn't force herself to smile as she usually did when someone tried to be funny.

Admiral Kalb continued. "How the hell can we protect the homeland when we don't even know where the attacks are coming from?"

None of them had an answer. Admiral Kalb shook his head and swung it toward Xandra. "What do you think, Ms. Strandlien? Help me make sense of this snafu."

She hadn't spoken since the meeting had started, and now eyes fell on her, all at once, perhaps waiting to see what idiocy would come from the mouth of this diminutive professor.

She returned their glowers, unaffected, and surveyed their crisp uniforms, clean-shaven faces, military haircuts, recognizing them for what they were: woefully inadequate for the current events.

They had never faced anything like this. They were cybercrime amateurs whose greatest successes had been hunting down insurgents on the dark web. They were spies, using rookie-level tactics to listen in on foreign dignitaries. They were military men foremost, who thought of cyber attacks as the weaker cousin of kinetic war. Who might deploy a cyber strike only in conjunction with a blitz from an armored brigade combat team. An average high-schooler trolling for ecstasy had more talent navigating the Internet.

Worst of all, they didn't see today's attacks as the catastrophe they were. And making no mistake, it was a catastrophe. Certainly enemy states, and even the US, had disabled the systems of other nations through cyber attacks. The Russians had taken down banking systems in Ossetia. The Chinese had disabled mobile networks across Taiwan. The Iranians had hacked American dams. The US had incapacitated the Internet throughout North Korea. But even taken together, those cyber forays paled in comparison to the widespread systems immobilization that had begun that afternoon and continued unabated ever since.

Every seventeen minutes, the boys at Fort Meade had reached out through the Department of Defense's classified information network, SIPRNet, to inform the Pentagon that another critical infrastructure had collapsed. And every seventeen minutes, this assembly searched for answers and came back with nothing but speculation.

Xandra doubted the timing between systems outages was a coincidence. The September 11 attacks on the World Trade Center had happened seventeen minutes apart.

As if on cue, the outer door opened and a uniformed OF-7 rear admiral rushed in to speak quietly with Admiral Kalb. A quick grimace and tightness around his eyes suggested the news was not good.

"An update, gentlemen," the admiral said. "The Chief of Naval Operations has confirmed that we lost communication with our carrier strike groups. We haven't been able to reach them by satellite since early this morning."

"How many carrier groups are affected?" an officer from Ninth Army Signal Command asked, sweat showing through his uniform at the armpits.

"All of them, I'm afraid."

"That's not possible." The captain from Naval Network Warfare Command stood, his seat sliding back, and leaned forward, palms on the table. "We've got eleven aircraft carriers across the globe, each with a half-dozen ships. What could possibly hit them all?"

"Sonofabitch!" Major General Nelson's eyes grew wide. "I refuse to believe we have eleven supercarriers—each with more firepower than the militaries of most advanced nations—just bobbing out on the ocean like limp dicks."

"The Navy—" Admiral Kalb began.

"Has its information wrong," Nelson finished.

Before the argument could continue, another uniformed officer from the Department of Defense rushed into the war room. He handed a sheet of paper to Admiral Kalb, who read it and crumpled it in a shaking hand.

"Gentlemen," he said after a pause, "I hope you've all found accommodations here in DC, because no one is flying out."

Twenty sets of eyes scrutinized him.

"Sir, no one is going home." That from the commandant of the Marine Corps.

"You misunderstand me," Admiral Kalb said. "Whoever these bastards are, they've scrambled our logistics software, military and civilian. Flights across the country are grounded."

That shut them up. But the implications were clear enough to Xandra. "Flights weren't going anywhere anyway," she said.

A throat cleared from the far end of the table. The captain from Naval Network pushed his stack of paper off the edge and swore. But she continued, "As we discussed earlier, our satellite network has been penetrated. Commercial airlines won't fly without GPS."

Major General Nelson's lips pressed together, almost impossibly tight, before exploding. "You're saying this is no big deal?"

"On the contrary, sir, it's a very big deal." Xandra ignored his scowl. "If they can scramble our logistics software, they can stop our trains, our trucks, *and* our planes. No medicine, no gas, no commerce."

Across the Pentagon war room no one made a sound. Twenty of the most powerful men in uniform stared at her. A pen snapped in someone's hands.

"And that's not the worst of it by far," she continued, without any trace of emotion in her voice. "In fewer than twelve hours, you can expect store shelves from Seattle to Sarasota to be bare. Because when this unknown enemy finishes undermining our logistics networks, they will have debilitated the national distribution of our food supply."

That got their attention.

Admiral Kalb swiveled, brow furrowed. "Say that again?"

Xandra met his gaze and held it. "Sir, with the amount of panic we should reasonably expect, and our collective inability to transport goods across the country, every store shelf in America will be empty by the end of the day."

Brendan started down the sidewalk, the Sparx headquarters door clicking shut behind him, into a scene more crowded than he'd expected and ever seen, except maybe during the Rose Parade. The atmosphere, though, didn't remind him of parade day. An electricity ran through the air, like a high-tension wire had snapped and was spitting voltage.

Along the Pearl District, ever more people exited their office buildings, talking excitedly in groups. The sidewalk teemed, almost at capacity. And the streets were more congested still. Cars filled the roadway, bumper to bumper, exhaust billowing. Rush hour had come early.

As Brendan passed the idled cars a radio blasted.

"…with critical systems exposed to the virus, the impacts are being felt across industries…"

The honk of a car horn drowned out all other sound. Another honk. A nearby motorist slapped his steering wheel in frustration. Up the street, a driver rolled down her window and leaned out, trying to see the source of the traffic jam. But the end was nowhere in sight.

"…trading on the New York Stock Exchange ended early after falling a record…"

Another honk.

Brendan growled in frustration. He'd taken an Uber to get to the interview, but there would be no way to hail a ride back home. Not even a cab. Traffic made that impossible.

His house was on the east side of the river, three miles away. He'd have to walk.

It would do him good, though. Might be able to clear his head. Vailea would ask him about the interview when he got home, and he wanted to tell it to her straight.

"Did you see that?" A shout brought Brendan's attention to a bald man with a cigarette who motioned at a traffic light. "There it is again," he said, falling in step alongside Brendan.

"What are you seeing?" The traffic signal appeared normal to Brendan. It had just gone from red to green. Cars weren't moving, so it didn't matter.

"Tell me I'm not crazy." The man rubbed his bald spot, dragging furiously on the cigarette.

"Not sure what—"

Then Brendan saw it. A flicker. Then another. And suddenly the traffic light went out.

Up and down the street, all the other traffic lights had also blackened. They swayed in the wind, drowned lanterns.

"Oh my," a woman said next to the bald man, moving quickly despite the extra pounds she carried. "Usually you don't see that except during a bad storm."

"Jesus Christ," Bald Man said, coughing a little at his own smoke. "That's not gonna help the commute."

Brendan shivered, speeding up. He needed to get home.

Without stopping, Bald Man faced the woman. "Can't catch a break today."

"No kidding," she said, blinking furiously. "I just went to the bank. They sent me away. Can you believe it? Closing early, they said."

"That's rough." Brendan didn't feel much like talking.

She shook her head. "It's worse than that. The manager said the interbank network is down. And just before they kicked us all out I heard a teller whisper that some accounts had been emptied."

"Hope it's not mine," Brendan said, not really meaning it. His bank account wouldn't be worth the effort.

"Mine either." The woman waddled to keep up. "That's my life savings we're talking about."

"Now that's a real shit show," Bald Man said. "But tell ya the truth,

I'm kinda glad the banks and stoplights are on the fritz. At least it's not just us."

The heavy woman arched an eyebrow. "What does that mean?"

"I work at Northwest Natural, and we're all gonna be puttin' in long hours. Double shifts. But we got a friendly rivalry with the boys over at Portland General Electric. It's good to know those assholes are gonna be workin' overtime, too, fixin' the traffic lights."

"What's got you pulling long shifts?" Brendan asked.

"Probably shouldn't mention it," Bald Man continued, "but we've been getting crazy readings today from the compressor stations. That's how the gas gets moved around. Need 'em every eighty miles or so. Anyway, it's got management going ape shit. We're gonna have to shut it all down if things don't clear up."

"Shut it all down?" Brendan couldn't imagine shutting the gas down in this cold.

"Yup. But we'll see." The bald man lit another cigarette. "I'll catch you later, folks. I gotta find out why these service lines aren't workin'." He disappeared into the nearest building.

Brendan continued beside the portly lady, east toward the Willamette River. They didn't speak. He was too busy listening to snippets from the radios of idled cars.

"...mayor's office asking people not to panic..."

"...major congestion..."

"...unconfirmed explosion at a refinery in Texas..."

"...Portland Public Schools announced closure of all after-school activities..."

"Where are you off to?" the heavy woman interrupted.

"Home. Across the river. You?"

"Grocery store. I don't like where this is going."

"Stocking up on food and water?"

She smiled. "Better safe than sorry. You might do the same."

"I gotta get back to my kids."

She shrugged. "Safe travels. You look like you can take care of yourself." And then she was gone, toddling to the Whole Foods that already had a line out the door.

Brendan pressed on toward the water. Every minute, more and more people came out of the buildings. The credit union across the street had a handwritten note on the ATM reading "Out of Order." The post office and library had shuttered early.

But all of that paled compared to what he saw before him, out across the river. As he reached the park at the edge of the Willamette, his heart took a dive on the canvas.

The bridges.

The Burnside Bridge stood closest, right in front. To the north, the Broadway and Steel bridges, and the Morrison and Hawthorne to the south. All five were up, raised as if to let a ship pass through. But there were no ships, just bridges, lifted to the sky.

And stuck that way.

7

"Kiri, grab us four ears of corn." Vailea pointed across the grocery store. "Hahana, go with her and pick out apples. You'll need at least six."

The produce section displayed dozens of fruits and vegetables arranged in bins and baskets. She liked this particular store, not just because it was in her neighborhood, but also because she had no trouble finding star fruits, taro, sour sop, and coconuts. American food was okay, but recipes from the Caroline Islands always brought comfort. She hoped to pass on that heritage to her daughters.

The twins skipped out of sight. Vailea trailed behind, following their voices. They were good girls. Noisy. Full of the restless energy of eight-year-olds. But good girls.

Hahana returned with her bounty. "Apples!"

"Corn!" Kiri dropped a bag in Vailea's cart.

"Almost done. All that's left is some bread," Vailea said. "It's over on aisle twelve."

The girls zigzagged toward their prize, dodging the dozen men and women who crammed the main aisle. *Why is it so busy?* Vailea always did her shopping after picking the girls up from school, and it was never this crowded. Maybe there was a promotion she didn't know about. Free hemp ice cream? A chance to win a goat? Portlanders went crazy for that sort of thing.

Kiri and Hahana came running with two loaves and a jar of peanut butter. Vailea eyed the jar but didn't scold them. As long as they didn't try to sneak candy into her cart. "Time to go."

Kiri wagged a finger. "Mom, you're forgetting something."

Hahana smirked. "We'll give you a hint."

"It's for our family," Kiri said.

"But not for a person," Hahana finished.

Vailea playfully slapped her palm to her forehead. "Ahh! Lykos! How could I forget? If you work together I bet you can bring me a bag of dog food."

They nodded in unison and ran off without saying a word. Vailea watched as they twisted around carts and disappeared.

The crush of shoppers had grown. Vailea started after her girls, but her path forward grew so cramped she could barely advance. Passing the beverage aisle, Vailea grimaced at the mad rush of people filling their baskets with drinks.

A teenager shoved past, juggling seven bottles of sparkling water. A group of children guarded their father's stack of a gallon jugs while he went back for more. An elderly lady struggled with an overfull basket of Vitamin Water, Kombucha, and Yerba Mate.

The shelves were almost wiped out. Water was essentially gone, except for a lingering bottle on the topmost shelf. The soda, too, was going fast, and the juice had vanished. Even the ranks of beer had been heavily reduced.

"Excuse me," Vailea said, picking out a woman about her age. "What's all the fuss over?"

"You haven't heard?" The woman's eyes shifted restlessly. "There's been some kind of computer virus. The Internet is out. The banks are closed. It's got a lot of people nervous."

Vailea could see that. The woman appeared pretty jumpy herself.

"Look at your phone," the woman continued.

"Thanks—" But the woman had already wheeled away, navigating toward the nearly empty beverages aisle.

Vailea pulled out her phone. Before she could check the Internet connection, a message appeared.

No force in the world can check the advance of our army and people. We rush forward like the blizzards of Mount Paektu. Final victory undoubtedly belongs to us.

It must be part of the virus the woman had described. Vailea swiped the message into the trash and was about to push her cart through the crowd when she noticed two unread texts from Brendan.

The most recent was a disappointment; he hadn't gotten the job. In a way, it was a relief. He'd make a fine security guard, but how could he ever be happy sitting behind a desk or standing for hours by a door? The man couldn't keep still for half a minute. No, if he could just be patient another job would open up. Something that would keep him on his feet.

Vailea scrolled up to read the first message.

`Babe, the Internet's down. Can you bring the girls home? Got a bad feeling.`

Brendan usually had sound judgment in practical matters. Maybe it would be best to head home a little early.

"Mom!" The girls each carried one side of a dog food bag. "Mom! A man ran his cart into us."

"He knocked Kiri over," Hahana said.

"Didn't even help me up, Mom. But I'm not hurt."

Vailea made a fist and suppressed a growl. "Put the bag in the cart. Let's check out before things get any wilder."

Just as she was about to slip the phone back into her pocket, she spotted the signal strength. "NO SERVICE" it said in capital letters across the top of her screen. Not only was the Internet down, but so was her cellular network.

There would be no way for her to write Brendan back, even if she wanted to.

8

"When are they coming down?" A nurse in scrubs scanned the raised and stuck bridges along the Willamette.

"They all went up about ten minutes ago," the man next to her said. "All of 'em."

Brendan leaned against the guardrail that separated the bike path from the water. On top of his galloping heart, his mouth had filled with the iron taste of a quarry lake. More painful still, a knot was forming in the muscles of his shoulders.

His first instinct was to panic, stuck on the wrong side of the water from his family. Caught in a downtown bursting with people. Trapped, with three hundred feet of icy water between him and the far bank.

He closed his eyes like he used to before a match. Panic wouldn't help him, and it wouldn't help his family.

The swarm of people in the park faded, the noise of traffic dulling with them. The anxiety of closing banks, blackened streetlights, and Internet outages thawed. And he could think again.

There weren't many ways to get home with the bridges up and traffic pinned back from the river all the way to the West Hills. But there was one that would do: the Tilikum Crossing, a pedestrian bridge a couple of miles to the south. While it was out of his way, it didn't have a center span, so it wouldn't be raised like the rest. He could cross there and double back toward home before sunset if he hurried.

The knot in his shoulders melted.

When he opened his eyes, the world came back into view—and with it the crowd and the noise and the metallic taste in the back of Brendan's throat. Somewhere in the distance, sirens shrieked. Dogs barked on the grassy stretches of the waterfront, biting at their leashes. A baby cried from a stroller.

He set off south.

Already, his shoes pinched his feet. Besides his suit, they were the cheapest and most useless article of clothing he owned. Black and scuffed from knocking around in the closet, they ostensibly matched the rest of his get-up. But he'd never had much use for dress shoes, and this was the only pair he'd ever owned. Hell, he'd never held a desk job and only brought these shoes out for weddings. And, much longer ago, for his parents' funeral.

Brendan loped down the waterfront, nearly a jog. The wind whipped cold against his suit jacket, the kind of late autumn breeze that said snow would be coming soon. Two days and it would be Halloween, with winter on its heels.

People covered the park. A group of high-schoolers trudged over the green grass. A man in janitor's overalls held his cell phone over his head, trying to get reception. Tourists leaned out over the rail taking photos of the bridges. Construction workers in orange hardhats and reflective vests huddled around a radio. "Shut up," one of them said. A plasterer, no doubt, judging by the chalky mess on his hands and face. "The President's talking. It's gonna be war when they figure out who the fuck did this."

Brendan approached, close enough to hear.

"...*a series of deadly and deliberate cyber attacks, perhaps the worst any nation has ever seen. But a great people will defend a great nation. Let me be clear: we will identify the perpetrators, hunt them, and bring them to justice. I, personally, will bring the full weight of the US military, law enforcement, and intelligence to this effort. Thank you. And God bless America.*"

Brendan set out again, watching the reactions of those around him. Folks who wouldn't normally make eye contact with a stranger now huddled close, speaking fast. Scores of people gawked at the bridges, spans parted in an upside-down 'v.' Baristas, lawyers, graphic designers, cooks—people from every walk of life—formed impromptu groups, some talking angrily, most frightened.

Brendan didn't stop to join them. He'd never felt comfortable in a crowd. Maybe it was because of how people wiped their eyes all over him, always the biggest person in the room, broken-nosed and awkward. Maybe he just liked open places. Unenclosed. Space to stretch.

He was jogging in earnest now. He needed to get home before dark. Before the pent-up energy of the city unleashed itself.

"Look at that!" A man in a business suit gasped, staring at the sky. "It's coming down."

A boy pointed. A fast food worker in a visor squinted and looked up.

Brendan stopped to see what had drawn their attention. At first, he didn't notice anything. The sky was clear, the sun low. There weren't even any of the contrails that normally pocked the sky like scars across the otherwise empty blue.

And then he saw it.

Miles above, the smoky signature of a falling object was clearly visible, fiery as it descended.

"Maybe it's a missile," the man in the suit said. "God, not now!" He smoothed his white collared shirt, in the exasperated huff of a real estate agent with too many listings.

"I hope not," a woman said, coming up beside them, in the autumn of her years, though long hair and freckles kept her in perpetual spring. "Hopefully just a comet."

"Do you think it's a jet?" the fast food worker asked, tugging nervously on a greasy apron.

Brendan thought that was the most likely. After all, Portland International Airport was up that way, at the edge of town. And farther north, a hundred miles or so, there was that joint army and air force base, Lewis-McChord. Maybe the plane came from there.

"It can't be a jet," a young woman said, joining them. Her PSU sweatshirt marked her as a college student. "That's atmospheric reentry, way up in the thermosphere."

"Could it be a meteor?" the fast food worker said.

"Or a spaceship?" the boy asked. A smile formed, dimpled and eager.

"No," the college student replied, biting her lip. "It's a satellite."

The man in the real estate suit didn't take his eyes off the sky. "How bad is this?"

"Satellites crash all the time." The college girl tossed a brown braid over her shoulder. "Out of fuel, and slipping gradually from their orbits. It's slow and then it's fast. The planet's pull yanks them into a sudden descent."

"Do you think it's an accident?" The fast food worker's eyes had started to tear from staring without blinking.

The college student shook her head. "No way to know. Sometimes it's unintended. Mostly, the companies or governments that launch them let 'em burn through the atmosphere when their useful lives are finished."

Brendan tried to tell himself that the young woman was right, that there were plenty of reasons why a satellite would come hurtling down. This was probably nothing, or maybe it was just a meteor after all. He hoped so.

Still, he couldn't shake a feeling of dread. He felt certain. Thousands of feet above, a satellite was falling to Earth. And, he felt equally certain, its maker had never intended for it to fail.

He wrenched his gaze away, hoping he was wrong. Time to get home. Past time.

But as he was turning to go, he witnessed a trail of smoke. Yet another satellite fell from the sky.

9

"Hahana, can you—" Vailea stopped and searched for her daughters. They'd been right next to her a minute ago.

"Girls?" Vailea called down the crowded aisle. Where had they gotten off to?

She tried to force her cart through the store as quickly as possible, but these people were as still as Rai stones. "Come back, girls." She stood on her tiptoes. While people were in a panic over a cyber attack, she didn't want her daughters running loose.

A hole opened in the crowd, just big enough for Vailea to muscle her cart through. With a last shove, she pushed into the cereal aisle. But when she got there, Hahana and Kiri were nowhere to be found. Instead, the aisle was filled with people grabbing boxes of cereal. A man and woman threw Cheerios into their cart. Another man was awkwardly climbing the shelving to get to a reserve pallet of Life Cereal at the top.

"Kiri! Hahana!" she shouted at the top of her lungs. Some of the shoppers scrutinized her, but most continued filling their carts.

An elderly woman close to Vailea, cataracts in both eyes, stopped long enough to say, "Better get those kids. Whole city's shutting down from what I hear." Then she swept the last of the Nutri-Grain bars into her cart.

The lights flickered. Vailea lifted her chin toward the high ceiling and watched as the fluorescent lighting sputtered again. *Flicker. Flicker.* And then darkness.

Gasps, followed by silence. For a few seconds, no one said a word. Small windows on the outer walls provided a faint source of light. Then, from the other side of the store, a woman shrieked. More sounds, fighting, pushing.

Vailea fumbled away from her cart and groped through the obscurity. She hated the dark. Worse, she hated herself for letting her babies go through the store without her. Panic rose even as she clawed desperately to suppress it. She gasped for breath, muscles straining like treading water.

"Girls! Where did you go?"

Nausea seeped to her core. A gut-tearing fear pulled her like a drifter into an alley. Her head spun, her heartbeat a turbine in her own ears. The girls. Oh, the girls in the dark without their mother.

"Kiri! Hahana!" she screamed.

As suddenly as they had gone out, the lights flickered back on. It must be the generators. Vailea recalled a conversation with one of her engineering colleagues who'd told her that every grocery store had an extensive system of generators that would kick in during a blackout, primarily to keep refrigerated and frozen foods from perishing.

"Attention shoppers." A young man's voice came through on the loudspeaker. He sounded nervous. "Our electrical system has gone out and we are now on backup power. In an effort to conserve energy, we'll be shutting down in ten minutes. Please stay calm. Thank you."

A tug on Vailea's blouse, and she spun around, ready to fight.

"Mom!" Red burst of excitement bloomed on Kiri's cheeks.

Hahana stood beside her, arms stacked high with bread loaves. "Did you see the lights go out?"

They were safe. Fear passed from Vailea with a shudder, leaving just the ache of threadbare muscles. She brought the girls close and shouted at them, making them swear they wouldn't leave her side. Tears ran down her cheeks, and she held them.

Hahana squirmed from her arms. "Mom, you're embarrassing us. You're dribbling snot on my skirt."

Vailea pushed herself up and wiped her nose and eyes, fingers coming away smeared in black. Eyeliner ran down her cheeks like ink from a broken pen. She swiveled around, self-conscious, to see if anyone was staring at her, but no one paid the slightest heed. Even the old lady who had taken the last of the Nutri-Grain bars had decamped to the Rise Raisin bars, focused on her own frenetic shopping.

"Okay, girls. We're going to play a game. You have to stay right next to me. Sound good?" When they had both agreed, Vailea continued, wiping her nose again. "You have three minutes. Put anything you want into our cart." If this really was an emergency, it wouldn't hurt to have supplies.

"Anything?" Hahana asked.

"Anything. Whoever puts in the most, wins. Now let's go!"

They stayed in the cereal aisle, grabbing everything they could get their hands on. Though Vailea felt ridiculous, it didn't stop her from thrusting shoulder-deep into the shelf and scooping scores of boxes into her cart, a heap of Corn Chex and Raisin Bran. The girls did their part, too. Hahana eagerly filled her arms with Clif Bars, Kind Nut Bars, Luna Protein Bars, and anything thoroughly covered in chocolate. If Vailea and Hahana seemed zealous about filling the cart, Kiri was fervid. She tore through the aisle, squeezing around the other shoppers, throwing in anything she saw. Fruit leather, cereal, oatmeal, maple syrup, and everything else she could reach. By the time Vailea told them to stop, both girls were out of breath, cheeks red from exertion, eyes gleaming.

"We've got to go."

"Mom! No!" they whined in unison. "This is fun."

"We've got to go. Now. And stay with me this time."

Begrudgingly, they obeyed. They held on to the cart, maybe afraid she would break down again and cry. Or maybe they thought this was a kind of adventure, a game. They put their feet up on the lower shelf and gripped the handlebar as Vailea drove them toward checkout.

There were nine lanes, each with a line so long it snaked into the aisles. The lines, though, weren't orderly like usual, but three-shoppers thick in places. An old man fell over beside Vailea's cart, pushed down by the forward press. Vailea stooped to help him, but a young man with a buzz cut scooped up the elderly gentleman before she could do anything.

"Thank you," the old man said, patting dust from a long, gray beard. "Are you a soldier?"

"National Guard, sir." The name "Czarnowski" was spelled out on the right breast of his combat fatigues, with "US Army" on the left.

The old man smiled, revealing gums the color of eggplant. "Has the governor activated you?"

"Yes, sir," Czarnowski said, his back a little straighter, chest pushed out. "Got called up by text message an hour ago. We're off to the California border."

"Aren't you needed here?" the old man asked, running calcite fingers over the helix of his ear. But the National Guard soldier had already disappeared into the crowd.

Vailea didn't have much time to wonder why the governor would send the National Guard three hundred miles south. The woman in front of her knocked her cart against Vailea's causing the girls to cry out.

Vailea pressed as far forward as she could. Eight other customers stood between her and the register, carts stacked beyond the brim. The fear that had gripped her earlier left her feeling weak, shaken. Even without looking in a mirror she knew her face was blotched and smeared. *Just hold yourself together long enough to get through the line. We can push this cart home.*

"Attention shoppers." Again, the young man's voice came through the intercom, more nervous now than before. "Our payment services system is experiencing an unexpected outage, so we're unable to process credit or debit cards, Oregon Trail cards, or gift cards. We can only accept cash or check at this time." After a loud gulp, he continued. "Also, please be advised the store will be closing in four minutes. You'll need to head to a register now."

For a few seconds after the announcement, the store was quiet. Almost peaceful. Then, the mood shifted.

"They've taken out the power grid!" a woman's voice said from the front of the store. "Look outside. It's all out."

"It's war!" a man near Vailea declared, talking to no one in particular. "This is it!"

On the other side of the store, a scuffle broke out. Shouts, the sounds of shopping carts colliding. Men fighting. It was coming from the bottled water aisle. Glass fell and broke against the ground. An endcap of Enfamil toppled over.

The lights flared and quivered, as if the generator was under some kind of strain.

Men and women bellowed at the far end of the store, some of them spilling into the main aisle as they wrestled over the few remaining water bottles. A man knocked another to the ground, while a third kicked at his curled up body.

The young man's voice came back on over the loudspeaker, but too many people were screaming and shouting for Vailea to hear a word. The sounds of more fighting spread to other parts of the store. People started wresting carts away from those standing in line. Some let their groceries go, some fought back. Dry goods spilled from toppled bins and shelves, and from overturned shopping carts. Customers snatched up the fallen food.

The lights throbbed again.

And then they went out.

Screams rose from every quarter, even from her daughters at her side.

"Hold onto the cart, girls," Vailea said. Up ahead the automatic doors of the exit had stopped, half ajar. Beyond, sunset spilled through.

"Mom, you're not going to pay?" Hahana said.

Kiri frowned up at her. "You have to pay before you leave."

She ignored them. The power was out. The store's generator had failed. Even if she did wait in line, they wouldn't be able to process her payment, and she didn't have enough cash for what was in her cart.

Maneuvering the cart forcefully around the line and toward the exit, she made her break. Other shoppers did the same. The surge took her through the half-open sliding glass doors and into the parking lot, breathing heavy, still pushing the cart as fast as she could.

Behind her, the grocery store erupted into a new kind of chaos.

10

Downtown went dark.

Brendan had been walking with a small group toward the pedestrian bridge when it happened. Every light from every skyscraper, every shop, and every window flickered and winked out. Up and down the skyline, street lights blackened. Bridge lights, harbor lights, streetcars, storefronts—everything succumbed to darkness.

There should have been a noise to accompany the blackout. A loud bang. The explosion of a transformer. The pop of electrical wire. But there was no sound of any kind. Just the gasp of people on every side of Brendan.

"I don't believe it." Tears rolled down the face of a dough-faced man in his middle years. "Who could have done this?"

The sky was rimmed with orange, cloudless except for the streak of satellites that continued to stain the dusk. The contrails gushed red, like an eyelid cut open in a prizefight. With night approaching, would the lights come back? They might just be out for a moment, a power-down before the restart.

A woman walking beside him stared at the city. She carried a box with a birthday cake inside, incongruous with everything around them. "First my car won't start, then my credit card won't work. Now this. What the hell is happening?" The cake jostled inside the box, frosting careening against the side. She didn't seem to notice.

Another man tugged at his thinning blond hair. "It's the hackers. That's what the news said."

A man with a briefcase kept pulling out his cell phone, as if by habit. He shook his head, seeing the screen still blank. "President had a press conference. Called it a cyber attack." By the crispness of his blazer, Brendan guessed he was probably a lawyer or accountant.

Across Naito Parkway, another wave of office workers poured out of the buildings. People streamed out of theaters, restaurants, and shops, moving quickly over the sidewalks and into the streets.

"But my car? That's not hackers." This from the dough-faced man.

"Could be," a woman said, voice calmer than the others. "What kind of car do you drive?"

"Cadillac Escalade."

"With built-in Wi-Fi?"

"Yeah."

"There you go," the calm woman said. "If it's got Wi-Fi it can be hacked."

The crying man kicked at the ground. "They got to us. Who do you think it was? The Chinese? Islamic terrorists?"

Brendan frowned. "Too early to know."

The small group continued their trek in silence. Up ahead, another satellite burned through the sky. Brendan rubbed at the badly-healed cartilage in his nose, trying not to worry about Vailea and his girls.

Someone flicked on a radio with the Red Cross logo on it.

"...and in New York, thousands of subway riders are said to be trapped in trains that have stopped between stations. Meanwhile, the mayor has asked for calm and warned that the National Guard will be out in numbers, and that looters will be prosecuted with the full force of the law."

The radio crackled.

"...F. Kennedy and LaGuardia airports are grounded..."

More static.

"...says cyber attacks...maybe war..."

Only bits of the broadcast came through now.

"...all off-duty personnel...report to..."

The woman holding the radio shook it. "Damn thing isn't finding a station." She spun the dial, but only static came. Finally, she flicked it off, and the group slouched on, shoulders stooped, a heaviness in their gait.

Brendan walked faster, pushing through the ever-growing crowd.

This was bad. He wanted to get out of town. It wasn't safe here, and it wasn't likely to get any better. In fact, it was likely to become a whole lot worse. He knew how people behaved when order broke down. There would be riots, if for no other reason than that the darkness would give cover to unleash pent-up rage. Property would be damaged. People would be hurt.

As soon as he arrived home he'd pack what he needed and he'd take Vailea and the girls out of the city. With his German Shepherd and a baseball bat, he'd walk out of town if he had to. And he pitied anyone foolish enough to step in his way.

11

Ireana Dunn still wasn't sure how she'd let herself be talked into this. Nearly November, muddy, cold, and here she sat roasting a hotdog on a stick. For dinner. In Oregon.

At least Jeremiah was enjoying himself, whooping and running circles around the yurts with his two cousins. Normally she'd shush him, but the campsite wasn't more than half full, and the boys were having fun jumping over ferns and fallen logs, chasing the squirrels that tried brazenly to pull hotdog buns from the picnic table and into the forest.

"Now, you have to admit you're relaxing." Annalore sat beside her in a folding camping chair, adeptly rotating her hotdog-on-a-skewer over the open flame.

Relaxation. There was that word again. The whole purpose of this trip was for Ireana to unwind, to forget the daily stresses of life and work and raising a third-grader on her own.

And there was plenty of stress. Between the HIV clinic and the urgent care center where she supervised triage, she was certain there was nothing in South LA she hadn't seen. Gunshot wounds, babies abandoned in the early morning hours, junkies with needles broken off in their arms. Hallucinating children, internal bleeding, eyeballs in Ziploc bags. A lifetime of vacation couldn't erase her stress.

That's why she sat here, a quarter mile from the gray ocean in a campsite at Cape Lookout. And this was supposed to be a vacation? The campground was so close to the Pacific that she could hear the waves smash into the rocks, depositing tiny jellyfish onto the sand-flea-filled shoreline.

It had all sounded heavenly when Annalore had proposed the two of them retreat out here for a sisters' getaway. The beach, the towering trees, cooking over a campfire and gazing at the stars.

Well, it would be dark soon, but she doubted there'd be any stars. Not that she'd see, anyway. The low-pressure system had brought too many clouds for stargazing. But she supposed what they lacked in celestial entertainment, they'd more than make up for in stink.

The nearby town of Tillamook smelled like the business end of a barn, with literally thousands of cows dotting the landscape. Methane rolled down the farmland, across the bay and on top of the campsite like a tarp pulled over a swimming pool. A giant fart-tarp.

Maybe the smell would not have mattered had the beach been warm. But if it was even forty degrees out here, Ireana would eat a bag of medical-grade nitrile gloves. Why hadn't Annalore mentioned that while the water from Southern California comes up from Mexico, the water in Oregon comes straight down from Alaska?

Ireana hadn't packed for this and was wearing a good portion of the clothes she had brought, layered on top of each other: three t-shirts, two long-sleeved shirts, a sweater, and a coat. Like a seven-layer burrito.

"So relaxing," Ireana lied, just as her hotdog burst into flame on the end of the stick. It popped and hissed, immutable against Ireana's efforts to blow it out. When, mercifully, the hotdog blackened to a shade never meant to be eaten, she slipped it off into the fire, just another lump of charcoal among the embers.

"Try again." Annalore tossed her a sticky package of Nathan's Famous hot dogs. "We've got all evening."

No kidding. They hadn't done anything since they got here. Jeremiah had woken up early, eager to rouse Royce and Eddie so they could all pee together in the frosty woods. Boys. Jesus.

After that, they'd made breakfast. A prolonged attempt at instant coffee and potatoes O'Brien cooked in a cast-iron griddle. Then more cooking for lunch. And on into sunset, just sitting and talking while the boys played superheroes and villains while trying to spear each other in the eyes with mossy sticks while running dangerously close to the fire.

So, no, it hadn't been a particularly relaxing second day of camping.

And Ireana didn't see how she could do this for another three days, shivering by a fire and listening to what a great dad Annalore's husband was, and how Ireana should find a strong man like him to help raise her son.

Annalore—the perfect one. With her perfect husband and her perfect children to whom she was teaching Russian because Annalore spoke four languages perfectly. Which was just perfectly perfect for a professor of lexical theory. Whatever that was.

Ireana needed some alone time. "I'm going to check my phone to see if I have anything from work." She stood and stretched.

"Sit back down." Annalore pointed a finger at the camping chair, every ounce the big sister. "You know we promised no work. You're on vacation."

Ireana decided she'd rather work herself to an early grave.

"No work, I promise. I'll just check to see if there's anything urgent in my inbox and maybe peek at the LA Times real quick." At least the yurt had electricity—a small concession to modernity.

Annalore guffawed, but said nothing.

Ireana's phone sat charging on the small table in the yurt, next to the heater. She splayed her fingers toward the vent where hot air should be coming out, hoping to fight away the cold a bit before withdrawing back outside. Nothing. She stalked closer. The thermostat was cranked up to eighty—as high as it would go. Still nothing. Not even a wisp of warmth.

"Jeremiah," she called out into the woods, "did you turn off the heater?"

He couldn't hear her, of course. He was probably up a tree somewhere, skinning his knees and wrestling with skunks, or whatever gross creatures they had here. She tapped on the thermostat again. Giving up, she grabbed her car keys and phone off the table.

"Shoot, my phone's dead," she said, stepping outside the yurt. She tried again. The stupid thing wouldn't turn on, even though it had been charging all day. "Hey Annalore, I think our electricity is busted."

She shivered. Could this vacation get any worse? If the heater was out tonight she'd ask for a refund. "I miss LA."

53

"What's that?" Annalore called.

"I said, I'm going to go warm up in the car."

"Just come over to the fire. That's the way you warm up in the woods."

The nerve! Ireana ignored her. Her sister could keep her woods and her campfire, the smoke and the dirt and all the rest of this sorry excuse for a vacation.

Cupping her keys in cold hands, she unlocked the car and climbed into the driver's seat. The trunk of her Buick Envision was still crammed with camping gear, mostly food and a cooler full of soda. She was proud of the car. It wasn't as nice as what Annalore drove, but it was still a new-model SUV. And so what if it was made in China? With a six-speed transmission, built-in Wi-Fi, and two-hundred-and-sixty pounds of torque, they obviously knew what they were doing.

She rotated the key in the ignition. Nothing happened.

There wasn't the raspy revolution sound that came before a flooded engine. There wasn't the clip-clip of a broken alternator or starter. The dash didn't even light up. Could it be the battery? She'd heard that salt air could cause corrosion, but she struggled to understand how it could have happened so fast. They'd only driven up yesterday.

She turned the key again. Still nothing. Just the empty sound of a vacation lost to disappointment.

12

Vailea slammed home the deadbolt. The metal clanged into the wood in a most satisfying way. They were home now. Safe.

She slid to the floor, her back against the thick planks of the front door, her daughters enfolded in her arms. Their hearts beat against her, twin shark-belly drums, chests heaving with each intake of breath. Hahana cried softly. Kiri's teeth chattered.

Lykos added himself to the pile. First, he came up to sniff the girls' hair, one at a time. Then, after touching a wet nose on Vailea's cheek, he lay down beside them. As usual, his tail didn't wag and he didn't bark. But she could tell he was guarding them. Nothing out there could reach them now.

Lykos had always been a strange dog, aloof and distant. If he hadn't looked like a picture-book German Shepherd, she'd have thought him a wolf. He had the eyes for it, certainly. Any normal German Shepherd had the brown eyes of a deer. A little lazy. A little simple. But not Lykos. His eyes were lighter, golden, unlike any she'd seen before.

Not that she was an expert on dogs. She'd never owned one herself until that day when Brendan had brought Lykos home after a long shift. He'd seen the dog while issuing tickets on what must have been one of the hottest days of the year. The animal had been panting, frothing, in the cab of an old pickup ditched on the side of the road. An abandoned dog in an abandoned car. Brendan had broken the window with his fist, apparently. He'd cut himself, even though he'd been careful to wrap his hand in his coat. A stupid thing to do. Even worse was that Vailea was sure he had reported himself for breaking the window. He'd always been honest—too honest. And the black mark on his record couldn't have helped when the layoffs came.

Vailea hadn't been thrilled at the new member of their family, either—patches of fur, covered in fleas. But the girls had loved him instantly and had begged to keep him. No, she hadn't been fond of him at first, but now she couldn't imagine this home without him.

Kiri ran her fingers idly through Lykos' thick, glossy coat. "What are we going to do with all this food?"

Hahana poked through the piles of unbagged groceries at their feet. "It's too healthy. I wish we'd filled the cart in the candy aisle."

Vailea ignored that. "We'll put it all away, of course." She pulled herself off the ground. "Come on!"

The girls perked up at seeing their mom in stronger spirits and jumped to obey, wiping wet noses on sleeves. Kiri ran to grab a chair so she could reach the pantry. Hahana scooped up an armful of cereal boxes.

As the girls dashed deeper into the house, Vailea flipped a light switch. Nothing happened. She toggled it up and down. Still nothing.

"It's cold, Mom," Hahana said. "The heat's off and Kiri says it's broken."

It *was* cold. Vailea could see her breath inside the house. She followed Hahana to the thermostat and pressed the touchscreen, hoping it would restart. It was one of the fancy ones, the kind that learned what temperatures the family liked and built personalized heating and cooling schedules. But even though she could control the thing from her phone, it was worthless right now.

Hahana's face crinkled into a pout. "This is a disaster, Mom."

"What's a disaster?" Kiri asked.

Vailea pulled her daughters in for a hug. "We'll be fine. It's not a big deal."

She knew a thing or two about disasters. She'd lived through Micronesian super typhoons, storms with names like Chata'an and Mitag. She'd seen how folks behaved when the police were busy. They acted out when no one was watching, when the emergency lines were down and no one was coming, when the shops were closed and food and medicine were in short supply. Neighbors who you should have trusted became fierce. People who you didn't know became dangerous.

When she was a girl, a typhoon had hit her atoll. Not an ordinary storm, not heavy rain and torn flags and leaky basements like Brendan associated with bad weather. The typhoon that hit them had made landfall like a war legion. Torrential rains had been the air force, landslides the ground troops. Winds so fierce the shingles blew from homes like shrapnel. In the low-lying island where Vailea lived, the sea had come to land and pulled more families back into its waters than it had left upon the shore.

Those lucky enough to survive had wandered the village in tattered clothes, soaking wet with no dry place to shelter. The island hospital, even if it had had electricity, couldn't have handled the influx of patients. The small Catholic church, even if it hadn't been swept into the sea, couldn't have handled the bodies that washed ashore. And even as a girl, Vailea knew they didn't have enough drinking water to last more than a day.

Her mother had once been strong, but that storm broke her. Vailea had walked behind, covered in the ocean's mire, as her mother cried into the receded winds, screaming at the typhoon that had taken Vailea's father, screaming to send him back. But he had never come, and Vailea's mother had never been the same.

For those next few days, before the lights came back and the food-ships docked, the island had turned on itself. Neighbors stole from neighbors. Grudges they had buried deep came out, with blood. Women couldn't walk alone. And when the first night came, the people of the atoll lashed out, bestial, while Vailea and her mother buried themselves in the mud, waiting for daylight and civilization to return.

So, yes, she knew something about disasters. She knew that when people acted crazy it was usually best to hole up. Until the crisis passed, they would have to make the most of it, curled up by a fire. Compared to hiding in the mud, it didn't sound so bad.

"Yay, I love fires," Hahana said when Vailea suggested it.

"I'll get the kindling." Kiri scampered out the back door toward the wood stacked against the side of the house.

"I'll get the newspaper and matches," Hahana said, running downstairs.

Other than the darkness and the cold, Vailea had few concerns about the lack of electricity. The food in the fridge would keep if they kept the doors shut. Her boss wouldn't expect any work to get done right now on the wall they were building downtown. And Brendan should be home soon.

All in all, it might be a kind of nice way to spend the evening. She rubbed her hands together, growing more excited about a night in with the family.

Ten minutes later, Lykos curled up in front of roaring flames, the girls sprawled beside him. Hahana had already opened a *Babysitter's Club* book and Kiri tickled the German Shepherd, trying to coax him to wrestle. For the first time in hours, Vailea relaxed.

Crack. Crack. Snap. Fire bit into the seasoned hemlock. The dance of shadows on the living room walls soothed her. They would be safe here, warm and protected. Vailea sat by the hearth as her daughters slowly fell asleep, feeding a log to the fire now and then. Kiri snored almost as loud as Lykos. Hahana had fallen into her book, drooling into the pages.

But as the evening progressed, Vailea glanced ever more frequently out the window. Soon the night would be here and she'd be alone in it. Alone in the dark without electricity. The kind of darkness that swallowed things. That swallowed cities. That swallowed children.

Brendan could never understand the danger of the darkness. He projected his power wherever he went, tall, strong, a boxer's body even after all these years. He didn't know fear. Even hurt, aimless, trying to provide for his family, he had never truly known fear. Not as she did.

She threw another split log into the firebox. She would not let it get dark. The dark and she had a truce, of sorts. They did not go near each other.

"Mom," a whisper came. "Mom, you're shaking." Kiri touched her knee. "Don't worry. There's nothing to be frightened of."

Vailea wiped her face. Had she been crying? "Sorry, baby. It's nothing. I'm just concerned for your dad."

"Don't worry, Mom," Kiri said. "Dad's okay."

"Oh, sweetie, I'm sure he is." She tried to sound confident, though the trill in her voice gave up the secret.

"No, Mom. He really is." Kiri pointed out the window and onto the blackness of the front lawn.

No sooner had she spoken than keys clicked in the lock and the door swung wide. Standing on the sill, Brendan's face came as close to relief as his stern features would naturally allow. "I'm so glad you're all here," he said, closing the door.

Vailea eyed him up and down in the light of the fire. His interview pants were filthy, the welts of his shoes had broken free, and his suit jacket had started to split down the back. His hair, which she'd been sure he combed before the interview, exploded across his head in an avalanche of tangles. "Brendan Chogan," she sputtered, before he could wrap her in an embrace, "what took you so long?"

He bent low, pulled her close, and kissed her. A deep kiss.

By the time Vailea resurfaced, Lykos had padded over to give Brendan a sniff in exchange for a scratch under the chin. Hahana rubbed the sleep from her eyes while Kiri gagged at her parents' affection.

"I'm glad to see you, too," Vailea said, only a little off-balance. But she was speaking now to Brendan's back since he'd already knelt at the hall closet, rummaging. "What are you doing?"

"We've got to pack our things," he said, casting a suitcase onto the floor, a thump across the hardwood. "We're leaving in the morning."

13

"We could find a cabin up toward Mount Hood," Brendan said, trying a new tack. "I used to work with a guy who has a place up that way. Right off Highway 26. Shouldn't be too hard to find."

Vailea scooted past him, arms piled high with flashlights. She set them on the kitchen table, atop the groceries she'd taken from the store yesterday. One of the flashlights fell to the floor, and rolled into the dining room. It came to rest against the hutch, where she'd stacked warm clothes and blankets.

Vailea hadn't stopped moving all morning. She'd pulled bottled water from the back of the pantry. She'd found sleeping bags for the girls in case they wanted to curl up by the fire tonight. But she hadn't awarded even the smallest bit of merit to his plan to leave.

"I know you mean well, Brendan," she said, flicking on a camping lantern, "but it's not getting any better out there. You didn't see the grocery store like I saw it. If you had, you wouldn't want to leave the house." She tapped the lamp off and put it next to the other flashlights. "Honestly, I've never seen people get so worked up about a blackout."

Brendan didn't mention that she wasn't great at handling the dark herself. Instead, he said, "It's not just the power grid—"

"I know, I know. You heard bits and pieces on the radio about a cyber attack. The Internet is down and the bridges are up. Some cars won't start and most every store is shuttered."

"And I saw satellites falling from the sky."

"Exactly. Which is why we need to stay put."

"The city isn't safe. It's bad now, but if the stores don't open up people are going to be hungry. It'll get worse out there." How could he make her see?

She pressed a red object into his hands, clearly no longer paying attention to anything he was saying. A Red Cross emergency radio, the kind powered by a hand crank. "Try to get this going." She patted him on the arm. "In an hour or so I'll see if I can get your dad's old shortwave working."

"We should be on the road in an hour."

She hustled off, searching for a first aid kit to add to her growing pile of supplies. "We'll reassess if you hear it's safe to travel," she said from the other room. "But find out as much as you can."

Brendan hefted the radio. Would it break in his hands? But after a couple of minutes revolving the crank he managed to keep it in one piece, and the battery charged enough that a little light appeared.

He scanned for a station.

The first one he tried—the Port of Portland emergency frequency—hummed with static. The second one—the NOAA weather all hazards station—buzzed inaudibly as well. As he rolled his thumb over the dial, he caught a few words on a station that he'd bypassed. He honed in on the frequency.

"*...the martyrs who laid down their precious lives in the sacred war for the freedom and independence...*"

Brendan had come somewhere in the middle of what sounded like a speech in heavily-accented English, some words so broken he couldn't understand.

"*...and in correcting for the Fatherland Liberation War, and in retribution for Imperialists whose treasons delayed but did not defeat our great nation, the just battles have begun. We, inheriting the heroic fighting spirit displayed by our forerunners, call on Imperialists to surrender their cities, surrender their arms. No harm will come upon those who do...*"

He listened, trying to understand the message and the context. Would some anonymous hacker group have overlaid the emergency broadcast networks in some bizarre performance art?

"*...You, the haughty, who had battened on aggression and pillage. You who* *fought a bare-handed man as brigandish robbers, fought rifle with atomic bomb. You have lived to see our country's glorious history and tradition of victory, our Juche-oriented military ideas, and outstanding art of command of the heaven-sent legendary generals, as well as the heroic spirit and indomitable struggle of our people who are boundlessly faithful to their Party and leaders. And now you have seen your Stars and Stripes burning and our flag flying high."*

The message ended there. After the final words came a military march with trumpets, cymbals, drums, and a chorus of rapturous male voices. After a few minutes of music, Brendan switched the radio off. It was good to know there was still a radio station working out there. Too bad it didn't have anything useful.

Then, out of nowhere, Vailea shouted, "We need to fill up the bathtub!"

Brendan peeked around the corner, just in time to step in her way.

"Move!" she said, suddenly frantic. She sped into the bathroom and out of sight, where he could hear her stoppering the tub and opening the faucet.

"Everything okay?" he asked, following her.

She sat at the edge of the tub, watching water trickle in. The pressure seemed low, but it filled steadily enough.

"No, no," she said. "I mean, maybe, I don't know."

"You … gonna take a bath?" She was fully clothed and the water would surely be cold without power to heat it.

She shot him the you-have-no-idea-what's-happening scowl that he'd gotten used to over years of marriage, then she sighed. "We get our water through gravity flow. About five miles east of here is a reservoir up on Kelly Butte that supplies the neighborhood."

"A reservoir? Sounds pretty big. Are you worried we're going to run out of water?" He sat down on the lip of the tub next to her.

"It is big. Something like twenty-five million gallons."

He put his hand over hers and squeezed, gently. "Then what's the problem?"

"Well, for one thing, that reservoir serves all of East Portland. Millions of people. But that's not really the point. The problem is that the water bureau needs to constantly refill the reservoir."

"Doesn't sound like a problem."

Her almond eyes stayed on the water flowing from the tap. "It normally isn't. But how do you think water gets up to the reservoir?"

Brendan thought for a moment. "They must pump it up."

"Yeah," Vailea said. "And if the electrical grid goes down they use a generator to run the pump …"

"And you said there's some kind of problem with the city's generators."

"That's right. No generator, no pumping. And when the reservoir goes dry, we'll be looking to the sky for water."

Brendan shivered. If she was right, the water would go dry eventually.

Just then, an air bubble gurgled out of the tap. A sputter of water gushed out. Stop and start. Then another gurgle, followed by a trickle. Vailea tried twisting the tap to open up more water, but nothing came out. The tub wasn't even a quarter of the way full.

Her eyes widened, black eyebrows curved not in surprise but in contemplation. Brendan was sure Vailea would be calculating how long the water would last them. But all she said was, "Go put some Tupperware out on the back porch and front lawn. We'll need to start catching the rain, if it ever comes."

* * *

An hour later, Vailea sat on the front step with her father-in-law's old shortwave radio. Brendan hadn't gotten much from his family when they'd passed. Most of their possessions had been lost in the same fire that had taken their lives.

"There we go," Vailea said as she put in the nine-volt battery. She flicked the on switch.

Nothing happened.

She sighed and pulled out her screwdriver. The radio had been sitting at the bottom of a box for more than a decade. Of course it didn't work.

The casing came off and she inspected the transistors, coil, air variable capacitor, and other common electrical parts welded to the circuit board.

Frowning at it, no obvious problem jumped out at her.

She clicked on the handheld microphone that came with it, attached to the radio with a cord. Without an antenna, she wouldn't be able to broadcast far, but if there was a working network of shortwave radio users she might be able to connect with them.

For now, though, the machine remained broken, with no easy solution.

She shook her head and peered down the block. All the houses on the street remained dark. How long would the lights be out?

Brendan had laid out buckets and plastic containers across the lawn to catch rain. And now he was down the way, talking with neighbors, trying to get a better sense of what was happening. People walked along the sidewalk like it was any other day, except, perhaps, that there were more on the street than normal for a weekday. Children played in the yard a few houses down. Smoke rose from half the chimneys on the block.

Every few minutes, a family walked or biked down the road. Everyone, even the kids, wore backpacks. Brendan had asked them why they didn't drive, and they'd said the roads were one big traffic jam. Many cars had simply stopped, broken down in the middle of the street. No one had been able to get through, apparently.

Vailea couldn't begin to guess where all her neighbors would be going. Hotels, she supposed. Scouting for a place where generators worked and taps hadn't run dry. She couldn't imagine walking out of town, though. Not with the girls.

But could they really stay here? The toilets didn't flush. They were eating meals by candlelight. The only heat came from the hearth. And she was covered in a patina of grime and wood smoke after only a day without bathing.

Maybe it's for the best the neighbors are going. If she ran out of firewood at least she'd be able to borrow from the stacks outside their homes. And if it really came down to it, they could find an unlocked backdoor to scrounge any other supplies they might need.

You're overreacting. Being around all these city people had her thinking the worst. No running water was hardly an emergency. Sure, it made life harder, but the water would be back soon. And the lights, too, within a few days. By Thanksgiving, everyone would have forgotten this had ever happened.

Vailea refocused her attention to the radio and checked the cables and adapters one at a time. *Czzshhshkkkzzshs.* The shush of static. She probed a wire and heard it again. Fastening the cable with a piece of tape, she screwed the case back on and searched frequencies for a broadcast.

After several minutes of trying, a faint, far-away British voice penetrated through the static.

"… no word from the Queen … her visit to Dublin Castle …"

Vailea manipulated the telescopic rod antenna to improve reception.

"… the streets of London are cleared except for Army personnel. And while no update has come from Buckingham Palace or Downing Street, it's clear that the city is shutdown for the foreseeable …"

Vailea glanced up. The scrape of a foot on the dry leaves made her jump. Down the avenue, a patch of yellow cloth darted behind a Halloween scarecrow. A person. Hiding.

"Hello," Vailea called. There was definitely someone there. "I see you."

Seconds ticked by, and Vailea started thinking her imagination had summoned ghosts. Then the patch of yellow emerged from its hiding place.

A woman, wearing a dandelion-colored dress and a fur coat, sauntered up the sidewalk. Boots clicked as she strode forward. "Hello." The stranger came closer. Her voice was deep and her hips swayed when she walked, in a way that made Vailea think of a cobra before it struck.

Vailea stood as the woman approached. There was something off about this blonde creature. A normal wariness of strangers she hadn't learned, perhaps. More than that, though. She undulated closer, almost as a seductress might.

"Hi," Vailea managed, weakly.

The woman kept coming, onto the autumn leaves of her front lawn. "That's a nice piece of equipment. Is it shortwave?"

Vailea clutched the radio. The boots, the dress, the furs—they didn't match. It wasn't the trashy outfit that made her nervous. Something else bothered her. Something she couldn't put her finger—

No. She saw it now. Blood stained the hem of the yellow dress.

Vailea backed up. Her heels hit the door. Reaching, her hand fumbled for the doorknob, though her eyes never left the stranger.

"Give it to me." The woman's hand thrust into a coat pocket and came out with a gun. She kept it at her side, half hidden. "Quietly."

A scream caught in Vailea's throat. She scanned the neighbors for help, but they didn't see. People continued down the street or sat on their porches, oblivious. Her hand left the doorknob and crawled up, as if on its own, to her sweater. Palm pressed against her heart, she felt it cantering beneath the wool.

She tried to scream again. Nothing came out.

The woman's expression changed. In the barest part of a second her face went from hungry, almost sensuous, to a frown and tightened jaw.

Walking up the front lawn, Brendan appeared, Lykos at his side. The German Shepherd slinked toward the front steps, hackles up, teeth bared. "Is everything okay here?" Brendan asked, cracking his knuckles against his chin.

He hasn't seen the gun. He wouldn't have asked that question if he had. She stammered, wanting to warn him. Nothing but a croak came out.

"Forget it." The woman in the yellow dress retreated across the lawn. When she reached the sidewalk, she trotted off, a clip-clop of boots on pavement.

Brendan squinted down the street after her. "What was that all about?"

Vailea's legs wobbled. She buried her face in his chest and shook, letting him wrap his bear-arms over her shoulders, shivering uncontrollably. That woman had come onto her property to rob her. Near her family. Near her children. And for what? A shortwave radio?

Would the police have come if she had called them? Was there even any way to call?

Questions tumbled through Vailea's head like the churn of waves on

66

the sand. Brendan held her all the while, soothing her. She didn't want to let go.

Several minutes passed before she finally disentangled herself. She lifted her chin to face his eyes. "You were right, Brendan. We should get out of here."

His thick lips split into a smile. "Let's get packed. We leave tomorrow."

14

"There you are."

Xandra scanned the darkness before landing on the shape of a man. The voice, come suddenly, should have startled her, but she was tired. Tired and hungry. Too tired to be surprised.

She put down the bag of chips. Dropped it, really. A crumpling noise followed as the package hit the ground. Her last four meals had come from the same vending machine, cracked open with a chair. She refused to feel guilty about stealing. Guilt wasn't one of the emotions she normally felt, anyway.

Over the past forty-eight hours, the Pentagon had changed dramatically. Of the more than twenty-three thousand military and civilian employees who worked here, only a fraction had remained. And who could blame them? What could they accomplish from their desks? No working Internet. No classified networks. The Department of Defense's secret Internet protocol router network, SIPRNet, had fallen to what the President had dubbed the "national computer silence event."

Before the broadcasts stopped.

Of course, it was much more than a silence event. Everyone in the building knew that as well as she did. They'd seen the cars marooned on I-395 and highways 110 and 27, all visible from the windows. Many of them had been watching out over the lagoon toward Washington DC when the power went out. The lights had flared and died in the capitol at exactly the same time as in the Pentagon. Everyone knew this wasn't just about computers anymore.

"I'm glad to see you, Xandra," the man at the doorway continued, stomping through the darkness. Admiral Kalb. She recognized his voice

...

as much as his silhouette. Despite his cheerful words he sounded like he'd slept about as much in the past two days as she had. Maybe less, which wouldn't have been easy. "Ms. Strandlien, I need you to go to Oregon."

"Oregon?" No one went to Oregon. At least not in her line of work. Not on purpose, anyway. It was the flyover state of the West Coast. A patch of green halfway between the headquarters of Apple and Microsoft.

"It's beyond the scope of your responsibilities, I know. But you're the only one who has the programming ability, the security clearance, and the capability to go."

This is going to be good. "You mean I'm the only person left in this place."

That wasn't strictly true. The Pentagon had emptied out when the generators blew. But there were still hundreds of Department of Defense employees left, though most of them were like Xandra—stuck, with no way to get home. She was actually surprised Admiral Kalb had come back. None of the other senior officers who had crossed the Potomac for the Capitol building had returned.

"No, I need you," he said, emphatically enough that she almost believed him. "I've already sent three of our other top hackers to the coast. And you're the fourth. Of all of my staff, you probably have the best background for this assignment."

"I'm not on your staff," she reminded him.

"You're my civilian advisor. And you've got the coding chops to do what I need." He smiled. "I'm sure MIT can spare you. I guarantee they aren't holding classes."

"What's in Oregon?"

He beckoned her to follow him into the hall. "Come with me. I'll tell you once we're outside. There's something I want to show you."

Throwing her coat over her shoulders, Xandra walked through the hallway of the "E" Ring and toward the north exit. The *clack-clack* of her heels echoed through the vast emptiness of the space, without so much as the hum of halogen lights or the voices of other people to muffle the noise.

69

Sunlight entered through the windows, and she could see him better now. Dark half-moons crouched under his eyes. Unless she was badly wrong, he hadn't shaved in forty-eight hours, or eaten much of anything. And the wrinkles in his uniform told her he'd slept in it.

Under his arm he clutched a military-grade "milspec" laptop. The device resembled a metal briefcase more than a computer, right down to the handle and lock. Built for rough terrain and hard use. Definitely not the kind of computer she'd expect the head of US Cyber Command to carry around.

Even though the Pentagon had more than seventeen miles of corridors, the architects had designed it so a person could walk between any two points in less than seven minutes. It was the kind of fact that brought Xandra as close to happiness as she ever came.

Outside, she could almost imagine there was no cyber war at all. Autumn birds chirped in leaf-bare trees. The sun shone cold through a clear sky. An officer of the Pentagon Force Protection Agency, standing stalwart by the door, nodded to them on their way out, just like any other day. *Does he have a family he should be guarding, instead of an empty building?*

"Homeland Security received a lot of intel over the past week," Admiral Kalb said. "Before the cyber attacks. Most of it made no sense at the time. Some of it seemed like fantasy." He sighed. "Not anymore."

They meandered through the half-full parking lot. A surprising number of vehicles, considering. Teslas and Mercedes lined up neatly in their rows, like an upscale dealership. Nothing like a crisis. *Give it another day.* When the Russians hacked Ossetia, civil unrest started within hours. She doubted she was the only one to have smashed a vending machine. And a hungrier woman wouldn't be above breaking into a Mercedes for a bag of chips left on the dash.

They exited the parking lot and entered an asphalt path across a field of neatly trimmed grass. Xandra knew this spot. It was the Pentagon's private airfield. Down the walkway there'd be a helipad, though unless you were a visiting dignitary or Air Force One you had to settle for a miserable commute like everyone else.

Admiral Kalb continued. "Did you read the classified report I sent you a few days ago? The one on Chinese-Russian joint military exercises?"

She'd read it all right, though it had been a waste of time. There was more classified information in an average C-SPAN broadcast than in that white paper. Everyone knew about the Sino-Russian navy drills—in the South China Sea this year, if she remembered right. Which of course she did. She never forgot a detail. "It's not news. The Nanhai fleet gets together with the Pacific Fleet every few years."

"Except when it *is* news ... or might be anyway. These aren't drills, Ms. Strandlien. At least not this time. We think it might be a buildup."

"A buildup?" Her words echoed through the empty, windy field. "Like an invasion force?"

"It's unclear. The updates are preliminary, and our satellites weren't in position before they went down. But with everything else that's going on ... it looks suspicious, to say the least."

"I still don't see how I can help, sir." A gust sent strands of shoulder-length chestnut hair into her mouth. She hawked it out, noisily.

He appraised her for several long seconds. Should she have spit more quietly? Her mother had always scolded her for not behaving like a lady.

Admiral Kalb cleared his throat. "You can go directly to the front lines. Make your way to the Oregon Coast. I've sent our other hackers to California and Washington. We don't know where the invasion is going to come from, but we know it will be the West Coast. Oregon probably isn't the most likely spot. But it's isolated and has no military bases nearby. They might make landfall there."

The suggestion that she go toward an invasion was ludicrous, almost insultingly pointless. "What could I possibly do to stop an invasion?"

"The military is under some strain." She could tell by his tone that this was an understatement. "We don't know where the landing will be. We're undermanned. Spread thin. And with our satellites and radar systems down we don't have any up-to-date intel on what's happening out at sea."

"And military communication, sir?" More hair infiltrated her mouth. This time she pushed it out with her tongue as subtly as she could.

"Despite our best efforts, we can't get a phone call out of Washington. We're all using shortwave radio, and even that's running into aggressive jamming issues."

When she'd first heard that most communication networks were paralyzed, she'd been uncharacteristically startled. In order to take out landlines the enemy had successfully neutralized the backup generators that kept those lines running during a blackout. It had been an impressive bit of cyber warfare.

"I need you to go to Oregon," he continued, "to provide malware for the Coast Guard to upload into the enemy's servers."

"What malware?"

"That part is up to you."

She stared at him, incredulous.

"Take this computer." He handed her the milspec laptop from under his arm. "Our boys have loaded it with every line of code we scraped from the attackers before they took us offline. We've also put in all the cyber weapons in the US Cyber Command arsenal. Some of those are zero-day exploits. Most of it, truthfully, is garbage. But I'm hoping you can look through and come up with something, anything, that will reverse the damage."

"That's a tall order."

He stopped and grabbed her forearm. It was the first time he'd ever touched her, and he seemed ... different. Maybe unsure of himself; though reading faces had never been a skill of hers. "I've been in communication with the Command Master Chief in Newport, Oregon. He's assured me that all we need to do—all *you* need to do—is come up with the code and hand it off to them. They'll take care of the rest."

"That won't be easy, sir."

"Will you do this for me?" He let go of her arm and smoothed out the front of his uniform. A wasted effort.

She hesitated. His request was nearly impossible. Even if she could somehow cobble a solution from random bits of code the enemy had left behind, she wouldn't be able to do anything except perhaps identify the source.

She almost told him she wouldn't do it. Almost. But, she wanted to help. And even more, she wanted to test her skills against the best in the world. Whoever had launched these attacks were the best she'd ever seen.

"Of course," she said, taking the computer. "I'll do whatever you ask." Two days of eating from vending machines and sleeping under conference tables made her eager for a change.

"Fantastic. Because it was no easy task finding you a ride." He continued walking, pointing down the green. "This is what I wanted to show you."

A plane—small and white, with a nose propeller and a single door on each side. It looked ancient, and she said so.

"It is. Probably older than you. And it's privately owned by the pilot. But it's one of the few serviceable aircraft within fifty miles. Ours are all tits up." He grimaced. "We're still narrowing down the possible causes for that."

As they approached, Xandra spotted a pilot in the cockpit. A Latino man in his mid-forties, with thick, dark hair. A fellow civilian; his hair too long for an air force pilot. She doubted there were any thirty-year-old Cessnas in the USAF, either.

"I know why the planes aren't flying," she said.

He rubbed his eyes, which only served to augment the half-moons below. "You do?"

"Of course. It seems fairly obvious that the problem comes from computer chips made overseas."

"Computer chips? Unlikely. The scale is too big. Too many devices are affected. Pretty much everything, really."

He really should realize by now that she was rarely wrong. Not when it came to the quantitative, anyway. "It's easy enough to engineer a backdoor into just about any piece of electronics, sir. A kill switch of sorts. The kind of intentional flaw that wouldn't be known to anyone except the factory that produced it."

Admiral Kalb waved her away. "Seems like a stretch."

"You know as well as I do, sir, that the integrity of our electronics has been compromised. Just last month I forwarded you my research on the number of Chinese computer chips in the F-35 Joint Strike Fighter. If I remember right, the number was in the triple digits."

"So you're saying any aircraft made with Chinese chips might be compromised?"

She wondered if he'd even read her report. "No. I'm saying that *any* electronics—from a generator, to a toaster, to a Super Hornet—almost certainly contains chips fabricated beyond the reach of our national control. And it seems likely, sir, based on what we're seeing, that all these chips have been simultaneously and remotely accessed."

"Wouldn't these chips need to be part of a device that's connected to the Internet to be accessed?"

"Not at all. They just need to be close enough to an Internet signal—" A crack in the path caught her shoe. She stumbled. Heels. Not the most sensible choice.

The Admiral didn't seem to notice her misstep and kept on at a brisk pace. "Any piece of electronics could be compromised? Generators even?"

Xandra shifted the laptop under her arm and hustled to keep up. "Every newer piece of electronics is probably compromised. Anything built in the last decade, I'd speculate. Those chips could have been triggered any time before the Internet went out."

"Triggered and shut down, you're saying." Admiral Kalb's eyes met hers, but he didn't slow his gait. "This only makes it more vital for you to get to the West Coast." He scratched at his chin as if just realizing the state of his stubble. "Under your seat you'll find a duffel bag. It's marine-grade and watertight. Inside are all the spare batteries and cords you could need. There's also a shortwave radio. I've written down the frequency we'll be broadcasting at, as well as the frequency for the Coast Guard in Newport. They'll have instructions for where and how to liaise when you reach the coast."

"Very good, sir."

"Is there anything else you require?"

"Nothing, sir."

"Good luck, then."

They reached the plane. The pilot hopped out and extended his hand. "Lorenzo Robles. Pleased to meet you."

Xandra shook his hand, beginning the absurd ritual of greeting and introduction. "Xandra Strandlien. Pleased, as well." She hated introductions almost as much as small talk.

"Off you go," Admiral Kalb said. "Good luck in Oregon, Ms. Strandlien."

She climbed into the Cessna.

A girl of about thirteen—dark hair and a dimpled chin—sat in the cockpit of the small plane. She waved.

"What is this?" Xandra asked.

Lorenzo climbed in and squeezed past into the pilot's chair. "What do you mean?"

"Why is there another person?"

The girl folded up the map that lay across her lap.

"This is my daughter, Carmen. She'll be making the trip with us. Couldn't leave her at home. Introduce yourself, Niña."

"Nice to meet you," the girl said. "You're the one we're taking to Oregon?"

"Yes." Admiral Kalb stuck his head into the plane. "Ms. Strandlien is a security expert, professor, and probably the best coder I've ever met." He closed the door and knocked twice on the side.

Xandra regarded Carmen's squishy little face, big brown eyes staring back at her. The girl probably hadn't washed her hands in days. Isn't that what kids did? Rolled around in the dirt and picked their noses? Xandra flopped back into her seat.

"Would you like a piece of candy?" the girl said, holding out a box of Milk Duds. "It's Halloween, you know."

Xandra waved them away, not bothering to reply. This was going to be a long trip. She hated children.

15

The girls sat in the back, on either side of Lykos, happily munching their way through a box of granola bars. "Everyone gone potty?" Brendan asked from the driver's seat. He didn't wait for a reply before turning the key in the ignition and backing the minivan down the driveway.

Pretty soon they'd be out of the city and into the country. Farmland and forest. All the way to the mountains if they were lucky. There'd be toilets that flushed out there. Running water. Maybe even electricity.

It was the morning of the third day since the lights went out, but already he missed the conveniences of life that he'd always known, theoretically, that he took for granted. Pooping into a plastic bag brought that theory into reality. He'd be willing to let some third-rate motel price gouge them as long as tonight he could read his phone on a working commode.

The Dodge Caravan was ancient. It was one of the older models, from the mid-nineties. Brendan had been saving up for something better, but money was tight, and a new car wouldn't be in the picture for some time.

The minivan puttered as he put her into drive and pointed east. Freedom was out that way. Open roads and small towns.

Despite the cold, Brendan rolled down the window. The fresh air smelled good, like a new cedar fence. Like pine trees and Lake Erie and woodsmoke all together. Crisp, clean. Maybe with the uncongested roads and dormant factories in the eastside industrial area, he noticed what had always been there.

The window wasn't halfway down when a new odor reached the car.

Faint at first, then stronger. Sewage, cheese, spoiled milk.

Kiri moaned, a hand over her mouth. "Do you smell that?"

Hahana gagged. "Smells like poop."

"Roll up the window, Dad!" they said in unison.

Toilets hadn't flushed since yesterday. He supposed it was inevitable.

"You're sure traffic jams will have cleared up?" Vailea asked after his window was up and the stench subsided.

"Absolutely," he said. "It's been days, and the city's emptied out. Won't be anyone on the road."

"Well, make sure to take the side streets." Vailea tapped nervously on the armrest. "Just in case."

The woman with the gun had scared her. Brendan supposed, in a backward way, he should be grateful. If she weren't frightened, she'd never have agreed to go.

"Hey, this is gonna be easy." He squeezed her hand. "We should be out of the metro area in no time, and we'll find a hotel well before dark." He'd meant it to be reassuring, but her eyes tightened at the mention of darkness. "Anyway," he continued, "we've got a full tank of gas and a trunk full of supplies. Getting out of here is the best thing we can do."

"It's going to be an adventure," Kiri squealed from behind them.

"Can we go camping?" Hahana asked.

"If we wanted to go camping we'd have just stayed home," Vailea snapped, one of her hands gripping the armrest. She'd feel better when they got out of town.

They drove through the small boulevards of the Ladd's Addition neighborhood, past homes with lights out and curtains drawn. It was hard to tell how many people were still here. A smattering of neighbors walked their dogs, and occasionally someone sat on a front porch, wrapped in a blanket. But mostly, the sidewalks remained empty. Here and there someone split or peeked out from a window. Once in a while folks with their heads together glanced sideways as Brendan drove by. But school was closed and the shops were dark. Even gas stations had shut down. There wasn't much reason to be outside.

And there weren't any cars on the street, except theirs.

"How long will we be gone?" Hahana asked. Brendan glanced back at her through the rearview mirror. Nose-deep in *The Babysitter's Club*, she flipped a page.

"In a day or two," Vailea said, folding her arms in tight around her winter coat. "When the electricity is back."

Brendan drove slowly, well below the speed limit. Not because he was afraid of being pulled over. He hadn't seen a cop anywhere in the last two days. It was that the streets didn't seem to belong to cars anymore. He felt like an interloper. At any moment, he expected someone to step out in front of him, no longer watching for traffic, no longer expecting cars on the roads.

A house caught Brendan's eye. A craftsman-style home with a handsome stone wall along the front, it blended in most ways with the others. The building itself wasn't out of place. But the door ... Now that grabbed his attention. Spray painted in red across the entrance, the words "Keep Out!" dripped like murder.

"Eyes on the road," Vailea shouted.

Brendan twisted back just in time to see a man in the street. "Shit!" Brendan banked hard to the right. The pedestrian dragged something behind him, a length of metal fencing perhaps.

Vailea pressed her fingers into his shoulder. "Keep. Your. Eyes. On. The. Road. You'll get us killed."

"He walked right in front of me," Brendan protested. Vailea said nothing, so he placed both hands on the steering wheel and glowered over the top. He'd keep his family safe. It wasn't his fault some moron wandered into traffic.

They'd gone less than a mile when they were forced to stop. Up ahead, along Cesar Chavez Boulevard, traffic snarled the length of the street from north to south, as far in each direction as he could see. While he couldn't spot the cause of the pileup, the cars had stopped so close together Brendan doubted anything bigger than a motorcycle could pass through. Vehicles filled the four lanes. And from what Brendan could see, there weren't even any people inside them, just an endless column of forsaken sedans, pickups, and semi-trucks.

Brendan stuck his head out the window. "What's happened to all the cars?" he asked a group of people walking down the street.

A man wearing an external frame backpack slowed, hands tucked into the straps, rearranging the pack without stopping. "Some of the cars just stalled. My guess, it's only the newer ones." He shrugged and kept walking. "Enough to make every road impassable."

"This is a mistake," Vailea said under her breath. Then louder, "I think we should go home."

Not a chance. Brendan shifted into reverse and started a three-point turn. "We'll just go around. I'm sure there's a way."

But ten minutes later, with plenty of stops and starts, they still hadn't found a route that would take them past the traffic jam. They tried Hawthorne Street and found it to be just as blocked. A TriMet bus had careened into a telephone pole, the right two wheels lifted a foot or more off the pavement. Glass covered the parking lot of the Grand Central bakery, pigeons wrestling over loaves too big to carry. And along the way, cars—too many to count. Cars that filled the street as far as he could see. Division, too, was choked with traffic. 12th Avenue. And, even some of the smaller streets.

The late-morning drive filled Brendan with a chill that had nothing to do with November. For long stretches they encountered no cars, just empty streets and vacant sidewalks. Broken car windows spilled glass across the ground. Some homes, too, seemed to have been ransacked, doors left open, kicked in, left in splinters. Trash blew along the street from overturned bins where garbage trucks had failed to collect it. The smell of urine occasionally wafted into the minivan. At least there were some people still around, forced to defecate in their own backyards.

Brendan spun the wheel and brought them west, almost in a circle. There had to be a way out of town. He just needed to find a break. A gap wide enough to drive through.

Out of nowhere, a brick crashed through their window.

The girls screamed. Brendan nearly ran them into a tree before coming to a stop. Small, square shards of glass flew everywhere. Vailea flailed, her eyes darting in all directions.

"Is everyone okay?" Brendan yelled, frantically searching his daughters for signs of injury.

Another brick came flying. It missed the window and instead bumped off the front quarter panel.

"Drive!" Vailea shouted. But Brendan had already pressed his foot to the accelerator, peeling down a side street. More bricks hit the top of the van.

"What the hell is happening?" Vailea shouted, while the girls screamed in the backseat.

Up and down the median, Brendan noticed at least six men, young, maybe in their twenties. One of them carried a television. Another carted a computer under each arm. A third held a tire iron in one hand and reached onto the ground for another brick.

"Don't know," Brendan shouted. He headed back toward the main road, still accelerating.

Up ahead stood the pedestrian they'd passed a while ago—the one dragging fencing on the ground. Except it wasn't fencing, exactly. It was a length of barbed wire, cut from a fence. And he was laying it on the street, directly in their path.

"Hold on," Brendan said, teeth set in a growl. It was too late to stop now. Too late to swerve. He accelerated toward the strip of metal spikes, his foot pressing down as much as he dared. They couldn't stop, but he'd be damned if he'd slow down.

The minivan flew over the length of barbed wire so fast he almost didn't hear the *tap-tap-tap* of the tires being punctured. For a brief moment he lost control and peeled out, sideways, the wheels leaving rubbery marks over the pavement. Only a few seconds, though, and he pulled them back on course.

Chancing a glance through the rearview mirror, he couldn't see the young men anymore. But he didn't hit the brakes. The *flop-flop* below told him the tires were losing air, but he wasn't planning on stopping. He'd rather drive on the rims than pull over.

"We have to go home," Vailea shouted. Only then did he realize the girls were still screaming. Lykos never made a sound, although the

German Shepherd was covered in glass. And Brendan had clenched the steering wheel so tight that it had bent under his hands. "We have to go home," she said a little softer.

Brendan nodded. He wanted to get out of town, maybe more desperately now than before. But he knew she was right. The minivan wouldn't take them far with blown-out tires. They needed to regroup and come up with a better plan. "All right," he said, taking the next left down a deserted side street, pointing them in the right direction. "But we both know it's not safe there, either. I'll take us home. But we can't stay."

16

The past three days had been some of the happiest in Han-yong's life. Never before had he worked so closely with his teammates. Never before had he enjoyed the comradery, the banter, the pure joy of his fellow officers. Never before had he labored with such passion. It was the kind of work he enjoyed. In a way, not even work at all.

On the same day that he'd deployed project *Sonnimne*, he'd gotten to finally see the scores of other projects that the warriors of Unit 101 had dreamed up. And he'd been more than a little impressed. There was project *Yongwang*—the five dragon kings—that exploited flaws in vehicle electronics. There was project *Sanshin*—the mountain gods—that opened the doors to every prison in Europe. There were projects to ruin generators, sabotage automobiles, empty bank accounts, and dozens more. But out of all of the projects, Han-yong's personal favorite was project *Chasa Bonpuri*—the death myth—that he had been working on in secret. It wasn't aimed at the Imperialists at all, but at North Korea's allies.

The first step of *Chasa Bonpuri* was already complete. He'd been able to hack into Chinese satellites. And what he'd found astounded him.

The late-afternoon standup meeting was about to start. The time had come for Han-yong to show the team what he'd learned.

"Junior Lieutenant Min. Give your report." The senior lieutenant stood across from a straight line of twenty-two junior lieutenants, their bodies rigid with perfect discipline as they waited to update their commanding officer. The senior lieutenant picked out the leftmost cyber warrior and motioned him forward.

Han-yong stood at attention among the group of his fellow officers.

This particular meeting included only the strike team assigned to North America. In an adjacent conference room, the strike team assigned to South Korea and Japan was giving its report. Throughout the hotel, the teams assigned to dismantle the enemy in Asia, Europe, and Israel would also, separately, be briefing their superior officers.

"Waterworks systems are still offline, sir," Junior Lieutenant Min replied, taking one step forward. He was a thin man, pimpled, and just out of his teenage years. "Potable water, waste water, and fire suppression infrastructure continues to be non-operational in all observable checkpoints. Additionally, any water treatment systems running on older-model generators—of which there are just sixteen in both countries—are under our operational control and continue to be managed under a contamination protocol."

The senior lieutenant nodded his approval. "Commendable. Next," he commanded. "Junior Lieutenant Wi. What is your status?"

Even three days into this war, a rush of satisfaction still surged through Han-yong every time his fellow officers gave their reports. For two years he had toiled in near anonymity, unaware of the broader picture. And now to learn the scale of the war effort—it was hard to overstate his exuberance.

Junior Lieutenant Wi advanced, hand to temple in salute. "Oil and gas systems in North America are still non-operational, sir," he said with the characteristically thick accent of a man who grew up felling trees in the Hamgyŏng Mountains of Yonsa County. "Petroleum refineries continue to be non-functioning with a one-hundred percent success rate. As are coal plants, natural gas pipelines, and hydroelectric plants. All systems that rely on these upstream factors continue to be defunct."

Han-yong had heard the same report for days now, though he fought to suppress a grin as he listened again. In every target country, all sectors of any importance had collapsed. Entire enemy nations had gone dark, paralyzed and ripe to be slurped like a ration-card beer. The Imperialist structure had fallen in on itself. Western civilization was destroyed by the very tools of its technological narcissism.

He almost laughed with glee, though that would be a punishable offense in the middle of a meeting. It took some restraint to hide his smile. The Imperialists had crumbled. Almost every hard drive connected to the Internet had been destroyed using a virus that over-exerted the central processing units. Nearly every server, too. And tens of millions of laptops, smartphones, and desktop PCs had been infected with an update to the motherboard firmware so that they couldn't even turn on.

The victory was complete. Almost too complete. The total collapse of the Imperialists had created a problem: without enemy computers or the Internet, it had become difficult to continue to sabotage or even monitor the infrastructure. A small matter in the great scheme. It was all destroyed. The nemesis was destroyed. The war was won.

"Next," barked the senior lieutenant. "Junior Lieutenant Ryuk. Give your report."

"Hospitals are all crippled, sir ..."

And so it went, each junior lieutenant reporting on his infrastructure target territory, detailing the damage, the unqualified destruction. Finance and banking, transportation, manufacturing, military, and cyber response ... the reports continued, with the same result. Total and complete destruction.

Han-yong's mind wandered to the larger war effort. He had heard that the Russians had rolled their tanks through Eastern Europe. And apparently the *Kantemirovskaya* Division had pushed even farther, all the way to the Atlantic Ocean, according to a recent edition of *Korean People's Army Daily*.

Just today, state media had reported that the People's Republic of China had expanded its territory into Laos, adding it to a growing list of conquests that included Taiwan, Myanmar, and Vietnam. And, far more importantly for the Democratic People's Republic of Korea, the newspaper reported that the entire Korean peninsula had finally been reunited under the Supreme Leader. It was the best news Han-yong had heard since yesterday's story about the incineration of Tokyo's metropolitan government buildings under a hail of Hwasong-12 missiles.

While Han-yong imagined Shinjuku burning, the conference door opened unexpectedly. Han-yong snapped himself from the daydream.

They had a visitor.

The colonel waddled into the room, resplendent in his medals.

Han-yong tried to hide his surprise, managing better than many of his comrades, some of whom had never seen the most senior officer in the flesh. To Han-yong's knowledge, the colonel had never even come to this floor before.

"Sir," the senior lieutenant sputtered, saluting. "We are most grateful for your presence. To what do we owe this great honor? How can we serve you?"

"Yes, yes." The colonel offered his own salute in reply and waved the senior lieutenant away. His voice was gravy-thick with phlegm, and pinpricks of sweat dotted his forehead, as if carrying his great bulk down the stairs had wearied him. "I must speak to the men directly."

"They are yours to command, sir."

"Of course." He faced the line of saluting junior lieutenants, returning their salutes so that they could stand once again at attention. "Unit 101, you have shown your ardent love for our cause through skilled warfare. You have shown iron nerves in order to achieve the final victory of the Juche revolution. And you have brought the allied Imperialist forces and their anti-socialist offensive to their knees. Our Republic, our Party, and our people thank you.

"I wanted to be the first to tell you. I wanted you to hear from my own mouth, rather than having my words filtered through your officers, the marvelous news which I am honored to deliver. The Supreme Leader himself has spoken with me. He tells me of his pleasure at your actions. He asked me—asked me!—to convey to you his fatherly pride in all of you. His thanks. Our nation thanks you. And I thank you."

As the colonel delivered his speech, the other officers glowed with pride. Some had tears in their eyes at the mention of the Supreme Leader. The same pride overcame Han-yong, but he strained to push it down. This was his opportunity to speak with the colonel directly about project *Chasa Bonpuri*.

"Continue on as you were," the colonel finished, saluting them in dismissal and waddling toward the stairs.

With his back to them, the line of junior lieutenants began to murmur among themselves, their discipline dissolving. But Han-yong strode forward, with more outward confidence than he felt, wanting to share his closely guarded information.

"Sir," he said, unable to keep a note of pleading from his voice. "I think you'll want to see this."

The colonel spun back, clearly annoyed. "What is it, junior lieutenant?"

Immediately, Han-yong realized he had crossed a line of protocol. The colonel had ended the meeting, and Han-yong, like a new recruit, had forced a much-superior officer into a new conversation. All eyes in the room glued on him. He had no choice but to continue.

"What is it?" the colonel said again, no longer affable.

"Sir, before you go, I believe you will want to hear my report." A lump of bile constricted in his throat. He swallowed it down, nose stinging at the taste and smell of vomit.

"All right," the colonel said, while at the same time the senior lieutenant said, "Make it quick."

Han-yong handed the colonel a thick, glossy printout, though he could feel his own face coloring to match a persimmon.

"What is all this?" the colonel asked, snatching the dossier.

"Sir. A satellite image of the eastern seaboard of the United States. It is a low-earth orbit photograph that shows the Imperialist cities of Baltimore, New York City, Philadelphia, and their capital, Washington D.C., among others."

"How did you get these?" the senior lieutenant demanded. "Our nation has no satellites in this area."

It wasn't the question Han-yong had expected. Who cared how he had gotten the images? Could the man not see what was in front of his face?

Instead of saying any of that, he replied simply, "I stole them."

The senior lieutenant's eyes bulged. "From whom?"

"From the National Astronautics Bureau." Bile surged up again, but he forced it down.

"You stole from the Chinese? From our allies?" the senior lieutenant stammered.

The admission sent shock through the room. Han-yong's fellow officers glared at him, but he refused to bow his head in shame. "I have not done anything that has not been done to us," he said. "Unit 61398 in China breaks into our servers all the time. It is a game they play and we play."

The only person in the room who did not appear shocked was the colonel. Instead, he nodded. "Explain this photograph to me. I don't understand what I'm looking at."

"The power in the United States has been out for three days, sir," Han-yong said, trying to keep his voice steady. "That means no generators, no electricity of any kind, anywhere."

"Yes," the colonel said. "But what does that mean for these satellite images?"

"Please let me explain, sir. There are ninety-nine nuclear plants in the United States, with almost all of those on the western side of their largest river, the Mississippi—"

"I'm sure the colonel knows all that," the senior lieutenant said.

"All of the nuclear plants have failed, sir," Han-yong said, continuing to address the colonel.

"The Imperialist nuclear plants have failed?" The colonel tapped his fingers over his chin, fat jiggling, a smirk appearing at the edge of his mouth.

"Yes, sir," Han-yong said. "Without electricity, the Imperialist engineers would not have been able to cool the fuel rods."

"You're saying the United States has suffered nuclear meltdowns at its ninety-nine nuclear plants?" The waggling of his jowls intensified.

"Not exactly, sir. It's only been three days since the generators failed. But as you can see from that first photo, the fuel rod storage pools have begun to boil. And in several of the photos smoke rises from reactors."

The colonel licked his lips as he nodded. "How long?"

Finally, the taste of vomit dissipated. In its place, the tang of satisfaction, like biting into a peach on a summer morning. "I don't know, sir. Weeks, maybe, before enough pressure builds up to break through the reactor containment structures."

"How do we ensure this happens?"

"If we can continue to neutralize reactor safety features and the corresponding power supply systems, a meltdown is inevitable. The result would be the release of massive quantities of radioactivity to the surrounding land. Fires, maybe. Radiation poisoning, certainly."

"And the scale of the damage?" The colonel's eyes glistened, and his hands rubbed together in the methodical hump of chubby fingers.

"Millions sick or dead, sir," Han-yong said. Yes, he tasted peaches so sweetly now. Peaches and the fruit of the jujube tree. "Smoke, craters, and—without a doubt—there would be millions of dead."

17

"I got one!" From the edge of the bay, Jeremiah waved the butter clam over his head and threw it onto the towel Ireana had laid on the sand. Not waiting for her response, he dipped the metal rake-head below the surface of the water and continued to scrape through the shallows. The mud smelled sharp and fishy in this part of the bay. Jeremiah didn't seem to mind. He waded forward, raking, in search of more clams.

Ireana watched as he stomped through the knee-deep water in a pair of grown-man's boots. She no longer felt the tight hands of shame around her neck, guilt for stealing those boots from the front porch of a yurt. The owner wouldn't be back. And they seemed to belong on her boy.

Food had become a problem. They were four days into the camping trip from hell, and their initial provisions had run out. Clams turned out to be one of the best ways to feed themselves. The critters tasted like slugs raised on mud and guts, but it was better than going hungry. If only barely.

"Another one!" Jeremiah held up the trophy before tossing it to the beach.

He'd already gotten dozens this morning. In fact, if Ireana were going to stick to the official catch limit, her son had probably well passed the allowable maximum. Not that she cared much for that. If the United States government wanted to slap her with a fine, they could do so—right after they airlifted her out of this sandy, salty pit of Gomorrah.

Any pretense at abiding petty regulations had become laughably quaint. She didn't care about the law right now. Not after Annalore had come back from a scouting trip to Tillamook, alone, drenched, and muddy. Humiliated. Afraid.

"Why didn't you send a cab?" Ireana remembered shouting as Annalore had slopped into the yurt, soggy from the thirteen-mile walk back from town. But before her sister had said a word, Ireana could see in her eyes that something was deeply, deeply wrong. She'd hugged her then, holding her as a story unraveled. Annalore told of the blackout that stretched across the Oregon Coast. She told of the looting and the gas station fire that ripped through town. And how no one would sell her water. And of doors slammed in her face when she asked for a drink.

Annalore told her about how she'd learned there had been some kind of a cyber attack. No one in town knew much, but they couldn't stop speculating about the fishing boats that had gone out and never come back. And the planes that had crashed into the sea. And the generators that wouldn't run.

None of the other campers had come back. Whether they had stayed in Tillamook or pioneered on to another town, Ireana wasn't sure. The five of them were all who remained at the campsite. Her sister, her nephews, her son, and herself. The only people, as far as she could tell, along this strip of ocean. Cold. Wet. With little to eat besides clams.

Initially, they'd been able to find some left-behind food and water in the yurts. Some hamburger patties in the coolers. Pancake mix and beef jerky. The first few days had been fine. There was enough to eat, and they'd been able to quench their thirst by melting the ice.

But they'd eaten the food and gulped down the easy drinking water. And recently, Ireana and Annalore had agreed their best chance of survival would be the two-day hike over the coastal range and into Portland. They'd stay here at the beach as long as they could. Then, when food ran out, they'd make the trip. Ireana didn't want to do it, but for some reason FEMA hadn't been able to find them here. The closest big city might be the best choice.

"Mom, there are so many!" Jeremiah shouted, pirouetting in the shallows. A clam in each hand had him jumping in the bay, a little caper that sent the brackish water spinning in all directions.

She wished she were finding the same success. While Jeremiah raked at the edge of the bay, his stack of butter clams and cockles growing ever higher, she dug in the sand, hunting for razor clams. So far, she'd only succeeded in ruining a couple of them and breaking half her fingernails. Not to mention soaking her pants to the waist in frigid water.

Early November, and it felt like it. The wind whipped cold against the edge of Netart's Spit, a peninsula that jutted out more than a mile from their campground at Cape Lookout State Park. From where she stood, Ireana could see the whole of Netart's Bay. Many people would find it beautiful; the way the receded water flowed, creating inlets, reflecting the cloudy sky. Birds of one species or another flitted about and dipped their beaks into the water. Dunes and wetland grasses framed the horizon.

A sludgy marsh, as she saw it. The muck at low tide out where Jeremiah found so much success glopped on interminably, mud and seaweed mixed in a massive blender and pooped out across the bed of the bay.

She'd had enough of this ordeal. Compared to eating bivalves over a campfire, triaging stab wounds at her urgent care clinic sounded like a spa package.

"I'm going to find a better spot to dig," she said, as much to herself as her son, and then set out slowly across the sand, toward the mouth of the bay. Keeping her eyes on the ground, she watched for the telltale dimple that would betray a razor clam. With any luck, she'd be able to shovel down faster than the clam could burrow, then gently work her fingers in it to preserve the somewhat-more-edible-than-the-rest muscle. The digging foot. It tasted like it sounded.

"Mom!" shouted Jeremiah. No doubt he'd added another clam to the pile.

Tracking bubbles in the sludge, she shouted back, "Great job, honey! Keep it up."

"Mom. Look!" he shouted again.

"You're doing great." She didn't want to take her eyes off the sand. She had a feeling a razor clam was around here somewhere.

"MOMMA! LOOK!" he screamed, voice cracking through the whip

of wind.

Ireana raised her head.

Jeremiah was jumping up and down and pointing out to sea. At first, she couldn't fathom what had him so riled up. The sea rolled in gray, the same color as the low clouds around them. The surf broke against the beach a hundred feet away at low tide. Seagulls and kittiwakes traipsed fearlessly in front of the crashing waves, then took flight in a group when the tide swept too close.

But he was right. There *was* something in the distance, a darker patch on the horizon.

"What is it, Momma?" Jeremiah ran up beside her. Muck fell off him in clumps as he pointed out toward the rim of the ocean.

"I don't know. Maybe just a trick of the light."

Jeremiah bounced with excitement. "I bet it's a storm. Momma, is it a storm?"

"I think it's a st—" Before she could finish he darted ahead toward the line of dunes at the mouth of the bay. Reluctantly, she followed.

Ireana picked her way over the beach. If a storm came, they would need to grab their clams and flee for camp. What they'd collected so far, along with the stream water Annalore and the boys were boiling back at the yurts, would sustain them for another day. She'd gag at every bite, but, better than hungry.

Up the white-sand path, Ireana wound past tall grass to the top of the dune. Jeremiah waited for her, eyes big as meatballs. "Boats, Mom! We're rescued!"

Cresting the dune, she peered out at the ocean. From this vantage she could take it in better, though it still took her a moment to adjust to what her eyes were telling her.

Near the threshold of the horizon she saw them. Ships. Jeremiah was right. They must be moving fast, because even as she stared they seemed to grow. No longer a gray line at the edge of sight, just below the low clouds. Now, individual ships stood out, a thousand silver thumbtacks pinned against the sea.

So many. Ships almost covered the expanse of ocean from north to south, more than Ireana would have thought possible. *All to rescue us.* She grabbed Jeremiah and started jumping up and down beside him, indifferent to the mud and grime that smeared across her clothes. "Boats! FEMA!"

Capering, hollering, waving their arms like shipwrecked sailors. Ireana didn't care. All she could think about was the shower she would take. Scalding hot. Coconut conditioner for her hair and a bar of soap, maybe with a great, poofy loofah. After that, she'd slurp a hot bowl of pho with chunks of beef and plum sauce. And she'd sleep. For a day at least.

Ireana was still thinking about the Egyptian cotton sheets she'd be nestled under tonight when Jeremiah tugged on her sleeve. He pointed to the closest, fastest boats. "Momma, what are those tiny ones?"

She wondered the same thing. Separated from the mass of ships at the horizon, hundreds of smaller craft closed in on the beach. Even from the distance of maybe a mile she could hear the roar of motors and hulls slapping against the water. There were dozens of kinds, varying in size. Some round, some long. Some skipped high on the waves, moving like quicksilver. Others had large fans on the back that reminded her of a swamp boat's twin turbines. There were too many types of watercraft to count, overwhelming the sea like dark stars on a gray sky.

Up beach, the first transports slammed into the shore, spilling troops out onto the low-tide sand. Farther north, another ship landed, larger, its bow opening like a ramp.

Ireana stared, her tongue stuck to the roof of her mouth, as a tank rolled forward from the gaping maw. The battle machine lurched onto the strand, throwing up waves of sand, its turret arcing from north to south. Men with guns followed. They ran along both sides, fanning out into the dunes.

This wasn't a rescue. She knew it then, in her core. No rescue had ever used tanks, or stormed a beach. This wasn't FEMA. It was an invasion.

"Run!" Ireana said to her son, as calmly as she could, grabbing him by the shoulder and spinning him back toward the bay. Even in this moment of panic, she knew what they needed to do. As a triage nurse, she'd learned how to focus her mind in an emergency.

"But Momma, we're saved."

She took her eyes off Jeremiah, just for a moment, and scanned the shore. The men that emptied from the transport ships waved each other onward. They sprinted from the breakers onto the beach, black weapons in their hands.

"Honey. It's not a rescue. It's not. We have to go."

They started to run, down the dunes and toward the campsite. All the while, more transports crashed into the beach, painted with flags she couldn't place. One was a blue cross on a field of white. The other, a white sun on a blue sky. Not American flags, that much she knew.

"What are we going to do?" Jeremiah asked, tearing along the edge of the marsh beside her.

"We've got to warn Aunt Annalore, and—"

An explosion cut off her words. Smoke and dirt cascaded into the sky. Then again. Sound pulsed from the blast, slamming into them, a hammer in the air.

A second blast struck inland, in the direction of Tillamook. The earth trembled. The hillside buckled and collapsed where a mortar landed short of the town, a landslide of clay barely visible through the cloud of dirt.

Then another explosion. And another.

"What are we going to do?" Jeremiah asked again, voice trembling.

"We're going to the campsite to get your aunt and your cousins. And then we're all going to run. Up and into the mountains. All the way to Portland if we have to."

18

They tramped along in haggard groups of three, five, a dozen, clothes smeared with dirt. Filth spattered their faces. Grime covered their hands and settled under their fingernails. Hundreds of men, women, and children skirted the abandoned vehicles on Interstate 5, parked bumper to bumper as far as Brendan could see. Some rode bicycles. Occasionally, an older motorcycle kicked up dust on the shoulder, though the throng of people made even that method of transport difficult.

Brendan waved to a woman, her dirty hair pinned in a bun. "Where are you going?" He didn't want to scare her, because, sometimes, he managed to frighten without trying. But the woman with the soiled hair barely winced when she took in his broken nose and oversized features.

"Going? I don't know. Anywhere," she said, shoulders sagged. "Can't stay here." The timbre of her voice held only weariness. She shuffled past him.

"How long have you been walking?" he tried, but by then she was too far gone and he didn't want to chase her.

He'd hiked down to the highway with Lykos, scouting for a way through the traffic, knowing the snarl of vehicles would be bad. This, though, was much worse than he'd expected. Not just the traffic, but the people. Their non-responsive eyes. Their plodding march north. Their despair.

A child bumped into him. The girl couldn't have been more than ten, just a couple years older than his own daughters. But she looked up at him and tears formed. Dirty tears that traced their way along the contours of her cheeks.

Before he could apologize, another person jolted into him. This time, a man on a bike.

Lykos yowled as a foot trod over his tail.

More people surged forward, a relentless crush along the highway.

The neck of Brendan's shirt felt suddenly tight. They were trapped here. Not just on I-5 but in this city. Stuck in a metropolis brought low by a war they couldn't see. He staggered, light headed. Was it getting hot out here, or was it just his imagination? No, he could still see his breath. *Maybe I should just sit down.*

He stumbled and caught himself against a large, sand-filled barrel at the corner of the off-ramp. Lykos stared at him with golden eyes, head cocked. Dizziness swept over him, a woozy vertigo that sometimes caught him in small spaces or when too many people pressed too close.

"Sorry, boy." He reached down and ruffled the fur on the animal's head when, after a few seconds, the spinning ebbed. "Just need a moment. Long as we're all together, we'll be okay. We can wait this all out at home."

He scraped his palm over the smooth curve of the barrel, the beginnings of an idea forming. The orange drum stood on a black base, filled with maybe eight hundred pounds of sand, set up to absorb the impact of a crash if a driver missed the off-ramp. "This would make a great rain barrel," he said. As much to himself as to his canine companion. "If rain would ever come." Though clouds dappled the sky, it hadn't so much as sprinkled in a week. Still, November should be a wet month in the Pacific Northwest. Rain would show up one of these days.

"Stand back," he said to Lykos and anyone else close enough to hear. Then he propelled his shoulder into the barrel. It didn't tip right away. His estimate of eight hundred pounds might have been optimistic. But when he put his full weight into the push, the barrel teetered and fell; the sputter of fifty-five gallons of sand spilled into the highway.

Refugees kept trudging forward without a second glance. The closest of them veered to either side, like fish parting for a reef. This time, though, Brendan didn't wonder at their glassy thousand-yard stared. He pushed the barrel upside down and shook out the last few grains, then raised the empty tub over his head. "Not bad, eh, Lykos?"

Hopping over the concrete Jersey barrier on the highway, he quickly left the stream of humanity behind. His heartbeat slowed when the mob of people dropped out of sight. His vision no longer pulsated in shades of crimson. Even surrounded by the emptiness of a city that should have been alive, he took in a lungful of clean air and let a smile spread across his face. "We're past it, boy. No more crowds. Not today."

Parallel to the Interstate, the Union tracks cut a straight line north and south. To his left, far up the way, a train waited. His first thought was it had stalled out like so many other vehicles, but as he approached he realized it hadn't stopped. It had come free. No longer on the track, the rear locomotive had toppled over, dozens of freight cars falling with it.

The accident shouldn't have surprised him. Not after the rest of what he'd witnessed since the lights went out. But it did. A derailment on this scale should have triggered every emergency service for miles. And yet, he and Lykos lumbered down the tracks, alone.

Corrugated well cars in blues and reds and white, tumbled down, misshapen from the fall. Some had broken open, spilling their contents across the ground. Nearest to Brendan, thousands of pairs of Nikes protruded from their swoosh-marked boxes. A group of boys picked through, searching for the perfect pair. But they were the only ones.

"We should get going," he said to Lykos, voice cracking somewhat. The derailment scared him. Maybe worse than the brick through his window. "Not too many hours until sunset."

He thought a lot about the train on the walk back. About the sneakers scattered across the track. And mostly about how no one seemed to care. Why hadn't the scroungers and the prowlers flocked in, like gulls to a dump? Thousands of dollars of merchandise had fallen, just waiting to be scooped up.

And yet those boys were the only looters.

Sweat ran down his forehead, hot fingers in his eyes, as he carried the tub through vacated streets, past cold, abandoned cars. Then down the empty sidewalks of his neighborhood, and finally home.

"What on earth is that?" Vailea asked when he dropped the barrel in the front yard.

He put his hands on his knees and offered her his best grin. "It's where our next baths are coming from," he said, a little out of breath.

She appraised the container, scratching her scalp with an idle finger. "Does this mean you've given up on wanting to leave town?"

He bobbed his head. "You were right. We've got to make it work here at home, until the lights come back."

Now her smile matched his. "And if they don't?" She poked him in the ribs, playfully.

He knocked on the top of the drum, a bongo reverberation. "Then we've got to gather more than just rain barrels."

She pulled a backpack from the porch and handed it to him. "Go on then. I can move this orange monstrosity under a downspout. Why don't you see if you can get us more supplies? Medicine. Food. Whatever you can find."

He nodded, throwing the strap over his shoulder. "We need information, most of all."

She tipped the rain barrel and rolled it toward the side yard. "Then go talk to the police. Find a station."

"All right. But I'm leaving Lykos here." The dog's ears perked up at his name.

She growled over her shoulder at him. "It isn't safe out there." He couldn't tell if her ferocity was for real or just show.

"It's not safe here, either. You need a guard dog more than me."

He expected her to put up a fight, but she said, "Be back before dark." And that was all he needed.

"Stay, boy," he told the German Shepherd. Then, with a kiss for Vailea, he nearly ran away from the house, before she could change her mind. In a couple hours the sun would set, and he didn't want to waste a minute.

Leaves wafted across the sidewalk and crunched under his shoes. The wind blew crisp. Clouds floated past, the crinkle-cut filling of a heavy bag. And the empty road opened up ahead.

He wanted to find a police station, but the closest one was the East Precinct, six miles away. The nearest fire station, though, wasn't more than a mile. He'd get some up-to-date information and be back before lights out. Maybe even bottled water and emergency supplies.

Rhubarb Street gave way to Hemlock Avenue, then Harrison Street, and still no other human joined him out on the road. He pulled his backpack tighter over his shoulders, shivering. On either side of the frost-covered street, bungalows and craftsman homes withstood the wind in silence, some with smoke billowing into the late afternoon sky, some with windows broken and doors thrown open.

Dusk approached, and he was alone. Most of his neighbors had left town. And he hadn't seen a police officer since the blackout. Hopefully the fire department would have some answers.

Trash blew across the concrete. Paper, mostly. Empty cans rolled past, a clatter of tin. Dust devils of red plastic cups. A cardboard box somersaulted into the gutter.

Then the glint of glass caught his eye. But this was no garbage.

Wine bottles in a half-empty case.

The wine had been looted, no doubt. Pulled out in haste and abandoned, probably for a richer prize. Yet here it was for the taking. Four bottles.

Brendan wasn't the type to steal. Yet, there was an argument to be made that the wine didn't really belong to anyone at the moment. Call it the law of salvage. Not stealing at all.

Before he could talk himself out of it, he slipped a bottle into his bag. Then another. Two bottles. He promised himself that when the lights were back on he'd find out whose wine this had been, and he'd replace the bottles he took, with interest. A whole case if they'd have it.

Brendan threw the backpack over his shoulder, more than a little pleased with himself. Tonight they'd drink wine, and let tomorrow care for itself

Tat. He paused, ducked. *tat-tat.* The crack of a gun. Someone was shooting.

And they were aiming for him.

* * *

Snow fell in the mountains—wet phlegmy snow, the color of an old lady's teeth. It gusted across Highway 6 without sticking, blowing tiny flecks against Ireana's face. She wanted to wipe the crust of sleet from Jeremiah's hair as he walked beside her, but found she could barely lift her arm. They slogged uphill on the highway. Away from the ocean. Away from the soldiers.

Ahead, with a pack of strangers, Annalore and her boys hiked up Highway 6, faster than she could. Ireana tried to keep up, but she kept falling farther behind, forcing herself to put one foot in front of the other. She couldn't let up. An army had amassed at the beach.

Her mind wandered back to the first minutes of the invasion. The shouts of soldiers on the shore, and the frantic sprint to warn her sister and her nephews. They hadn't had time to grab anything from the yurts. Just their clothes and their lives.

But that was enough.

They'd joined the hundreds of strangers who'd come running from the small seaside towns, weaving past lanes of stalled cars in both directions. So many abandoned vehicles. But the farther they got into the mountains, the fewer cars they came across. Until, in this part of the state forest, they saw none.

"It's getting dark, Momma," Jeremiah said, breaking through her thoughts.

"I know, honey. We'll find shelter soon," she said. But Tillamook was miles behind them now and who knew where the next mountain town might be? "There'll be a farmhouse somewhere. If not, we'll get a fire going to keep us warm."

Finding fuel might be hard. Even Ireana knew the wood on either side of the highway was too green to burn. But the road was littered with clothing, papers, golf clubs and even furniture, discarded by those fleeing, their loads grown too heavy. If Annalore could get any of that to burn, they might stay warm enough for the night.

Bom-bom. A faint explosion echoed dozens of miles behind them, ringing through the mountain pass. Ireana flinched, and the strangers along the highway did the same.

It hadn't been a true battle. Only attackers. No defense, as far as she had seen. Where the Coast Guard and Navy were, she couldn't guess. Why weren't they protecting the shore?

"And why isn't my phone working?" Or her car, or any of their phones? And how could a foreign army make landfall on a nearly empty beach in Oregon? And where would their next meal come from? Where were they going to sleep tonight? And how many days of cold and hunger would it take to get to Portland?

"What did you say, Momma?"

"Nothing, honey. Keep walking."

* * *

The bullet struck Brendan from behind. It knocked him forward onto the frosty sidewalk. Stunned, he was sure he'd been shot. His stomach lurched as red liquid pooled around his torso, for all the world like blood.

Was this death?

Breathe. His senses came back with every lungful of air and his vision began to clear. The houses on his block slowly came back into focus, dull colors in the fading day. The pool of red liquid reached his face. Pinot noir. Not blood after all.

Except for a ringing in his left ear, his hearing was coming back. The only other sound was the scrape of approaching footsteps.

"Is he dead?" A man's voice.

Brendan froze on the ground. His heart seemed to be trying to escape out his mouth, gone dry. He couldn't swallow down the taste of wine and bile.

"Shhhh ... Yeah, he's dead." A second whisper, nearing, careful.

"Is there always so much blood?"

They stopped just feet away. Quiet for a moment, standing over him. Then, in a croak, the closer one broke the silence. "He's bigger than I thought."

"Shut up."

"He's like ... a giant."

"Shut up."

"We shouldn't have done it. I told you, we shouldn't have done it. There's plenty of good shit in the houses."

"Shut up. Get his backpack and wallet and stop being a pussy."

Brendan stayed still, mind racing. Had the bullet missed him? There were still a lot of ways this could end with him dead.

Feet shuffled closer. Fingers slipped under the shoulder strap of his backpack, delicately, as if to avoid the blood.

Now or never. Brendan sprang to life.

He wasn't particularly fast. In his boxing days, he'd been slower than most. Stronger, sure. But never fast.

And yet, the prospect of taking a bullet in the back put a special urgency into his jump. In an instant he was on his feet, spinning, catching a wrist in his massive paw and twisting an arm. The killer shrieked and dropped to his knees.

Not men. Boys. Maybe sixteen years old. Boys with guns.

Tears welled up in the eyes of the one on his knees. "Lemme go," he screamed. Brendan had probably dislocated his shoulder, though not on purpose. Small things sometimes broke in his hands.

Even as the boy cried out, the second one raised his gun. A Browning A-Bolt II Medallion rifle, the same model that, as a kid, Brendan had brought to Oxbow Lake for blackpowder deer season with his father. A fine weapon. The kind that could take down a 280-pound white-tail from across an open field.

The boy aimed, squinting through a scope, even though there was no need at this close range.

Brendan dropped the first boy's arm and fled, abandoning his backpack on the street. They won't shoot, he told himself, sprinting over the cold, hard lawns. They have my bag. They have what they want.

So when the crack of the rifle sounded, it took Brendan by surprise. Hedges came to meet him as he flipped into a frost-covered lawn. He patted his hands across his body, fingers feeling for an injury. Nothing but the scrapes on his face and palms. But no blood on his body and no hole through his clothing.

When, with a flush of relief, he realized that he'd again been spared from death, he dashed for home, thinking that Vailea was right. It wasn't safe out here.

19

"Four days down." Kelly Seong focused on the Pacific Ocean growing darker in front of them. They had been long days, standing on the deck of the Japanese cargo ship *Yodohashi*, watching the sun rise, burn across the late-autumn sky, set in a splash of pink, and give way to the stars. Over and over for four miserable days.

"Bored as hell," Orion groaned beside her, leaning against the fiberglass rail.

"Lucky to be alive," she reminded him.

It was a minor miracle that the crew of the *Yodohashi* had been sailing close enough to see her maritime distress flare in the water. A miracle that they'd plucked Orion and her from their crash site a hundred miles off the coast of the Hawaiian Islands.

"We're going to die," she could remember Orion saying, after she'd swam to him, finding him in the darkness of the ocean purely by listening to his splashing and whining.

At the time, she'd agreed with him. They probably were going to drown out there. But all she'd said was, "Stop being such goddamned shark chum." Then she'd broken open her offshore distress kit and passed the maritime flare to Orion. "Unscrew the top, and point it away from your face."

While he'd struggled with the maritime flare, she'd pulled out a smoke flare of her own. Fire had sparked from the top of it, followed by orange smoke. She'd kept it above the water, easily swimming with her legs and free arm.

Orion had dropped his into the ocean.

But, sometime in the next hour, fortune had smiled on them in the form of a passing cargo ship. Kelly had been exhausted by that time, not from treading water, but from the extra work of holding up Orion's head every time he'd slip beneath the gentle chop of the Pacific.

A call had come down from the gunwale. "*Mukō o mite. Hitobito wa mizu no naka ni iru.*" A life preserver had hit the water beside them. And minutes later, Kelly had found herself breathing heavily on the deck of the *Yodohashi* while Orion puked seawater at the feet of an astounded crew.

They should have died. Survival odds for ditching during a controlled flight were low, even before you threw in the nighttime hot switch. Even before you threw in the complete and inexplicable combat systems failures of the Super Hornet aircraft.

Not to mention the power outage on the supercarrier. *What the hell had happened on the* Gerald R. Ford? It was a question she'd asked herself again and again for these last four days.

God, they just needed to get off this ship and back on land so they could get some answers. If only the captain would change course for Pearl Harbor. But there wasn't much she could do about her present situation. The captain didn't speak half a word of English, and seemed more than content to keep going east, toward the US mainland.

"Are you sure we're alive? This is just what I imagined hell to be." Orion shook the railing in frustration. As stir crazy as Kelly felt, she knew Orion was worse. Without so much as a deck of cards to pass the time, they'd mostly stood at the bow, wrapped in their blankets amidst the freight containers.

"I'm gonna hit the mess," Orion said. "See if there's something to eat that's not noodles. Coming?"

"Nah, I'll stay here. I think we're going to make landfall soon."

"You're lucky," Orion said absently. "You can eat all the shit they serve."

"The fuck is that supposed to mean?" He'd really begun to get on her nerves. Most days, she thought about throwing him overboard at least once.

Her weapons systems officer stood there with that stupid fucking grin, wearing the reflective orange uniform that the cargo crew had offered them when they'd fished them out the Pacific. It looked ridiculous. He looked ridiculous. And the blue hardhat that he insisted on wearing made it even worse.

Kelly didn't care what she smelled like; she wasn't going to abandon her flight suit with her squadron insignia unless someone pointed a gun at her. Maybe not even then. She was a Black Ace fighter pilot, and if she had to stink like a spaniel in a skunk fight to show it, well, some things were worth smelling for.

"Which do you like better?" Orion laughed, trying hard to get her goat. "The ramen, the rice, or the raw fish?"

"I'm from Georgia, ass rod. I like grits and collard greens cooked in bacon fat." She balled her fist, daring him to continue.

Orion swallowed with a dry-mouthed gulp. He'd been on the receiving end of her fist more than once this voyage.

Kelly showed him her back and observed the eastward sea and the way the sunset changed its hue. But the calm that she usually felt watching the ocean eluded her. Could she have been stuck on a ship with anyone more annoying than this dicksock?

The only thing worse than confinement with Orion was her complete lack of contact with the outside world. The radio onboard the *Yodohashi* wasn't working, for some fucked-up reason. Which meant she couldn't call in her status to the Jerry, which meant she was absent without leave. AWOL. They would think she was dead. And, since it had been days of sailing east across the Pacific Ocean, there'd been more than enough time for the Navy to deliver the news to her parents. Hell, they'd probably already started planning a funeral in Duluth.

The other technical malfunction, beyond the radio, was the GPS. It was shot, as far as she could tell. And every time she peeked into the bridge, she saw the captain and first mate with a humongous map spread across the table. She couldn't be sure, but she thought they might be charting their way by the sun and stars.

It was a hell of a way to sail, but the captain seemed to know what he was doing. He was a grizzled old mariner on a cargo ship that had been built well before Kelly was born, and seemed as likely as anyone to be able to chart his way across the Pacific.

"Hey," Orion said. "What did you cluck about earlier? About making landfall soon?"

"That's about the sum of it," she said, her back still toward him. If she saw his face right now she might put her boot through it. "Should be in the next couple hours."

"Says who? You suddenly learn to speak Japanese?"

"I don't need a translator for basic math." Her temper flared again. "We've been holding steady at twenty-five knots, day and night. And the captain said Portland—"

"The captain?" Orion sputtered. "The Old Man of the Sea said a whole bunch of gibberish and you heard what you wanted to hear."

"Well, I fucking heard Portland, Oregon." She gripped the rail tight enough to whiten her knuckles. "And anyway," she continued, trying to regain her calm, "they have a deep-draft container port in Portland. One of only five on the West Coast. Makes sense we'd be going there."

"When did you become the fucking expert on container ports?" It almost seemed like he'd put in extra effort to making his ordinarily insufferable voice an extra level of obnoxious.

"My mom brings in combines and tillage equipment from overseas for the family business—"

"Whatever." He slumped forward on the railing. "At the rate this rusty scuttle is going, we'll die before we see land." Despite his obstinacy, Kelly could see that he was paying more attention to the horizon, squinting into the distance.

"Yeah, well, twenty-five knots isn't so bad for an old ship like this. If I've calculated right, we'll end this long-ass trip real soon. A couple hours or less, I'm pretty sure."

"I'm pretty sure you're full of shit," he shot back. "Are you telling me you know, by memory, the distance from where this cargo ship picked us up and some random US commercial port?"

She could feel her face getting red, but she shoved her hands into the pockets of her flight suit so she wouldn't punch him again. He seemed to have forgotten what the last one felt like. "Well, I have a pretty goddammed good idea. Didn't they teach you a fucking thing at Nugget University?"

"Nugget University? That's fucking *it*. You're dead."

She pulled her hands out of her pockets, ready for whatever weak-ass attack he could throw at her. They faced off. Kelly was sure it would be a fight. *Well, he'd better start liking miso soup, because he'll never chew a steak again.*

She put up her fists.

Orion crouched, preparing to tackle her.

"*Ohayōgozaimasu, kaigun shikan.*"

They both spun. The greeting was coming from aft, between the rows of man-height shipping containers. Captain Nakata emerged, dressed in the same orange uniform and blue hardhat as his crew.

"Good morning, Captain," Kelly said, trying to imitate the bow she'd seen the other crew members give him. He deserved that respect. If it weren't for him, she'd still be floating in the open ocean.

Orion just stood there, not even managing a military salute. He leaned against the rail doing his best impression of a meatloaf sandwich, clearly unimpressed by a civilian captain.

The captain nodded politely to both of them, and then pointed past the bow into the shrinking light, out to sea. "*Anata ga* kiri *o mite imasu ka?*"

Kelly shook her head. "I don't understand."

Orion just snorted.

"*Kiri, kiri,*" the captain said, pointing again out to sea.

She shook her head again.

The captain bowed, clearly knowing he'd not been understood. "*Sayōnara, kaigun shikan.*" He took his leave back toward the bridge.

She followed the direction where the captain had pointed. There had to be some *kiri* beyond the bow. She strained her neck.

"Something's out there." She squinted against the rising darkness, at the blurring along the edge of the horizon. "Sonofabitch, you seein' that?"

Orion leaned out toward the bow. "Not a damn thing but the same fucking view we've had for a hundred hours. Sea and sky. Enough to

108

make a man shit himself."

"Shit yourself all you want," Kelly said, rubbing the back of her neck with one hand. "But I'm telling you, if you look out far enough you'll see what the captain was talking about. Fog. There's fog and we're heading into it."

Orion's face fell. "Fog. Jesus, I hate fog. Now I'm definitely going to the mess."

"Go if you want. But—not that I expect you to remember this from the million-dollar military education you slept through—I'm pretty sure that's *advection fog.*"

The Navy devoted considerable resources to ensuring its pilots knew as much as possible about weather systems. Everything from the derechos that can accompany a thunderstorm, to the downdrafts from a squall line, to the telltale signs that auger a haboob. She knew it all. And the knowledge had saved her life and her plane on more than one occasion. "Weren't you ever paying attention?"

Orion rolled his eyes. "Yeah, I guess I might have skimmed the book on *bullshit things I never need to know.* But I learned one thing: you can't see your dick in your hand when it's foggy."

"Look, Beetlejuice," she said, using his call sign as a sort of truce. "I'm not going to lecture you on your dick or your hand. But do pay attention once in a while. That fog out there means there may be land ahead." She paused for effect. "But, sure, go below if you want."

For once, Orion didn't seem to have anything to say. He looked at her, then back at the horizon. Frowning, he leaned forward against the rail. He must have decided it would be worthwhile to see land after so many days at sea, despite the fog, because he stayed where he was.

An hour later they were in the thick of it.

The fog approached slowly, then all at once. One minute it spread across the horizon, filling a fraction of their field of view. And then, suddenly, it was all they could see.

The cargo ship sliced into it, fog on every side so thick Kelly might have been in the middle of a loaf of bread. The minutes passed in silence. It wasn't even possible to see if they were moving. All she knew was the dampness across her face and the presence of the ship. There was nothing else in the world.

The fog began to lessen. She could see the water at the bow. A minute later her world expanded again—maybe as far as a couple hundred feet and no more.

"It's dissipating," she said to no one in particular.

"How far does the fog go from the shore?" Orion asked, now that the silence was broken.

She shook her head. "No idea."

Orion pulled in his chin and lowered his brows. "So, we could pretty much slam into the shore at any time right?"

"There are lighthouses. Plus, Captain Nakata knows what he's doing." She hoped he did, anyway.

"C'mon, Moonshot. You've been with the Navy a hell of a lot longer than me—"

"No shit—"

"And even I know we're going to get ourselves shipwrecked by this civilian captain with his slide-rule—"

"It's a sextant."

Orion continued. "Shipwrecked on this grand-pappy junkboat without GPS or a working radio—"

"I get it." She was starting to see his point on the hazards of the situation.

"—in the fog, past sundown—"

"I said, *I get it!*"

"Just sayin'. If we're as close to the shore as you think, maybe it's time to drop anchor and wait until the ovation fog passes."

"Advection fog," she corrected him. *He's not wrong.* She'd always had an innate distrust of hierarchy, whether with the Navy, or her school years, or back as a kid when her mom used to make her cold-call farmers for tractor parts.

"You know I'm right," Orion continued.

"Yeah, shut up. I know you are."

"God damn. There's a first time for everything." He did a little hornpipe on the deck, grinning like a nugget piss-drunk on shore leave.

"Even when you're right, you're an annoying shit. Shut up and let's think about how to voice this up the chain of command." Their situation *was* dangerous. Fog and nighttime sailing had caused more than one shipwreck. Hopefully they'd be able to see the lighthouses before it was too late.

"I love being right."

She was about to slap him just to shut him up when she saw something. "Holy shit!" She grabbed Orion's collar and pointed straight ahead, across the bow.

Orion's jaw dropped as he let out a slow, "Fuuuuuuck."

A shape materialized out of the fog. A dark patch. Or, rather, many dark patches. What might have been a hundred reef rocks in the distance. Dark and hazy, just barely visible.

"Are those … is that the …?"

Up in the bridge, whoever was steering the ship—the pilot, Kelly supposed—must have seen the dark shapes, too. With a heavy *thu-thutt*, the ship's main engine switched off. Without any more warning than that, the pilot put the helm hard to starboard—a maneuver something like a hockey player pivoting sharply and sending a spray of ice into the air.

Except with the ship, the yaw was slower. Much slower. There was no way to instantly stop a 200,000-ton container ship.

"We're going to hit," Orion screamed as he and Kelly rushed to the starboard side of the bow.

The ship was tilting slightly as it circled, causing Kelly to lose her footing. She stumbled and fell. And when she regained her footing, she saw they were still moving toward the black, jagged shapes outlined in the fog.

"We're slowing," Kelly shouted to Orion over the sound of the engine shifting to full astern. The entire ship rattled. They were gliding toward the shapes more slowly now, but would it be enough?

"Jesus, the rocks! We're going to hit them," Orion squealed. "We need life vests."

"Those aren't rocks," Kelly said. The shapes were coming closer just as the fog was dissipating, a combination that allowed her to see more clearly. She gasped, her mind working in overdrive to compute what she was seeing. Ships. A hundred ships in the fog.

The *Yodohashi* was slowing rapidly, but they were gliding inevitably toward the armada in front of them. Cruisers, destroyers, transport docks, frigates, and countless landing ships. All clearer by the second. And closer; perilously close. Close enough to see the flags and markings on the fleet. The yellow star on a field of red for China. The blue cross of the Russian navy.

"Not rocks at all," she said, just over a whisper. "We're seeing what our radar sweep picked up four days ago. The invasion force of our enemy. And they've already landed."

20

Xandra flipped on the shortwave radio, hoping she could finally get it to work. She hadn't heard from the Coast Guard in Oregon or Cyber Command since they'd left—two days ago. But she was optimistic that this evening might be different. At dusk, changes in the earth's ionosphere allowed higher frequencies to travel farther.

She held the longwire antenna over her head that would allow her to broadcast her voice, and she scanned through the channels Admiral Kalb had written down. "Hello?" She put the microphone to her mouth. "Anyone?"

Still nothing.

"Worthless," she muttered, throwing the radio back into her bag and glowering out the window.

They were flying over the middle of nowhere. Not nowhere, exactly. But the closest thing to it. Nebraska. Somewhere west of Broken Bow, if Lorenzo was reading the chart right.

Xandra would have thought the pilot could be more specific, given he was the one entrusted with shuttling her safely across the country. Apparently not. It had been difficult for him to get his bearings, even in the daylight. And now they were pointed into the setting sun, he seemed to have almost no idea where they were.

"I'm going to put us down," he shouted from the cockpit.

She squinted into the fading daylight. Below, the fields whizzed by, muddy and cold, as unbearable as everything else they'd flown over for the last day and a half. She was tired of the dirt and the small towns. Tired of the local population's fear she witnessed at every landing spot. Tired of beef jerky and pretzels, and the pain in her feet, and the smell of engine oil and unleaded gas. Tired of her own stink and the suit she'd been wearing since that first meeting in the Pentagon.

"Can't we go a little farther?" she asked.

More than anything, she was tired of failure. The milspec computer lay open on her lap, hundreds of files, millions of lines of code. The quantity of it was daunting. And so far, despite going through more than half of the extra batteries, she'd learned nothing of any use.

Certainly, after hours of running through the enemy's executable commands, database triggers, and malicious functions, she now had an idea of what some of the files were meant to accomplish. The file in front of her at the moment had been designed to target America's chemical sector. Specifically, the toxic release of pesticides from a New England manufacturing plant. Another file included code inserted into a wastewater treatment facility. And yet another targeted hospitals. There were thousands of files, more than she could analyze in a year.

Where had it even originated from? The digital fingerprints she recognized made her wonder if it hadn't been launched by a single enemy as everyone seemed to think, but by several. Markers abounded in Arabic, Cyrillic, simplified Chinese, and even Korean. Perhaps the cyber attacks were the product of many nation states, working in tandem, hard as that was to believe.

She bit her lip, frustrated by her failure. No vulnerabilities in the enemy code presented themselves. And, worst of all, she'd audited the code written by US Cyber Command to take out Russian power grids or Chinese banking. And it was hopelessly outdated. The enemy that had taken down so much of America's critical infrastructure possessed significantly more sophisticated cyber weapons.

The Cessna flew fourteen-hundred miles from the Oregon Coast—about halfway there—and she hadn't achieved anything. If there really was an invasion in the Pacific, she could do nothing to stop it.

That was the other problem: the slothful pace of their transcontinental flight. Delay after delay had kept them from moving faster. The reason came down to refueling. Flying was fast enough, but fuel was hard to come by, siphoned from the underground storage tanks below gas stations. Most of the time they struck out, or were chased off, or couldn't even break the manhole cover that separated them from their prize. And when they did manage to get through, often the hose wasn't long enough to siphon more than a half-dozen gallons—when there was even any gas in the storage tank.

"It'll be dark soon. Can't fly at night," Lorenzo said.

Yet another problem. She couldn't argue with the need to stay grounded at night, as much as she wanted to. As much as she wanted to scream at him that they weren't going fast enough, that she was failing in her mission. There was no use arguing because he was right. Even with the moonlight it was hard to tell sky from earth. They might slam into a tree or the side of a mountain. Navigating at night would be impossible. Landing could be deadly.

So she continued to plow through the code, searching for something, anything, that would help her unravel the hundreds of individual infrastructure attacks. But, as always, she saw nothing.

Giving up for the moment, she pressed her cheek against the window as they straightened over a highway and eased in for a landing. Below, there were no cars on this part of the road. She'd found that to be true almost everywhere—few vehicles in most stretches, and elsewhere traffic jams that went on for miles. The bigger the city, the worse the snarls.

"There's a gas station," Carmen said, pointing out the front of the plane. "Put down here, Pop."

In front, a lonely Whoa & Go sprang out from the sunset. Lorenzo brought the Cessna down for a landing as quickly as he could, overshooting the gas station by about a quarter of a mile.

"That's close enough, Pop," Carmen said as they came to a stop. "I'll grab the pump, you get everything else, okay?"

In no time, they were out of the plane and onto the highway, bringing along the tools for fuel extraction. Carmen had built a hand-pump that she was especially proud of, made from PVC pipe, O rings, caps, and plugs. Lorenzo carried the hose, fuel can, and crowbar. Xandra didn't carry anything, which she considered fair. As the passenger, she could take the opportunity to stretch her legs.

The evening breeze blew cold, and their breath escaped like the last wisps of a fire extinguisher. Lorenzo and Carmen raced forward, no doubt hoping to begin before the light was completely gone. Xandra clomped behind them in her heels. She tried to keep up, but her feet ached, and she fell farther and farther behind.

"How long can we keep doing this?" Carmen asked, well ahead.

Lorenzo ran a nervous hand through his black mane. His shadow stretched in front of him as tall as three men. "The gas? It's been working so far."

"You know it'll ruin your gaskets, Pop. And there's always the possibility of vapor lock. We should be using 100LL, not auto gas."

Xandra only heard parts of what Lorenzo was saying now. "... less octane and is designed for low altitudes. But it's cold out, and we're not flying too high ... Premium if you can."

Xandra stopped trying to keep up. Even though they hadn't been walking much over the past two days, her feet were killing her. Why had she decided on heels for that meeting with the admiral? When she taught at MIT she always wore something more sensible, black loafers or wedge sandals.

Pulling off a shoe, Xandra rubbed her bare foot. A red welt had formed along her tendon, the beginnings of a blister. The other foot was no different.

"I need a new pair," she said to herself, dropping the heels onto the pavement. She'd rather go barefoot than spend another minute in those things.

The quarter-mile walk to the gas station took longer than she'd have liked, tiptoeing over gravel and bits of broken glass she normally wouldn't even have noticed. By the time she arrived, the sun had set and only a white afterglow remained. Carmen was kneeling over a pried manhole cover while siphoning fuel into a six-gallon can. Lorenzo stood next to her, directing the flow of gas into the canister.

"We've got a lot here," he said to Xandra as she approached. "Might be able to fill up the tank halfway." His gaze dropped to her feet. "What happened to you?"

"The shoes were unsatisfactory. I'm going to procure a new pair."

Carmen peered up at her like she was crazy, but Xandra paid the girl no mind. Many people glanced at her sideways. Singled her out as the odd one. She'd gotten that look since grade school. It was as if no one ever stopped to think that maybe they were the strange ones. They were the ones who cried when their pet birds died, or fought over petty insults. They laughed even when a joke wasn't funny, or blushed at a compliment, or sobbed in a movie theater.

Other people behaved unpredictably—not her. She was calm, rational. And if she decided her shoes no longer fit her situation, why was it so odd to jettison them along the wayside?

But Carmen had stopped staring, and Lorenzo just shrugged and handed her the crowbar he'd used to pry open the manhole. "You could take a look in the store," he said, nodding toward the Whoa & Go. "Get us some food while you're at it."

Now *that* was a reasonable reaction to their situation. Much better. She thanked him and took it. At this point, it would be illogical *not* to break into a store for much-needed dry goods. If she was willing to smash a vending machine in the Pentagon, a Whoa & Go out in nowhere wouldn't be any harder.

Holding the crowbar in front of her, she tiptoed carefully across the pavement to the little concrete building. Face to the glass door, she squinted. It was hard to see much in the darkness. There might be shoes in there.

Holding the crowbar like a bat, she swung.

The glass broke easily. In the stillness, the noise echoed across the fields and highway, the only sound for miles except for wind over fallow fields. The shattering rung in her ears, and then all fell quiet. There was no alarm, of course—four days without power. And even if there had been, no police would come. No law in four days, either.

The only trouble came from her bare feet. Glass had scattered across the inside of the darkened shop, too sharp to wade through. She thought about jumping over, but the shards had spread in an arc twice as far as she could leap. It had been premature to throw away her heels.

Xandra sighed at the glass strewn over the floor. For some reason, this little obstacle made her feel defeated. More than the hunger in her belly, or her stink, or being trapped for days with the pilot and his child. More, even, than the delay in reaching the coast. It was as if the glass represented all of her problems. She needed shoes, but to get them she needed to get into the store. To get into the store, she needed shoes.

She lifted her face to the stars. Since the lights had gone off, she'd seen more stars than at any other time in her life. A sextillion points of light fell down upon her. Until now, she had ignored starlight altogether. And it was actually kind of beautiful.

Even now, surrounded by a primitive darkness, Xandra had trouble imagining the totality of civilization's dissolution. What was it like on other continents? Had the United States managed to retaliate? Had darkness spread across Asia and the Middle East? Perhaps she would learn when the systems came back online. If they ever did.

"Whatchu doin' here, miss?"

She spun and came face to face with a bearded man, half hidden in the darkness.

"I'll ask you again. Whatchu doin' in front of my store?" A shotgun held low and pointed away told her he expected an answer.

Behind her, the shattered door told the story. It should be obvious what she was doing here. But she supposed he wanted details.

"I was hungry."

He sized her up, from her bare feet to her dirty suit jacket. She had no idea what he must have thought of her, but all he said was, "You ain't from around here, are you." It wasn't a question.

"Look," Xandra said, gently laying the crowbar on the ground. "I'm just trying to get something to eat."

She could smell him better than she could see him. He reeked of alcohol as he lurched nearer. Unshaven. A Cornhuskers cap and denim overalls. "Now, see here. I don't know where you're from but around here folk don't take what's not theirs." He raised the shotgun to his shoulder, unsteady. Visibly drunk. "Makin' a citizen's arrest. We'll see what sheriff has to say."

Xandra's mouth had gone completely dry. Her knees and hands shook. No one had ever pointed a gun at her.

But one thing she knew without a doubt was that she wasn't going anywhere with this man.

"Come on," he said, a little wave of the shotgun to speed her on the way.

That's when she bolted.

It was a gamble. The store owner wouldn't shoot her in the back, would he? She had some notions of conduct among rural men, and she was pretty sure that while she had failed at playing the damsel in distress, he wouldn't take that shot.

The pump of the shotgun as he chambered a round. The click of the safety as it switched off. She was wrong; he was going to shoot her.

"Unreliable damned piece of jammed shit shotgun," he shouted.

Still running, she heard him pull the action release and eject the jammed round. The slug rattled onto the concrete. "Dammit, you come back here!"

Barefoot, she sprinted toward the gas station, indifferent to the gravel and splinters on the way. "Lorenzo!" she said with a hiss. "Carmen!" She peered around the fuel dispensers and pay stations. They weren't here.

Behind, she heard the man pump another round into the chamber. "Don't take another step."

She ran, faster now, as fast as her legs would move. Through the parking lot and onto the highway. Boot-steps pounded behind her, giving chase.

The moon and stars helped her along as she raced the quarter mile to the plane. How many minutes it took to reach the plane, she didn't know. It felt like seconds.

Breathing hard, she jerked to a sudden stop in front of the Cessna.

"Xandra?" Carmen said. "You startled me." The girl was pouring gasoline into the tank opening at the side of the plane.

"We need to go!" Xandra shouted. She knew she sounded hysterical. That couldn't be helped. She grabbed the fuel can out of Carmen's hands and shoved the girl toward the plane. "We're leaving now! Where's your father?"

"He's inside," Carmen said, crying out at the rough treatment.

Lorenzo was sitting at the controls when she pulled herself through the door after Carmen. "What's the fuss?" he said. Then his eyes fell on his daughter. Putting a gentle hand on her cheek, he brushed away a strand of hair. "Why are you crying?"

Xandra watched the accusation escalate across his face. A fatherly ferocity; the first time she'd seen a storm in his eyes.

"We've got to go. He's right behind me," she said. They didn't have time for his paternal instincts. "Now!"

"What's she talking about?" Lorenzo asked his daughter. Then back to Xandra, growling. "Who's behind you?"

Xandra reached over to close the door to the fuselage. "The store owner."

"I don't think—" began Lorenzo. But he was interrupted by a blast. Shotgun pellets peppered the plane, the metallic song of a hundred tiny balls smashing into the side.

The three of them gasped.

And all at once they were in absolute agreement.

"Hold on," Lorenzo shouted, louder than he needed to. The gunfire had stopped. "We're taking off."

Not bothering to buckle in, he slammed the key into the ignition and twisted.

And nothing happened.

From the window, Xandra watched the store owner, teetering drunkenly.

Lorenzo tried the key again. The engine sputtered like a dry cough. "Come on," he urged it. "You can do this." The engine made a ticking noise. *Tick, tick, tick, tick.*

"You're going to flood it," Carmen said, face red but voice calm.

The store owner loaded another shell into the shotgun. Stumbling, he raised the gun again and fired toward the front windshield. A dozen tiny spider webs of glass formed, but the windshield held.

Lorenzo turned the key. A soft oscillation and the engine turned over, bellowed, and came alive. The propeller spun. They taxied forward.

"He shot my window!" Lorenzo said.

They were moving slowly down the highway now. They were going to make it.

The far fuselage door opened.

A Cornhuskers cap poked up, followed by the face of the store owner. Faster than Xandra would have thought possible, the man pulled himself higher, one hand on the lip of the entrance, the other holding the gun. He was almost inside the cabin.

The Cessna was gaining speed quickly. In another few seconds, they'd be going fast enough to take off.

Xandra kicked at the store owner, but he grabbed her bare foot. "No one outruns the law, lady." He yanked at her leg, strong, meaty fingers trying to wrench her out of the plane.

She threw herself backwards. But the store owner held on and hoisted himself on top of her. They wrestled for a moment, though Xandra didn't have much fight in her.

He punched her across the face.

The blow came so hard, so unexpectedly, that Xandra saw pinpricks of light. She stopped hearing any noises but the buzz of her own skull. And when she shook herself back, she saw Carmen standing over her, fighting the man with all her strength. The blows of the thirteen-year-old couldn't have been much, but the store owner had turned all his attention to the girl.

"Take it up, Pop," Carmen shouted.

Xandra shook her head. Some of the stars faded.

The store owner swatted Carmen with a beefy paw, hard, knocking her backward. The girl tumbled into the seat behind her, rolling across the floor. Then she stood, slapped her palm against the cabin wall, and screamed. Rage traced every angle of her face. Ears pink. Nose dripping blood.

The Cessna lifted off the ground. Xandra could feel the ascension of wheels lifting off the highway. It felt like an elevator moving up, but faster, and through darkness.

Carmen was still screaming when she threw herself at the man. She ran into him with such force that she knocked both him and herself out of the open door. Both man and girl tumbled into the night, just seconds after the Cessna's nose wheel lifted off the ground.

"Carmen!" Xandra scrambled to the door.

Down below, she watched as the store owner fell, thirty feet at least. His body hit the highway, bounced, and disappeared behind them as they ascended. No one could survive that fall.

But Carmen was still holding on to the lip of the cabin. "Help!" she screamed, hands clutching the edge, legs kicking into the open air.

Xandra grabbed Carmen by the elbows and hauled her into the interior of the plane. She was crying, of course. But unhurt.

"Thank you," Carmen said, between sobs, prone on the floor.

Xandra stretched toward her, fingers almost reaching the girl. But she couldn't quite bring herself to touch the child. "You're alive," she managed. It was more than she could say for the store owner.

21

Kelly stood next to Orion at the bow of the *Yodohashi*. Waves slapped the side of the ship, *whap-whapping* in an off-beat rhythm. Other than the wash of water, the night was still. Eerily so.

Fog and darkness enveloped them. She pressed her back against a wall of shipping containers stacked three high. The corrugated metal seemed the only solid thing in the whole world.

Across the bow, the night revealed little and the fog less. There was no lighthouse to cast its light. No stars above, or moon. Only the beam from the cargo ship's searchlight, mounted on the bridge castle, revealed what lay in front.

Ahead, and behind, and all around, was an armada.

From north to south, the ships filled the nearshore. There were guided missile cruisers, recognizable by their long, thin hulls and the full armament of surface-to-air missiles, torpedo tubes, and anti-ship missiles. There were smaller destroyers, specialized in finding and sinking submarines. There were Corvettes, with a shorter range that usually meant they never left their own coastal waters. And, though it was far behind them now, Kelly had spotted an aircraft carrier before the sun had set in the west. The Liaoning—unless she missed her guess—a Soviet-built, Chinese vessel that could launch thirty-six fixed-wing and rotary aircraft into the skies.

And then there were the landing craft. *Serna*-class, *Dyugon*-class, *Ondatra*-class, *Yuzhao*-class, and more. Before darkness had obscured the coastline, she'd seen them in neat rows on the beach, like so many dump truck beds. Those craft had brought soldiers.

But, more than anything, Kelly had seen amphibious warfare ships—

amphibs, the Navy called them. They had one main purpose: to support ground forces during an amphibious assault. Directly astern, outlined by the searchlight, sailed an *Ivan Gren*-class vessel. That thing, Kelly remembered, could carry thirteen battle tanks.

The *Yodohashi* sailed slowly north, carefully, fearfully. Engine power was cut to keep them quiet, and the only other mark they made on the ocean as they passed through was the sweep of the searchlight, just enough for the captain and pilot to navigate through the ships and away from here.

"Why aren't they firing on us?" Orion asked.

Kelly shushed him. He asked the right question, of course, but he needed to keep his mouth shut. Not only did they need to move quietly, but every damn Navy man should know not to question Lady Luck out loud if he could help it.

"It's the flag," Orion said, answering his own question.

Kelly let out a low whistle when she spotted what Orion was pointing at. Up the mast fluttered the green, white, and red tricolor of Iran. The captain had swapped out the Japanese flag.

"Do you think it will work?" Orion whispered.

Kelly didn't know. The fog blew thick enough to make seeing difficult. But there was no hiding a cargo ship of 30,000 deadweight tons floating like a turd in the head beside these ships of war. If anything, the Iranian flag would only give them short pause before they saw the Japanese markings on her side.

And when that happened it wouldn't be long before a boarding party stormed the *Yodohashi*. Or sunk her.

Kelly watched, breath held in, as the cargo ship completed its turn away from the closest battlecruiser. It was *Kirov*-class, one of the heaviest surface combatant warships anywhere in the world. The vessel had—among a host of other armaments—a six-barreled Gatling gun, which could direct a maelstrom of fire across their bow if it so chose. But the ship made no move to sink them as they drifted away.

"How could this happen?" Orion said, red face visible even in the mounting darkness. "How could they be here? On our shore?"

Kelly just shook her head.

They stood in silence at the bow as the cargo ship dipped and rolled in the chop near shore. It wasn't safe to sail this close to the beach, but Kelly didn't care anymore. If they sunk here she'd swim ashore. All she could think about was finding a plane and raining brimstone down on the invaders.

Seconds became minutes, then more minutes, and still the *Yodohashi* floated slowly up the coast, without interference. The ships grew sparser, then disappeared behind them. It didn't seem possible that the flag had fooled them.

The only explanation Kelly could think of was confusion. The US Navy befuddled itself with simple operations, taking damage in shipping lanes, colliding with oil tankers in peace time. Compared to that, a multi-nation invasion must be difficult. And perhaps the ships had run into communication challenges that kept them from hailing the ersatz Iranian vessel. Maybe their radios and GPS weren't working well either.

Behind her, Kelly heard the flag of Iran snap as the wind picked up. Fog licked across the water. The tide rolled up the sand. And soon it was just them cruising beside an empty beach, the armada behind.

Hours later, when the *Yodohashi* finally entered the mouth of the Columbia River, Kelly let out a breath. She was shaking. But they'd made safe passage and she was back in her homeland.

She couldn't help but wonder, though, if this was still her homeland. Or maybe an occupied America.

22

"Please!" the woman sobbed under the beam of the flashlight. Not for the first time, Sierra Eigelb paused to consider her situation. The scenario that was playing out had done so a dozen times since the lights went dark. And, surely, in the history of the world, it had played out thousands of times. Hundreds of thousands of times.

It was a struggle of life and death. Where she was both life and the bringer of death. Where she was the strong and at her feet squirmed the weak.

"Please," the woman said again. Sierra ignored her.

There was the question of morality. Ethics. Norms of behavior. Sierra had never held fast to any ethical code. In fact, if anything, she'd always felt that her code was really just a lack of code. Working in retail at a clothing boutique hadn't required any kind of moral compass. Just smile and ring up the customer. Tell them that shirt really shows off their curves. Cute. Maybe just try a size up.

In the old world—the world that existed up until five days ago—her lack of code kept her free from bullshit like church or political affiliation. But in the new world, a province of real freedom from authority and institutions, her knowledge that there was no objective morality became a superpower. It's what separated her from this woman at her feet.

The bitch sobbed again, clutching the body of the man who was presently bleeding out on the kitchen floor. Sierra sneered at the children, shaking beside their mother. And then she laughed, a low cachinnation. Loud. Concussive. Why hide her exhilaration?

The first time Sierra had killed a man, she hadn't been able to suppress her giggles, her euphoria. It was as if her whole life had been leading up to that moment when she pulled the trigger, not at a target—which she had done countless times—but at another human. And then another. And another.

The elation had consumed her. A new drug. An aphrodisiac. The opening of a portal in her mind she'd never known existed. So she had continued. And each time she hoped, increasingly, that the lights would never turn back on.

In the first hours after the cyber attacks she'd wandered aimlessly through the streets. Everyone else had been so panicked, so afraid. She'd meandered the boulevards and observed the fistfights, the mobs of people trying to get home. Then, as the days wore on, she'd seen the population of the city dwindle when residents could no longer flush their toilets or heat their homes or get water from the tap. She'd seen the ones who stayed, suffering, stealing from each other. She'd seen them board their windows and lock their doors.

And none of that had kept her out.

The first time she'd killed a man it had been in self-defense. A would-be rapist. The first night of the blackout. Then she'd killed for food and water. Then a warm place to sleep. And then, around the third or fourth night, when she had all the water she could drink, all the canned pears she could stomach, and a choice between any number of homes that she'd emptied to lay her head, she'd kept on killing.

Now she'd established three safe houses in three different neighborhoods, all spray painted with warnings across the door. Each house contained a stash of food and water, gasoline, and other useful odds and ends. It was the perfect setup. She could prowl the neighborhood, taking whatever liberties she liked, and return to whichever home suited her best.

She hoped the phones all stayed off forever, and the police continued to hole up wherever it was they'd slunk off to. Sierra had learned that in darkness she could get away with anything.

"Please!" The woman no longer draped herself over the man. He was a lost cause. Instead, she scooped up her brats in a sort of protective embrace.

The woman's blubbering snapped Sierra back to the present. That had been happening more and more, her mind floating after a kill. She liked the floating, the drifting, the chemical surge of hormones and endorphins, like the relaxation after sex.

"Take the food. Take anything you want," the woman cried. There were three children, a girl and two boys, all of them too young to survive on the streets. A pity, really, that they'd have to try. Sierra wasn't going to kill a child. That was a code of sorts, she supposed.

The weeping whore glanced furtively at the body on the floor. The husband had blubbered more than the wife, which was why she'd killed him first. That, and because he'd reminded her of her own first husband. That bastard had been a bawler, too.

"Tell the kids to leave," Sierra said to the woman, motioning toward the door with the flashlight. They were the first words she'd spoken to any of them.

The children ran out of the kitchen and into the street. Sierra didn't watch them go. The oldest was maybe ten. Not old enough to make it out there, but such was life. Such was death.

Now she was alone with the slut. It would've been perfect, except for the howling and blubbing. The woman was on her hands and knees, face pointed at the Marmoleum flooring, drool falling in a stream from both corners of her mouth. Pathetic.

"Let me go," she pleaded, between hiccups. "I won't say a word. I won't tell anyone about this."

Sad, what people would say before they died. "You know what I've observed?" Sierra asked, but not waiting for an answer. "I've observed a sort of dichotomy over the last five days." She walked in a semicircle, SIG Sauer loose in her hand, no longer pointed at the pathetic hussy. "There are two reasons why people have stayed in the city. Either they're strong—like me—and thrive in the new order. Or they're too feeble to flee. Too incompetent, or stupid. That's the second group. The weak ones who stayed."

She clicked her tongue at the woman—the mother, the wife—in a pool of her husband's blood. More blood would stain Sierra's furs and yellow dress. She couldn't bring herself to care. A little blood on her clothes might add to her reputation. "Which are you? The weak who stayed or the strong who will thrive? I have a guess, but why don't you tell me?"

The bitch didn't reply, just kept moaning on the floor. Contemptible. She reminded Sierra of her oldest sister, Donna. Donna was weak. Living in Nevada with her brood of children, letting some man tell her when to wash dishes and fold clothes. Yes, this woman was definitely a Donna.

"I think you know the answer," Sierra continued. "There's a new world order forming, and you're not part of it, Donna. You're all alone."

"My ... my name's not ... I'm Meredith." Spit flew from the woman's mouth, tendrils of drool connecting her top and bottom lips.

"You're either part of the new order, or you're a loner, an outcast. A bandit, Donna."

The woman sobbed. "I'm not who you think. My name is Meredith. I don't know any Donna. Please, let me go!"

The sobbing was starting to get out of hand. Sierra would have to end it.

"Donna, I'm going to kill you now," she said, lifting the SIG Sauer and lining up the sights on the woman's temple.

She reminded Sierra so much of her oldest sister. Donna should die badly.

"Please, I have children." An unbroken stream of drool formed a bridge between the Marmoleum and her mouth.

"Donna, Donna, Donna. Your children are just as safe as they can be," she lied.

And then she pulled the trigger.

Her weapon recoiled in a slight kickback. Heat flooded her, a sexual warmth. She closed her eyes and breathed deeply through her nose, head tilted slightly back, lips parted at the joy of it.

But her bliss didn't last.

A noise in the kitchen spun her around, searching through the darkness with the beam of her flashlight. Boots clomped on floorboards, a shoulder pressed through a doorway. Someone else was in the house.

Sierra raised her pistol and cursed herself. She should have heard the intruders coming into her kill spot. She shouldn't have let herself get carried away by the nirvana of death. It was stupid. It might even cost her life.

But what she saw across the kitchen wasn't what she'd expected. A man's face. Blue eyes like the taiga, close-cropped white hair like a tundra. Strong, heavily muscled. Beautiful.

He didn't blink, nor did he reposition the Grach semi-automatic pistol from where it was pointed at her breast.

"I ... I was ..." Sierra stammered, terribly aware of the dead man and woman spread before her, the backsplash of their blood on her yellow dress. On the floor. On the kitchen wall.

She had seen a lynching yesterday. A man kicked and punched in a mall parking lot, then dragged to a tree where he was hanged. No one seemed to know what he'd done, why he'd been killed. But that hadn't mattered to Sierra. She had stayed awhile, after nearly everyone else had gone. Stayed to see the face turn purple and the tongue turn black.

Now it would be her turn to hang.

Sierra lowered her gun, but didn't drop it. "They had to die," she offered. It was weak.

The man stayed silent. That blue-eyed stare appraised her, cautious, curious. She'd have expected anger, or revulsion at the very least. Any man who came upon a red-handed murder might feel these things.

"The woman stole from me."

Could she run? The kitchen exited into a backyard. She could make a break for the rear door and hope the man couldn't shoot a moving target in the night.

Before she could decide what to do, two more men walked into the room. They wore identical black clothing, tight fitting, almost like uniforms. Their clothes weren't the only matching things about them. They wore their hair close-cropped, and shared unflinching stares.

The white-haired man studied her so deeply she felt herself melt. Then he ran his eyes over the bodies, judging her and the kills. Impassive, emotionless.

"Let me join you," Sierra said, forcing a confidence she didn't feel. "You're a killer like me, I can sense it. We could be a team. I can help you."

For a moment, the only sound was the after-ache of her voice in a kitchen that felt both very full and very empty. Then, the white-haired man spoke in a guttural, heavily-accented rumble. "You may join us. We are looking for chaos."

He told her what she must do to be part of them. He told her of the invasion. Of the death they'd already unleashed as forerunners of the attack. Of the force that was coming behind them. And, best of all, he told her how she could live if she became part of it.

At first, she was horrified by what they proposed. But there was another part of her that listened and smiled, aroused by the audacity of the plan. It was that part of her that said, "Yes. I'll do it."

She held up a blood-dotted hand as a sort of pledge and swore herself to him and his army. The hand that she raised to the ceiling was about to do a lot more killing. This wasn't just murder. It was killing on a grand scale.

Everything had changed. For the better. A new era of freedom had started for her now that the Russian naval infantry had come to Portland.

"Do you understand what you are to do?" Gavriil asked after he finished.

Sierra nearly laughed. "Yes," she said. "I get to keep killing, house by house. Killing and burning. Stealing if it sows chaos." And she knew just what she would steal, and who she would kill to get it.

23

Brendan's eyes shot open, but his mind trailed behind. He'd heard something. The crack of a branch, perhaps. Coming from somewhere outside.

He sat up in bed. *This isn't my bedroom.* It took him a moment to remember they'd pulled the mattress into the living room to be closer to the fire. Vailea and the girls were still asleep beside him. Lykos had woken, though, ears erect and pointed toward the sound.

The dying embers added only a trace of warmth to the otherwise wintry room. They threw a patina of reddish light across the walls, shadows diving and pouncing like a second man in the ring. Brendan pushed himself off the mattress and tried to remember what day it was. Five days since the cyber attacks.

Lykos stood with him. The dog appeared as eager as he to investigate the source of the noise.

"If it's a squirrel, you know I'm not going to let you chase it, right?" He patted Lykos on the withers. "We're not that hungry yet."

Food was definitely running low, but water, more than anything, worried him. They'd drunk nearly everything in the bathtub, and if it didn't rain soon he'd have to search the empty houses.

Brendan slid off the bed and picked up the baseball bat he'd started sleeping next to, since the boys had shot his backpack in the middle of the street. "Tomorrow, we'll go looking for water. A gun, too."

Just as he hefted the bat, another noise came from outside. Either he was imagining things, or people moved out there, whispering, sneaking around to the side yard.

For a few seconds, he just listened. Lykos panted quietly beside him, hackles up, yellow eyes glowing. The protest of a window sliding up, ever so slightly. Somewhere below them.

The basement.

Lykos growled; a guttural noise far deeper than that of a normal dog. More primal. Muzzle crinkling, his lips curled back to reveal pink gums above bared, canine teeth.

From the basement, a footfall tapped against a floorboard. A small sound this far away. But Brendan and Lykos advanced together, hunting, bare feet and paws inching into the dining room and through the kitchen to where the stairs led downward.

A woman whispered something indiscernible from below. Then a man's voice, hissing in reply. "Tsssst. Voice down."

Brendan tiptoed down the stairs, bat held high. The slide mechanism of a semi-automatic pistol cocked back with a click.

A flashlight swept through the darkness. The creak of a floorboard.

What he wouldn't have given, at that moment, for a working phone. A phone with an emergency operator at the other end.

Holding the bat in front of him, he reached the bottom of the stairs. Lykos stalked forward even more quietly than Brendan.

Without warning, the beam of a flashlight fell on them.

At first, Brendan had no idea what to do. He squinted, bat raised.

A gunshot.

Brendan put his free hand over his ear, flinching. The bullet had knocked a chunk of drywall into the air, just over his shoulder.

From the living room, his daughters screamed. Brendan forced himself to focus on the woman standing in front of him, holding the smoking gun. He recognized her—yellow dress, fur coat. Blood at the hem. The one who'd frightened Vailea on the lawn. The one who'd tried to steal their radio. "Get him," she shouted to the man beside her.

The man came at him without hesitating, fast and thick, with cropped blonde hair. The kind of man Brendan might have faced between the ropes. With a sidearm still holstered, his first strike caught Brendan by surprise. The blow wasn't aimed to hurt him, but instead, with military efficiency, the man disarmed him of his bat.

It clattered on the floor by Brendan's bare feet. But he couldn't stop to pick it up. His attacker was pressing forward, punch after punch aimed at his head. It was all Brendan could do to dodge, to fall back against the onslaught.

The blonde man brought elbows and knees into the mix, in a style Brendan vaguely recognized but had never encountered. Not the kind of fighting he was used to. Not that he was in any shape to be fighting a younger man, clearly prepared, with bad intentions.

Brendan took a hit in the ribs and winced. He threw a combination, two jabs and a right hook. Nothing connected. *I'm going to lose this fight.* He had the weight advantage, but that wouldn't matter if he couldn't land a hit.

It would have been over in seconds, except for Lykos.

The ceiling spun when the man head-butted Brendan from below, up to his chin. He fell to one knee, reeling. But in that instant, an opening appeared. And in that opening, Lykos pounced.

From the dim beam of the flashlight, Brendan could see only shapes and the blurred path of the German Shepherd as he jumped. Lykos hit the man hard, more than a hundred pounds of muscle and teeth projected at full force.

As the man and beast tumbled, the woman screamed and ran. Her flashlight hit the floor.

The man screamed, too, as Lykos' jaws clamped onto his wrist. The snap of bone, like a stick broken over a knee. His gun landed near the flashlight.

"Off," shouted Brendan over the screaming. "Off, Lykos."

Almost reluctantly, the animal obeyed. It backed away from the intruder, bloody muzzle bared.

Brendan picked up the sidearm. His head hurt. He wanted to throw up, but he tried to stave off the nausea. "Get out of here," he said to the blonde intruder. Already, the woman in the yellow dress was pulling herself through the open window. "Get out," he said again, waving the gun.

To his credit, the man didn't make a sound. His wrist was a bloody, broken thing, cradled in his other hand. But he didn't speak as he stood. For a moment, he fixed Brendan with a blue-eyed stare. And then, dashing in the other direction, he was gone, up and out the egress window, following the woman into obscurity.

Brendan stood at the base of the stairs, panting. Lykos panted, too. The light from the fallen flashlight brightened the far wall, but cast everything else into shadow. He put his head between his knees, letting the breeze from the open window whisk away his sweat.

"Are you okay?" Vailea stood at the top of the stairs, holding an iron fireplace poker. She walked down, sharp breaths wheezing through her teeth. "We heard fighting."

"It's over," he said, trying to sound more confident than he felt. Then he told her what happened.

"We need to defend this place," Vailea said.

Blood still pounded in his ears, but he shook it away. "We need to leave."

"I'll board the windows," she said, as if she hadn't heard him. "More will come. We need to protect the girls."

He didn't agree. They needed to pack their bags and travel east, where psychopaths didn't break into your house and try to kill you. Where, maybe, they could find a country sheriff who didn't cotton to midnight burglary. Only then would the girls be safe.

Instead, he just nodded. He'd help board the windows if that's what she wanted. He'd build a wall if she asked. But even as he nodded, he could feel a new nausea creeping up. A sinking, colossal stone in his stomach that told him his chances of escaping this city were quickly slipping away.

24

Morning light skipped across the river like a stone, pale at first, purple and faint. The fog was lifting with daylight. Every minute brought more light until the Columbia River revealed itself, shoals and reefs, rocks and tributaries, illuminated enough for the *Yodohashi* to push forward once again, navigating the river inland, away from the armada that waited on the coast.

The booming voice of one of the ship's officers resounded behind Kelly, on the other side of the blue shipping containers. His words were foreign, but it was clear his directions were to pull anchor. They were underway again.

She frowned down at Orion beside her at the bow rail, wrapped in a blanket, still wearing that ridiculous blue hardhat even as he lay sleeping. She almost kicked him awake. Almost. But she let him sleep a little longer. At least one of them would be rested.

Slowly the cargo ship glided upriver.

A port town emerged through the fog on the Washington side. Nothing and no one stirred on its banks. The bulk terminal sat empty, devoid of freighters. The parking lot beside it brimmed with cars, but none drove. Not so much as the revving of an engine or the flash of headlights. The wharf should be hopping with activity. It might've even reminded Kelly of her hometown, in a blue-collar sort of way. But as it stood, the harborage had more in common with a graveyard than a shipyard.

They passed a coal export terminal, which, like the bulk terminal, lay empty of both people and ships. Beside it, the paper factory wasn't running. The wharf, too, was still. The waterfront was vacant. No stevedores, no longshoremen. The container cranes sat motionless, neither loading nor unloading. And every space where there should have been people had none.

The *Yodohashi* slipped past the town, under a bridge with no cars. A riverside Mexican restaurant revealed broken windows, looted pantries, and a parking lot empty except for diamonds of glass on the blacktop. A pilot boat on the dock took on water, scuttled, only its bow visible. A set of apartment buildings displayed shattered, boarded windows. None with lights on.

What had happened to this place? *Have the troops from the armada made it this far east already?*

"Ehhhm." Orion shifted beneath his blankets. He pitched and tossed, opened his eyes. "Where—" Pushing himself up, he sucked in a breath. He'd be wondering where he was. It happened every morning.

"We're a couple hours from Portland," Kelly said. Then added, charitably, "Go back to sleep."

He smacked his tongue and mussed his hair. "We're not going to let this happen, are we?"

She knew what he was talking about, but didn't say anything. He continued anyway. "How can you be so calm about it all? Goddam Chinese. Goddam Russians. This is America. They've fuckin' invaded us, Moonshot. And you don't even seem to be the slightest bit pissed."

A smile crossed her lips. She was anything but calm right now, but it wouldn't hurt to let him stew. All she could think about was how to find her way back into the saddle of a Super Hornet to put some real hurt on this invasion.

But she said none of that. Instead, she flipped her smile into a grimace. "Lieutenant Bether, you goat-herdin' raisin. You may not have a plane to fly, but you're acting like a midshipman on liberty. You have a job to do."

His eyes widened.

She continued, doing her best to imitate her one-time drill instructor back at Officer Candidate School—a Jarhead who would've made nugget stew out of Orion. "Get your ass off that deck and into your flight suit.

We're at war and you're a Black Ace. I want you back here in ten minutes, dressed like you mean to participate."

He scurried aft in a most satisfactory way, making her smile. The grin broadened when she reminded herself that soon they'd be in Portland. Soon she'd make her way to a base. And soon the fight could begin in earnest.

* * *

Ireana blinked and stretched. She'd been dreaming. Or had it been a nightmare? She couldn't quite remember.

They were in a car. No, a van. To her right, Annalore dozed in the passenger seat. The boys were jumbled in the back like a litter of puppies. Ireana remembered now, her mind pushing away the haze of sleep. Late last night they'd found the van here, unlocked at the west edge of Portland, where Highway 26 breached the city. So many abandoned cars. Thousands, spilling onto the sidewalks, filling the streets, making passage even by foot difficult.

Six days since the power went out. Six days since her own car wouldn't start. After so much time, no one stayed in their own cars. Everyone else was like her: traveling by foot or bicycle, with an occasional older motorcycle puttering along the shoulder. No one seemed to know where they were going.

"Did you sleep?"

Ireana twisted back toward her sister. "Yeah, a couple of hours."

Dirty and tired, Annalore looked like Ireana felt. Her skin was sallow from mild dehydration, lips beginning to crack.

"We should wake the boys," Ireana said. "Keep moving east."

"Let them sleep a few more minutes," Annalore said. "Then we'll go." And she added, almost as an afterthought, "There's got to be someplace in this city that's safe."

* * *

The cargo ship passed from the wide Columbia River, forest and farmland on either side, to the slightly narrower Willamette River. Farms gave way to industry, hills to starboard and mills and factories to port. In no time, they were sailing through the heart of the city.

But it didn't look like a city. Not to Kelly.

It looked like a shell.

Portland should have been bursting with activity. Traffic and noise, commerce, people along the waterfront. But it was empty. The buildings hulked, tall and dark. The cars didn't traverse the roads. The bridges seemed to be stuck upright, allowing the *Yodohashi* to pass easily through the waterway. A ghostly quiet hung over the city.

Standing beside her, Orion fussed with the zipper on his flight suit. "Have the Russians and Chinese come this far already?"

She didn't know.

The ship glided forward, quiet. To the east, on the other side of Interstate 5, a freight train, 53-foot containers double stacked in well cars, stagnated on the tracks. One of the containers had fallen off, iron ore scattered across the way.

Kelly felt a chill that had nothing to do with the cold. The city was in collapse. An American city, fallen.

A magazine inserted into an automatic rifle clacked from the riverbank, faint, close by.

"Get down." She grabbed Orion's arm and hauled him to the deck.

"What—" A spray of bullets. Seconds later, another. Shooting at them.

The helmsman must have heard it too. The ship veered hard to the port side. Kelly shifted her weight, riding out the turn, then swung her gaze to the left. They were approaching the shore, and more immediately, a pedestrian walkway that floated along the rim of the bank. Too close.

The pilot had overcompensated.

"Watch out!" Kelly shouted up to the bridge, though she knew no one would hear her. And even if they could, they wouldn't be able to react quickly enough.

The *Yodohashi* was going to crash.

She didn't want to be on the ship when that happened. Here on the bow, they'd be easy targets for the sniper.

"Come on," she shouted to Orion. When he didn't respond, she gripped his arm and pulled him toward the port side, where already the shrieks of metal on concrete boomed as the ship sidled up against the walkway. More shots from the automatic rifle punctuated the rasp of the ship going aground. Bullets ricocheted among the cargo containers.

"Come on," she said again. "We've got to get off."

"How?" he managed, eyes wide.

Another spray of lead careened into the side of the ship. Sparks flew. The *Yodohashi* scraped the walkway. A bullet whizzed, nearby, a metallic ping as it hit somewhere behind her. Adrenaline filled her, rushing into her heart, arteries, and muscles.

"Time to show me if you've earned that ace," she said, strong now. Confident. "We're gonna have to jump."

25

They were out of water.

Brendan scooped the last of it from the bathtub, halfway-filling three plastic bottles. The girls would each get one. He wasn't going to let his daughters go thirsty. Vailea would get a bottle, too. That left no water for him. But he'd be fine. And anyway, with luck he'd soon have something to drink.

"Just what I needed," Vailea said when he handed her the bottle. She put her hammer down and drank deeply. She'd finished boarding the windows, and had now set in on nailing shut the front door with pallet scraps. Head tilted back, eyes closed, she finished off the bottle in one long drink. He watched her, hoping his prolonged stare didn't betray his own thirst.

"Lykos and I are going out for a bit," he said, slipping around her. "Be back soon."

Before she could reply, he escaped out into the afternoon sunlight with an empty duffel bag thrown over his arm.

Smoke swirled in the air. It made his parched, cracked lips feel even drier than normal. They were all thirsty. Thirsty as they'd ever been.

If it would just rain, they'd be fine. Or even snow. Heck, he'd drink river water if he could be sure it was clean. But the rain hadn't come, and he didn't trust the river, not since everyone's toilets had stopped flushing.

Lykos padded silently beside him, tongue lolling from his mouth, just as parched as the rest of them. The German Shepherd's gums were dry and his eyes sunken. Brendan hadn't refilled his water bowl since this morning.

"I'm sorry," he said to the dog. "I should have gone out for water sooner. I just thought … we don't usually go so long without rain. And I don't feel great about … what I have to do." Breaking into houses. He didn't even want to say it.

Brendan's parents hadn't raised their boys to be thieves. They'd been small-town people, hard-working and honest. The kind of folks who struggled at a working-class wage and visited the Methodist church on Sunday. The kind who'd say, "A Commandment is a Commandment." Not the kind who stole.

"I'll do what I have to."

Lykos cocked his head.

"Let's just try not to get shot at."

The walk was more nerve-wracking than Brendan had expected. They kept to the alleys of Ladd's Addition, staying away from open streets.

They'd gone about a quarter mile when Brendan felt they were far enough from home to start scavenging. He pointed to a two-story bungalow, pale green with chocolate trim and a chocolate door. "Let's try this one." Neat camellia bushes edged the foundation, and new shingles covered the roof. A small, blue sign in the yard proclaimed, "Protected by Brinks home security." A laughable pretense. The sign had stopped meaning anything six days ago.

Brendan knocked on the door and peeked through the front window. Drawn curtains and darkness obscured the interior. No smoke rose from the chimney. He knocked again. Still no response.

"Are we going to do this thing or not?"

Lykos lolled his tongue out, ears alert, and waited.

Brendan was about to circle around to the back when a lock clicked and the door opened a crack. "What do you want?" came the call from the other side. A face, lined and old, squinted out at him. The loose skin of a man with more days behind him than ahead.

The man's sudden appearance caught Brendan off guard. "I'm … just looking for water. Do you have any?" He hated begging, but it was a far cry better than stealing.

The old man smacked his lips together. "We don't have any to spare. Running low ourselves."

Brendan stood on the stoop, not sure what to say. Finally, he managed a weak, "Sorry to bother you."

"Hold up there," the old man said. Brendan could see him better now, as he approached the gap. Hair poked out in irregular clumps, white and thin. Mottled pigmentation across his forehead complemented the wrinkles on his face. "I do wish I could help." He sucked on a front tooth. "Hey, how about this. I know a guy named Michael. Old poker buddy. End-of-the-world type. Always put away a little extra. Lives a few houses down. Stone wall and red painted door. Try him. Tell him your story and he might have what you need."

The door shut in Brendan's face before he could get out a "thank you."

He winked down at Lykos and grinned. "That's something. Not too many red doors. We can find that."

The air tasted smokier than before as Brendan continued down the street. Had the wind shifted? Maybe a neighbor had put green wood in the fireplace. He didn't pay it much mind, though. He had a lead to follow.

But after meandering up and down the block, he couldn't find the house with the red door. Wooden doors and white doors lined the street. An occasional blue one. Nothing red.

Brendan was about to give up and try begging off another neighbor when he spotted the house. It had a stone wall. And the words "Keep Out!" had been sprayed across the entrance. In red paint. Could that have been what the old man meant?

The grin fell off his face. "What do you think, boy? Should we try it?"

Brendan trotted up the steps that led past the stone wall, up to the entrance and knocked. A lump rose in his throat that he struggled to swallow, parched as he was. He didn't even know if this was the right house, and the warning on the door worried him.

But then he thought of his family. They'd be shuffling around for something to drink right now, maybe wandering to the tub to see how much was left. They'd find it drained. And he didn't want to return with an empty backpack.

Brendan knocked on the spattered wood. "Hello? Michael?" Then a little louder. "Anyone there?"

No answer. He tried the knob. Locked.

"Come on, boy. Let's check the back."

Lykos sniffed the ground as they walked around the house. An odor in the grass sent his nose to work. When they reached the back patio, Brendan saw what had caught his dog's attention. Blood in the dirt. A path of blood and soil, as if a body had been dragged through the backyard.

"What happened here, boy?" Louder. "Is anyone here?"

No reply. Brendan stood on the back patio, coughing from the smoke in the air, wishing he could go home. Wishing the tap ran. Wishing his biggest problem was supporting his family, not stealing for them.

He tried the door.

It opened without resistance. Brendan tiptoed into the kitchen. Enough light shone through the windows for him to see the red smear across the floor. More blood.

Lykos pushed past, nose down, doing laps. If there was anyone here, that dog would know.

Crimson footprints caught Brendan's eye. They covered the kitchen floor, tracks from dozens of bloody boots that muddied the Marmoleum. People had come in after all the blood had spilled. Many people.

He gagged. The stench reminded him of offal and chum. Nose burning and eyes watering, he wanted to get out. There were other neighbors to ask, other ways to find water.

He put his fingers to his lips, beginning to whistle for Lykos.

But an open cupboard door made him pause. Pushing it open with one hand, he held his nose with the other. What he saw inside almost made him glad he'd come to this place, no matter the smell and the blood.

Canned pears, beans, chili, tuna, and a dozen other rows of tin filled the shelves. And that was the least of it. Row upon row of Evian and Icelandic Glacial filled the cabinet. Fiji Water, Aquafina, Arrowhead, and more. Brendan filled his bag, stopping only to drink some himself, not caring about the stink of death and bile. Liquid ran down his chin and onto the floor, mixing with the dried blood to form a tiny puddle. He hadn't drunk this well for days.

"Lykos. Come here, boy," he called, filling a bowl for him.But a few laps of water was all Brendan allowed him. This kitchen turned his knees to soup. They couldn't stay.

He pushed the kitchen door open, staggered outside and took a breath. Dried blood cracked under his shoes. He took another deep breath and kept moving.

Had the air quality gotten worse over the minutes he'd been inside? The clouds of smoke blew thicker now, bitter on his tongue. Gray cinders drifted past like floating tissue paper. He jogged around the side of the house to the front yard, trying to get a sense of where all the ashes were coming from. It didn't seem like wood fire. It didn't seem like chimney smoke.

Hopping up on the stone wall, Brendan scanned the horizon. Almost immediately he saw the source. A fire raged. Downtown.

All along the skyline the city was burning.

* * *

From across the river, Sierra watched fire consume the forty-two-story office building locals called "Big Pink." Normally, she liked fire. She liked watching it dance and flicker, lick and caress, groping, swaying. A sexual being, fire had appetites that could never be sated.

Today, though, the fire only annoyed her. Arson was all part of the plan. But it wasn't her plan. The Russians had commanded her to join them as they "put the city to the torch." Their words. A bit melodramatic, she thought. Her plan had always been to kill. Not to burn. Not to take women as prisoners for their soldiers. That was the Russian directive. All Sierra had ever wanted to do was kill, because it was fun and because it was easy.

She'd rendezvous with them later. She'd play their games—capture women, burn and destroy. But not right now. Now she was hot for murder. She'd make a quick stop at her nearest safe house, then off to find an easy kill. Maybe someone who reminded her of her second husband, short and impotent. Shouldn't be too difficult.

One of her safe houses was close, in the Ladd's Addition neighborhood. The most recent of her safe houses, founded just yesterday. The one where she'd killed the little Donna-lookalike. The one where Gavriil had found her.

She thought of him a lot. So strong. And quiet. She liked her men quiet, she decided. Both of her past husbands had been loud. Loud but frail. Gavriil was everything they weren't. Everything she'd always wanted in a man.

Trash blew down the street. Glass from broken windows covered most of the lawns. Fewer and fewer houses had smoke coming from their chimneys. So many people had left town, and the ones who stayed had locked themselves in their homes. Except for a man and a dog she saw in the distance, the streets were empty.

A minute later, Sierra walked up the steps of the stone wall, past the spray-painted door, and around to the back where she'd left it unlocked. She didn't have a key.

The door was open.

An almost instant rage grabbed hold of her. Someone had broken in. Violated this place. New tracks covered the floor—big footprints. And animal tracks. By the fresh puddle of water, they'd just left. Maybe only minutes earlier.

Her anger reached new heights when she saw the cupboard door was open. Half her water had been stolen.

"I'll kill them!" She screamed, smashing her fist into the cupboard. But she knew it was an empty threat. Whoever had entered her sanctuary had gone, and she doubted she could track them farther than a few feet from the house, even with blood on their shoes.

But wait. Hadn't a man and his dog been walking down the street just minutes ago? She tried to recall what they looked like. A large man. A German Shepherd.

She remembered them now, recognized them even. They'd been in the basement of the house with the shortwave radio she'd wanted to steal. The man was the same one she'd tried to shoot. The one who'd snapped Evgeny's wrist.

"A tooth for a tooth," she said to herself. "That man's life for his violation."

But how to do it? She wouldn't want to involve the Russians. They didn't have time for petty vendetta. She'd have to do it herself.

"How am I going to kill you, my little water thief?" she said, stretching. "And, how about your family?" The Russians always wanted prisoners, but if Sierra acted quickly, she could do this on her own. No need for prisoners. Just the rush of the kill. No one would even need to know about it.

Darkness would serve her best in this. The sun would set soon enough. Perhaps she could sneak in a quick cat nap before the fun.

"Save some water for me." She suppressed a yawn as she wandered upstairs to Donna's bed. "I'll be by soon to quench my thirst."

26

On the other side of the wall, Hahana and Kiri pounded nails. Vailea listened to the hammering from the frosted grass of the front lawn, a smile on her lips. Not just because the girls had nearly finished reinforcing the door, but because of how they thrived, even in the un-ideal circumstances.

Vailea couldn't wait to get them started on her next project.

She stood back, appraising her handiwork. Boards covered the living room and dining room windows. Wood, from a pair of reclaimed pallets, fortified the front door, sealing it shut.

Tomorrow she'd start in on the perimeter.

The back door creaked opened, and Brendan loped around the side yard to join her.

He put his arm over her shoulders. And for a several minutes they stood together in the smoke, not talking. To the west, the sun hung low over the smoldering city, visible above the trees. Crows scratched through the leaves in the street. Far away, a dog howled, forlorn. No barks came in reply.

Finally, she broke the silence. "Do you think it will cross the river?"

He massaged the broken knot in his nose with a forefinger. "No. It won't cross. The river's too wide." He smiled down at her. "Come on inside. It will be dark soon."

She wiped the soot from her face. "I'll be just a minute more."

White ash mottled her brow. It stuck to the sweat on her skin—sweat that covered her despite the chill. Blotting her forehead with the back of her arm had only managed to smear the cinders across her face. Sweating didn't bother her. Ash didn't bother her either. But darkness, that was another story.

As Brendan disappeared around the side of the house, Vailea heard the squeak of the back door and the patter of feet as the girls ran around to the front lawn. Hahana crept cautiously onto the grass. "Oh, wow! No one's getting through that door."

Kiri ran out behind her. "Is your part done, Mom?"

"For today," Vailea said. "But you girls have to get back into the house. You can't be out in the smoke."

The fire wasn't close enough to be a direct danger, but the acrid stench was everywhere. It clung to her hair and clothes, irritating her nose with the smell of burning synthetics. The real danger, though, wasn't the smell. It was the fumes. Who knew what was in that soot?

When the fire had started, the girls had begged to come outside. They wanted to see the glow of smelting steel smoldering, light that filled the day and night. Despite their pleas, she had stayed firm and they'd mostly been content to sit at the upstairs window, watching the blush from their city burning to the ground.

"Bedtime, girls." Vailea shooed them around the side of the house and followed through the back entrance. "And change those clothes," she called after them as they ran ahead. Their outfits were doubtless covered in toxic fumes.

"It's gotten worse out there," Brendan said as Vailea entered the house. He handed her a towel. The terrycloth was soft against her face, even though it hadn't been washed. "We could try again on foot," he said. "There's got to be a way out."

Vailea didn't say anything. From the back window she could see the smoke and cinders sweeping through the air like silver snow. Black smoke billowed over all of it.

"No," she said.

"No?"

"We can't go out there, Brendan. The girls can't breathe that air. We can't either."

"But the fire—"

"It won't cross the river. You said so yourself."

He closed his eyes like he was going to disagree, but instead stomped off into the other room. The man didn't know how to have an argument. It was probably because he was so big. He thought he'd scare her. As if she frightened as easily as that!

She shivered and went to the hearth to throw another log on the fire. In no time, flames lapped at the hemlock with a satisfying sputter and pop. She picked up another log for good measure and was about to maneuver it onto the fire when Lykos came into the living room, ears pricked. He slunk forward, lupine, moving toward the door. There was someone out there.

"Brendan," Vailea hissed. He didn't hear her. "Brendan!"

"What is it?"

Vailea set down the log. "There's something outside."

A knock came from against the planks on the front door. A timid knock. She barely heard it over the crackle of the fire.

Brendan bounded into the room, a baseball bat in his hands. "Get back," he said.

The knock came again. On the other side she heard a woman's voice. "No one home. I told you this part of the city's almost empty. Let's keep going."

"There's smoke coming from the chimney," a second woman said. "Someone is definitely home."

Brendan sidled up to the front door. "Who's out there?"

Excited chatter on the other side. The two female voices spoke at once. "Thank goodness," one exclaimed, while the other said, "We're looking for help. We have children."

Always the tender heart, Brendan called out before Vailea could stop him. "Come around the back." He patted Lykos on the withers. "It's okay, boy. We'll be good hosts."

Vailea met the strangers at the rear of the house. A black woman, about her own age came inside first, layered in dirty clothing, made dirtier by the smoke and the road. Then three boys, all within a few years of each other. They didn't make eye contact, and instead huddled by themselves in a corner of the kitchen. Last came the sister of the first, unless Vailea missed her guess. The two women were of an age, equally exhausted, filthy.

All five of them had the same drained, heavy curve to their mouths. Faces hard and tired.

"I'm Ireana," the one in layers said. She introduced the rest by turn, her sister, son, and nephews.

She held out her hand. "Vailea."

"And I'm Brendan." He handed them each a plastic bottle.

Vailea didn't want to part with the water, but the smiles and glassy-eyed gratitude the women beamed toward them mollified her somewhat. "We'll get you some clothes, too," she said. "They won't be clean, but better than what you've got. You're both about my size."

"Thank you," Ireana said, tears appearing in the corners of her eyes.

Excusing herself to the bedroom, Vailea returned a minute later with sturdy clothes for the women. Kiri, too, pulled white shirts and gray sweatpants from her dresser for the boys. And soon their guests were wearing fresher clothes and sitting together on a couch. Their eyes had a faraway tilt, and they shivered despite the fire.

"It's bad out there," Annalore said, studying the floor, foot tracing an arc over the hardwood. "There's no power in any of the towns. Hillsboro looks like an earthquake struck. Beaverton and downtown are so burnt out we had to walk miles out of our way to avoid the fire. The stores are all closed. We had to walk around south of the city to find a bridge that wasn't up." She took a long drink of water. "And there are a lot of people walking on the highways—"

"We tried to tell them they're headed the wrong way," Ireana cut in. "We tried to tell them not to make for the coast. Most wouldn't listen." She wiped her eye, sending little flecks of tears over her shoulder. "They're fleeing Portland, but they're going the wrong way."

"Why?" Vailea asked. "Is there a problem with going toward the ocean?"

"Because of the invasion—" Ireana's words were cut short when Lykos jumped to his feet, hackles springing up, yellow eyes glowing in the firelight. His lips pealed back in a snarl.

"Do you hear that?" Brendan asked. "Outside."

Through the cracks in the boarded windows, Vailea saw a streak of flame. Glass shattered, followed by a small explosion. Fire erupted against the side of the house.

"Get up!" Brendan jumped from his seat. "Those are Molotov cocktails!"

* * *

"It's a lost cause," Orion said, kicking the tire of the Toyota Corolla. "None of the cars at the front are starting."

Kelly couldn't disagree with that. They'd spent the day wandering down the east side of Portland, foraging for a vehicle to take them out of town. North, to the nearest military base in Washington. But the roads were so jammed it seemed improbable that they'd find a way through. And when they did come upon a car with open road ahead, it wouldn't start.

Orion threw himself down on the curb in front of one of the abandoned houses. "What's happened to this city? No cops. No firefighters. It's chaos."

She just shook her head. Darkness had taken over, streetlights cut off, power grids down, almost every engine and generator defunct. And six days since a similar outage had happened on the Jerry.

They'd both seen more rats than people over the course of the day, and more flies swarming over human waste than she'd ever expected to see outside of a warzone. Though, she supposed, this probably was a warzone—or would be soon when the troops that had landed made it over the coastal mountains.

If nothing else, the fire proved that.

Downtown Portland, across the river, was ablaze. How it had started, or why, or by whose hand was a mystery. But the flames had come quickly, flaring up just this afternoon, and now spread over blocks, igniting skyscrapers and filling the dusk with smoke.

Another reason to get out of here. "We need to keep going,

Beetlejuice. We're AWOL and there's a battle to join. Somewhere the good guys are still fighting."

He pushed himself up, sighing heavily. "They can't blame us. We never deserted."

"Yeah, we just dropped a seventy-million-dollar aircraft in the Pacific. I'm sure they'll give us a promotion and a Silver Star for valor."

Long shadows trailed behind them in the dying day. If they couldn't get a car to start soon they'd have to make the trip to McChord Air Force Base by foot. A hundred-mile trip.

"Maybe there's something that will start up on the bridge there," Orion shouted.

Ahead of them, a plaque marked it the Sellwood Bridge, of a deck-arch-type that didn't have a center span. So at least they could cross it, unlike almost every other bridge she'd seen today. Not that she was terribly excited about wandering to the west side of the river with its growing fire. She'd give this spot a last try, then they'd better start walking north before it grew too dark.

"I think I see some older models," Orion said, loping forward. "I'll bet we can get one running."

Rows of cars crammed Tacoma Boulevard. Some had shattered windows, but most remained untouched, pristine and motionless. From what she'd learned from the few people they'd come across today, the vehicles had all stopped at once.

"What happened here?" Kelly had asked a group of men and women, picking their way south along a side street. One of them had been pushing a bicycle packed high, three or four bags strapped to the frame. Road dust had covered them, head to toe, like street urchins out of a Hugo novel. And by the smell, none had showered in recent memory.

They hadn't wanted to talk at first. Big mistake. Kelly had had enough of people ignoring her, and she'd followed them down the road, shouting until they stopped.

That's when they'd made their second misstep.

The man, a thick fellow who looked like he'd spent too much time in the weight room and not enough on the treadmill, had laughed. Then he'd pointed a gun at her. A Smith & Wesson double-action .45.

If the gesture had been meant to frighten her, it missed. Badly.

She had put up her hands then, as if to surrender. But instead of complying, she'd launched a left cross toward the barrel of the gun, grabbed it, and had left the bodybuilder with a broken nose and an empty hand.

"Will someone give me a rundown of what the fuck has happened in the last six days?" she'd asked, the .45 pointed at its former owner.

Then they'd all started yammering at once. Cascading systems outages. Networks around the world. A brother-in-law gone missing.

"One at a time!" she'd shouted. "You." She'd pointed at the woman holding the bicycle. "Talk."

The young woman had gulped. "We, uh, we first realized something was wrong when the Internet went out. Then the traffic signals went off and my manager told the wait staff to go home. Told everyone. The restaurant was shutting down early.

"But we didn't go home. Not at first. CNN took over on all the channels. A live feed from their headquarters in Atlanta. Madness. People were just standing in the dark and they were saying that the grid had collapsed and satellites were falling out of the sky—"

"Then it started happening here," the muscled man had interrupted, hands above his head. "I was in the Bank of America building, and we could see them, out over the water where the bridges were all lifted up. Satellites falling. Then the President got on TV. But the lights went out here, too, and we turned on the radio. And the city went dark and we didn't know what to do. We couldn't drive out and couldn't leave my grandma."

"I don't see any old lady," Orion had said.

Kelly had kicked him in the shin to shut him up, but the bodybuilder had just looked down and said, "She was on a respirator. Held on for a few days, but without the machine and her meds …" He'd trailed off.

"Hey Moonshot, check this out," Orion said, pulling her from the memory. "There's something in the water."

To the west, the sun was setting over skyscrapers darkened by blackout. Some of the buildings were on fire, though sunset camouflaged the flames, and only the smoke was truly visible, painted with yellows and oranges. Across the water pealed the occasional burst of gunfire. Otherwise, the city held its breath.

Kelly approached Orion where he stood at the apex of the bridge, leaning out over the walkway. Staring north into the river, his breath sent motes into cold air. "How deep do you think the river is?" he asked.

Sunset sparkled over the water. On the near shore, the defunct Ferris wheel of a carnival sat silhouetted against the beach, surrounded by other rides. All dark. "This time of year? Fifty or sixty feet in the middle. Why?"

"That's deep enough," he said to himself.

"For what?"

"Don't you see it?" he said, pointing furiously. "There, at the shore."

Kelly heard a noise from the river below. It started as the grinding of a gear and the trickle of a waterfall. Then the noise grew louder, a metallic crescendo; an enormous displacement of liquid.

Orion's hand fell to his side at the same time his lips puckered open.

Black metal emerged from the river. A conning tower and sail planes. And water running off the hull of the *Borei*-class nuclear submarine as it rose.

27

Another Molotov cocktail smashed into the house. First came a shattering, like a wine glass dropped onto a blacktop. Then the whoosh of flames, lighter fluid squeezed onto a campfire. Upon impact, fire burst from the bottle. Glass flew in all directions. Flames scattered across the lawn below the explosion, rising and burning.

"Get the girls to the basement!" Brendan faced the newcomers. "Your kids, too. Go!"

He needed something to smother the fire with. From the gaps in the boards he could see the fire growing, climbing up the siding. A comforter lay across the mattress on the floor by the fireplace. He tore it off the bed and threw it over his shoulder.

Lykos pawed at the front door. Vailea stood in the middle of the living room, wide-eyed, gun in hand. Shaking.

"Go downstairs," he said, firm but gentle. "I got this." Then he rushed into the kitchen and out the rear entrance. Lykos sprinted after.

A Molotov cocktail smashed into the front of the house, glass exploding. He crouched behind the empty rain barrel and peeked out from the side yard. In the fading light, the shape of a woman appeared, furs and a yellow dress. She bent down and picked up a bottle. Casually. Then lit it and threw it against the side of the house.

Her! That was the woman who accosted them the first day after the collapse. She'd threatened Vailea on the front lawn. The same lawn she advanced over now.

And worse, this was the woman who'd tried to shoot him in his own basement.

"Come on out," she shouted, waving a pistol. "See what happens to those who steal from me."

Fire licked the side of his house, burning with sudden ferocity as alcohol ignited, then dying down to smolder on the grass. Brendan clutched the comforter. He needed to put the fire out before it engulfed the wall beyond repair.

Lykos growled beside him.

"Stay," he said, placing his shaking palm on the dog's rough topcoat. "She's got a gun."

The weapon glinted in her hand. If he went out there now she'd make easy work of him. But he needed to do something. He couldn't just crouch here and watch his home burn to the ground.

"What's happening?" Brendan heard the words over his shoulder and swiveled to see his wife ducking low and edging along the side yard toward him.

"Vailea, go back." His voice broke. "It's not safe."

She didn't reply and made no move to obey. Instead, she took up a position beside him, inspecting the woman on the sidewalk. "Has she stopped throwing the bottles?" Vailea whispered.

"Yeah. But she's got a gun."

"So do I." Vailea creeped forward, around the side of the rain barrel.

"What are you doing?" he hissed. "Get back." The woman in the yellow dress strode closer.

Vailea ignored him.

Brendan glanced back to the woman. Her boots crunched over glass as she marched toward the front door.

From the corner of his eye, he saw Vailea shift. Slowly, she raised her gun and aimed.

Four short bursts from the pistol. The muzzle flashed in the fading light. *Pop-pop-pop-pop.* Each time she pulled the trigger, the gun recoiled, but she held it steadily.

Gunshots reverberated through the neighborhood. Inside the house, children shrieked. Brendan couldn't separate his daughters' voices from the boys. They were probably all screaming. He realized he was also screaming, yelling at Vailea.

The woman screamed, too, and fled back the way she'd come.

"What was that?" Brendan demanded, pulling her through the side yard and into the house. When they were safely inside, he latched the back door and peered out the window, probing for signs of another attack.

Vailea shook her head. "Four shots. And now we're out of ammunition."

"Forget about the ammo," Brendan said. "We need to get help!"

She didn't seem to be listening to him, so he said it again, louder.

"You can try broadcasting out over shortwave," she said, pointing him to where it sat on the table. "I haven't had much luck, since the signal won't travel very far."

He picked it up and began to scan for a working station, face flushed. His wife had shot at a stranger in the street! It didn't seem possible.

Vailea sauntered from the kitchen, talking to herself. "Four bullets. I can't believe I missed everyone."

* * *

Sierra fumed as she ran through the dusk.

"I'll kill that bitch," she screamed. With her SIG Sauer and a pocket full of ammunition she had more than enough firepower to kill everyone in that house.

But that wasn't the safest approach. She wanted to punish the water thieves, but she also didn't want to die. There was a better way. So she continued south, toward the amusement park where the Russians had set up camp. They would help her. If nothing else, they would want that radio destroyed as part of their operation to upset every channel of communication.

Gavriil probably wouldn't let her kill the woman. He'd have his own designs for her. But he'd let her kill the man. And one itch scratched was better than none.

She ran through the vacant streets of Ladd's Addition. The emptiness made her pout. She wished someone would stop her, ask her where she was going in such a hurry. Maybe even try to get physical with her.

The need to kill had intensified. Where before it had been an ache, a dull throbbing, now it was a toxin in her blood. She needed it. But she didn't really want some fool to jump out at her. That killing wouldn't satisfy her. She needed to kill the people who hid behind their boarded windows and shot at her.

The Russians would help with that.

28

"We can't keep going," Lorenzo said from the pilot seat, four-thousand feet above the river, focusing on outside, through the spider webs of cracked glass on the windshield. Lead shot rolled on the cabin floor.

Xandra guffawed. "We're almost there. We've got a full tank of gas. Just push it." They were close, maybe only a hundred miles away. Already well into Oregon.

She still hadn't been able to send or receive a broadcast to the Coast Guard station in Newport. But they'd find the Command Master Chief when they landed. "Keep going," Xandra continued. "We've crossed the Cascades. You said yourself that was the hardest part."

Almost no light remained in the day, but that didn't matter. Even in the dark Xandra estimated Lorenzo should be able to land on the beach. How hard could it be to tell sand from water? It was worth the risk, anyway. She didn't want to take any longer than absolutely necessary to reach the coast.

"Nope," Lorenzo said. "My plane, my call. I didn't spend four days flying across the country just to crash-land into a snuffed-out lighthouse."

Xandra frowned. More delay. That was the theme of this trip—long periods of boredom, hopping from one town to the next in search of fuel. Delay after delay. And for what? She'd tormented herself trying to find a solution in the enemy code. But the code was clean. Simple. Deadly.

"It's all a giant waste of time," she muttered.

"Xandra," Carmen said in a soft voice. "Are you okay?"

The girl had been mercifully quiet for the past forty-eight hours, ever since she'd almost fallen out of the plane. So when she spoke it took Xandra by surprise. The girl should stay quiet. It made the trip less tedious.

"Forget it," Xandra said, pressing her forehead against the window.

They flew over the Columbia River, the most visible landmark from their altitude, glimmering in the last light of the setting sun. Though the river flowed into the ocean, it snaked north at Portland, which meant soon it would be impractical to follow. Fortunately, the Cessna had a built-in compass. The coast would be a straight shot west from here.

"Why isn't it flooding?" Carmen asked, staring down at the river.

Xandra sighed. For some reason she didn't mind answering questions from graduate students, or even—at the worst—undergrads. But a thirteen-year-old just didn't have the same foundation of knowledge. Children asked so many questions, but never really understood the answers.

It seemed that the break she'd enjoyed over the past two days had come to an end.

Xandra didn't bother to keep the exasperation out of her voice. "Why should it be flooding?"

Carmen blushed, but plowed ahead. "Well, it was flooding when we stopped in Idaho. And you said all the dams had been hacked."

The flooding at the American Falls Reservoir on the Snake River had been extreme. They'd spent several hours there, near Blackfoot, procuring shoes to replace the ones Xandra had lost and refueling the plane at a gas station. And though the station had been five miles from the reservoir, the floodwater had come so close that by the time they evacuated, the rising Blackfoot River had nearly consumed the highway.

Carmen continued, twirling a lock of black hair between her fingers. "There must be dozens of dams on the Columbia River Basin."

"Sixty," Xandra said, offhand. Numbers had a way of sticking in her head.

"There you go," Carmen said, bouncing up and down in her seat. "With sixty dams, the flooding should be epic. But it's dry down there."

This was the first major waterway west of the Rocky Mountains that hadn't been flooded. Elsewhere, reservoirs had spilled into floodplains and townships, fields and suburbs. Quite a mess, really. No doubt more than a few people had died as a result.

"What do you think makes the Columbia different?" Xandra knew she shouldn't encourage more talking, but she was still a professor at heart. Challenging students came naturally.

Carmen tapped her fingernails on her chin. "Maybe the hackers didn't get in?" she said hopefully.

"Small chance of that." Xandra paused for effect. "No, you can be pretty sure whoever it is who's behind all this has managed to hack the Columbia Basin dams, too. It just didn't get them anywhere."

"Why not?"

Xandra yawned. "Because the Columbia dams weren't built for flood control." The setting sun made her tired. "They're hydroelectric. All you manage to do by hacking them is shut down the grid. And that, as you can see, has already happened." If she'd wanted to fill young minds she would have become a middle school teacher like her mother. Dreadful woman. Fat and loud, too free with her affection, too easily hurt by words. Xandra hadn't talked to her in years.

"Has anyone ever died from a dam bursting?" Carmen asked.

Xandra stretched, tired of sitting, tired of this plane and this girl. "Lots of times," she said, not trying to keep the boredom from her voice. "The biggest one in history killed more than a hundred and seventy thousand people. The Banqiao Dam on the River Ru."

"In China?"

"Yes—" Xandra stopped. A thought formed just across the horizon of her mind, spurred by what Carmen had just said. She opened a file on her laptop and began searching furiously. This was it. She'd been thinking about the problem all wrong.

"What is it?" Carmen asked.

Xandra was too excited to shush her. Instead, she said, "We may not be able to reverse the damage done by the cyber attacks, but that doesn't mean we're helpless."

Carmen canted her head to the side. "We're not?"

162

"It's like what we were talking about, with the dams. Ours are already breached. The water has already spilled. But we can still fight back. We might be able to redirect the code against whoever did this to us."

"I still don't understand."

Xandra typed furiously. The enemy's code was both extremely sophisticated and highly targeted. Each file was meant to take down a single piece of infrastructure. And, crucially, the authors of these viruses had gone to great lengths to make sure their code only targeted, for example, American banks, and not their own financial systems. But by combining the American code with the more sophisticated enemy code, along with some creative editing, perhaps she could build new cyber weapons.

"If the Chinese hacked our dams," she said, finally responding to Carmen, "then we'll give them a new Banqiao." If she could customize this code to enough computerized control systems, she might be able to affect more than just a single dam. "Maybe hundreds."

"But how do we know it's the Chinese?"

Xandra pursed her lips. "We don't know who it was. But if there's an invasion on the Oregon Coast, we'll know exactly who to target: whoever's ships are on our beaches."

Carmen slouched, chin on fist. Finally, she spoke up. "You told me your laptop doesn't connect to the Internet. How are you going to deploy the code, even if you know who to aim it at?"

Xandra stared out the window. "I don't know," she admitted. Something would come to her. She just hoped she could figure it out before it was too late.

Outside, the sky grew darker and farmland became exurbs. The Cessna dipped forward, starting its descent.

"Where are we going to land?" Xandra shouted up at Lorenzo, over the buzz of the engine.

"We're coming up on Portland. Might be cutting it close, though. Night's coming fast."

It was true. Already, the only light came from the thin pink line that marked the afterglow of a sun that had sunk below the horizon. Soon enough it would be dark.

"We should land now, Pop," Carmen said. "Every passing minute it's going to get harder."

Lorenzo pushed down on the yoke. Below them, the outskirts of the city rushed by at ninety knots. Block upon block of houses vivisected by highways rushed by, an occasional park thrown in. The arterial roads were jammed with cars, more here than anywhere they'd seen.

But what drew Xandra's attention was the fire.

At first it was hard to spot, with the ground below growing darker and darker. But as they descended, boundless swaths of black appeared— charred homes, burnt warehouses and box stores.

Within seconds they found themselves surrounded by smoke.

"I can't see a thing." Lorenzo gripped the yoke so fiercely the veins stuck out from his hands.

"Pull up, Pop!" Carmen shouted.

As quickly as it had come, they flew out of the haze. A sudden shift in the wind took the smoke north, and all at once Xandra could see the city below them, the fire, and the ruin.

"I've got to take us down now," Lorenzo shouted. "The smoke will come back any second. It's now or never."

Xandra could see it, too. The window to land was closing fast.

"Seatbelts on!" Lorenzo pushed the yoke farther forward. "This is going to be bumpy."

They came in low, ash whipping past, fires raging to the north and across the river. Carmen screamed at her father to slow down.

At street level, cars blocked the major roads so Lorenzo veered toward a lesser street, two lanes in each direction. The roadway was clear and straight, but Xandra didn't know how long that would last.

In front, ever closer, the skyscrapers of downtown Portland burned. Nearer still, the Willamette River blocked their path, with a toppled train on a rail line and congested highway in front of that. If they didn't land in the next few seconds, it would all end in a fiery wreck.

The front wheel of the Cessna touched down, bounced, and went up. Xandra's stomach lurched as they hopped down the street. She couldn't look away. There could be a pileup in front of them, and they wouldn't know until it was too late.

Brakes screeching, they slowed, weaving left to right. Houses zipped by, shops and darkened streetlights and useless power poles, all too fast to see the inevitable looting and ruin.

Mercifully, they slowed. And, finally, came to a stop.

"Is everyone all right?" Lorenzo asked. "Carmen? Are you okay, honey?"

"I'm okay, Pop."

Xandra thought she was going to be sick. She tugged on the door handle and stumbled into darkness, lighted by the faraway blaze of fire. Deep shadows flickered over the street as she faltered toward a grocery storefront and puked against the side of the wall.

The smell of burning homes—the soot and the chemicals—caught her nose and she puked again. They should be flying to Newport right now. She wiped her mouth with the sleeve of her suit jacket. They should never have landed.

"Xandra, can I get you anything?" Carmen said, joining her by the defiled wall of the grocery store. It had been ransacked, every window broken. Almost unrecognizable as a store, except for the unlighted sign high above.

"Get me the radio," Xandra said. "We need to check the Coast Guard frequency." Maybe they were finally close enough, now that they were in Oregon.

Carmen returned with the duffel bag. And Xandra had just enough time to flip on the radio when a noise erupted in the distance, a familiar sound now. Too familiar. Gunshots.

She grabbed the girl's arm. "Run," she whispered.

29

"You can't be sure, though." Orion's voice had come to sound ever whinier over the course of their time together. "It could have been any submarine."

They walked north on I-5 as it cut through the city of Portland. To Kelly's left, the downtown burned in a massive conflagration, smoke exhaled into the afterlight of sunset. To her right, industrial buildings and warehouses pushed up against the interstate.

She coughed at the fumes that wafted across the river. In a few miles, they'd be past the worst of it. She refused to think about the more-than-hundred miles that separated them from McChord Airforce Base.

"I *am* sure, nugget. And maybe if you'd spent more time with the spotter cards and less time with the nudey ones you might learn to recognize enemy subs, too." The Navy issued decks of playing cards with images of ships, aircraft, and submarines from adversary nations. A good pilot needed to know the difference between a North Korean *Nampo*-class frigate, and the South Korean *Ulsan*-class, unless they had a boner for court martial. "I'm telling you, that was definitely the *Alexander Nevsky*, out of the White Sea port of Severodvinsk. Russian. Nuclear. Bulava missiles—"

A fuel tank exploded on the other side of the river. Then another, somewhat nearer. These detonations had been happening a lot.

"I don't doubt that there *is* a sub called the Alexander-whatever-you-said. I just doubt that you coulda told the difference between it and an American sub. The sun was setting."

Kelly's eyes stung and her nose burned, but Orion annoyed her most of all. She wanted to scream at him, or abandon him on the interstate, or punch him. But she did none of those things. Instead, she wiped ash off her face with the sleeve of her somewhat-less-sooty flight suit and said, as calmly as she could, "It wasn't an American vessel, Orion. There was a crest that must've been ten feet tall. In Cyrillic. You know, the Russian alphabet."

"Hrrmm," he said, a noncommittal grunt.

She'd seen the crest on the conning tower clearly enough. A golden man with a downward pointed sword, Cyrillic below. It was the *Nevsky*, without a doubt.

They reached a section of the road where cars filled all four lanes, with more crashed or stalled along the shoulder. Anything bigger than a bicycle would find this way impassable, and even Kelly had to walk on the hoods of a few cars in order to keep moving north.

"I think you're wrong," Orion continued. "But, sure, report your suspicions when we get to McChord Airforce Base. They'll probably blow a gasket over it. If they believe you."

She ignored that last part. "The 62d Airlift Wing at McChord would have every jet scrambling over a nuclear submarine parked in the center of a major American city," she said.

"If there even is a 62d Airlift Wing left."

"What does that mean?" A rush of anger set her cheeks burning.

"You're joking, right? We haven't seen any sign of American military since we made landfall." He swept his hands across the skyline of downtown. "How many other cities have fallen, Moonshot? If they can take out a supercarrier and a city, what can't they take out?"

She stopped in the middle of the interstate. Not because she was angry, but because he might be right. She wanted desperately to report in to the nearest military base, but who knew if that base would even be standing?

Before she could put her fears into words, a sound echoed above. It wasn't the distant crackling of fire, or the occasional explosion on the far side of the river. It was something more familiar, more remarkable.

A plane flying through the night.

"It's coming toward us," she said, rubbing her hands together in excitement. She hadn't heard the sound of an aircraft since her own had disappeared below the chop of the Pacific Ocean.

She could see it now, to the east, approaching for landing, low beneath the rising smoke. A Cessna, probably a single-engine model. An older one, she guessed by the clunky hum of the engine.

"What is it?" Orion asked, wiping his nose on the nape of his flight jacket.

She wanted to punch him in the shoulder for not recognizing the aircraft immediately. How many flight officers couldn't identify a Cessna on approach less than two miles away? But all she said was, "Let's go see where it's putting down."

Vaulting over the concrete highway barrier she sprinted across the train track just south of an overturned freight train, and found herself surrounded by warehouses and darkness. Through the vacant industrial streets she ran, past empty roadways, and into a neighborhood.

When she did stop, finally, Orion came up behind her, panting and coughing from the smoke. "You're nuts. We're never going to find where it landed."

She was about to tell him to shut up and follow her when another familiar sound rumbled through the night. Not the noise of the plane, this time. The sound of gunfire.

Someone was shooting. Four distinct shots. And it wasn't clear what direction they were coming from.

* * *

Lorenzo ran. Past stop signs and piles of autumn leaves; past houses with broken windows and doors. Past the stink of human waste and trash heaped at curbs, floating down the streets.

He rushed through the darkness.

His daughter sprinted in front of him. He needed to keep her safe.

Xandra and Carmen sped through the smoke and the fire-wrought shadows. They ran fast and had a head start. But he was gaining.

Toward the gunshots or away from them, he couldn't be sure. And so he followed, racing into the quiet, smoke-filled apocalypse that was once a neighborhood.

"Stop," he called out as soon as he caught up with his daughter. Hands on his knees, breathing heavily. "Slow up a bit." *I'm too old for this.*

Xandra leaned against a street sign. Carmen swiveled her head, searching for the source of the gunshots, even though there hadn't been any since those first four.

"Where are ... we even ... going?" Lorenzo asked between breaths.

"Keep your voice down," Xandra hissed.

"Do you even know ... which way the guns were fired?" Lorenzo continued, still trying to catch his breath. His teeth hurt from breathing in the cold air, and the skin on his face burned from exertion. "We could be heading ... right toward it."

For the first time since he'd met her, Xandra shifted her eyes and shrugged. "I apologize," she said, though it didn't show in her voice. "I heard gunshots and I ran. But you're right. I have no way of knowing where they came from."

"We should go back ... to the plane," Lorenzo said, remaining bent over. "I can take us up. We have enough ... fuel to get to the coast." He took a deep breath. "The landing will be dangerous, but no worse than whatever's here."

Xandra arched her eyebrow. "You're willing to take us to the coast? Tonight?"

"Yes," he said. *Anything to get Carmen out of here.*

"It's good that you've seen reason," Xandra started walking. "Coming, Carmen? We have a mission to complete."

"Sure." But Carmen made no move to follow them.

"Niña?" Lorenzo whispered. "Is everything okay?"

"Fine." But she still didn't budge.

Xandra stomped her foot. "Then let's go."

"Pop, what's that?" Carmen pointed to a burned out church. Fire gutted the inside. Maybe an accident with a gas stove. Maybe arson.

"It's nothing. We need to go. It's not safe here." Up the street, a moving truck's doors splayed open, dark legs sticking out in the shadows and a black puddle beneath. It might have been motor oil. He knew it wasn't.

"There might be people inside," Carmen said, tugging his arm toward the burnt-out building.

Lorenzo squinted into the blackness. "More reason to go."

"Pop, that's St. Sharbel, A *Catholic* church. This is a neighborhood. Look around!"

"We don't know anything about who lives around here." He pulled his arm free. "If anyone even does. We don't know what's in there. What's in any of these buildings. Come on. Back to the plane."

"Will you just listen to me?" she shouted, plopping down onto the trash-littered street. "I'm tired of being treated like a child."

Lorenzo could see Xandra stiffen as the words ricocheted through the street. More outbursts like that and someone would hear them.

"Carmen, you *are* a child," he said, as softly and kindly as he could.

"Pop. You don't listen. Why aren't we helping more people? We could fit another two or three in the plane. More if we had to."

Lorenzo couldn't see his daughter's face very well in the darkness, but he was sure it was flushed. He had only heard her voice break with fury once, and that on the day before the cancer had taken Abril.

He remembered Carmen, just a slip of a girl. A girl who'd done a lot of growing up as her mother lay dying. Carmen had occupied the bedside chair more than he had. She'd cleaned bedpans more, even, than the nurses. And when she saw him that morning she'd shouted at him. He didn't remember the words, just the anger in them.

What he did remember was bumbling from the chair to pour himself another drink.

Carmen had pushed him then, knocking the bottle of Fernet from his hand, with him teetering to the ground after it. She'd just turned eleven that month, but she'd stood over him like a giant while he sobbed on the floor. Too drunk to stand, he'd cried as if she were the adult and he was the child. He'd cried on the sticky vinyl while she screamed at him, and he'd promised to God to stay sober this time.

"Are you even listening, Pop?" Carmen continued, snapping him from the memory. "There are probably people in all these houses. Maybe even kids. They might be hungry. It's the least we could do to see if we can help." She rounded on Xandra. "And *you*. You can't take even an hour away from your precious mission to see if you can help them."

"Niña," Lorenzo soothed. He tried to shake the memory away. "We—"

"Both of you," Carmen interrupted, pushing herself back to her feat. "You only care about yourselves. You just want to fly away, and damn the people burning on the ground."

"They're not my family," he said, working to keep his tone as gentle as he could, though he hated when she swore. "*You're* my family, Carmen. All that's left of it. I just care about you. Only you."

"Pop, I'm going. You can come or not. And you, too, Xandra. Come or not. But I'm going to see if they need help."

Lorenzo stared helplessly as his daughter stormed toward the stone church. "Wait," he called.

She faced him. He could see her silhouette etched in red like a full-body halo. "I'm coming with you," he said with a sigh.

"Good," she replied, huffy, as if she expected nothing less. "And you, Xandra?"

The night was still. Lorenzo couldn't hear anything but the amplification of his heart drumming its way out of his neck. He whispered a prayer for safety, intending it only for himself though it magnified in the silence.

"Xandra?" Carmen asked again.

Before she could answer, their conversation was cut short by the clip of footfalls on the sidewalk. A man's voice, then a woman shouting back in response.

Strangers approaching, running toward them through the night.

"Hide!" Lorenzo said as panic took him. These people might be the same ones who fired that gun. "Quickly!"

But he was too late. The strangers appeared around the corner, dark shapes moving fast. All he could do was put his body between them and his daughter as they sprinted near.

"Hold up," a woman said. She skidded to a stop, almost bowling them over. The man beside her stopped, too, falling backward slightly as he tried to avoid running into the group.

In the flickering light, Lorenzo could tell there were just two of them—a man and woman, as he'd suspected. But he was no longer scared. Not when he saw what they were wearing. Flight suits. They were pilots, like him. And not just any aviators. American military. He could have cried with joy.

"Pop, they're fighter pilots," Carmen said from behind him, echoing his own thoughts.

The woman stared at Lorenzo. She stuck out her hand. "Lieutenant Kelly Seong. And this is Lieutenant Orion Bether. Good to meet you."

"Lorenzo Robles," he said. "And this is my daughter, Carmen."

Xandra stuck out her hand. "I'm glad you're here," she said, without preamble. "I'd like to learn about the situation on the ground—"

"Do you hear that?' Carmen interrupted.

Xandra glowered at her, still holding out a palm to be shaken. "Let the grown ups—"

"I hear it," Kelly said. "It sounds like a news report."

"...*broadcasting from Portland, Oregon. If you can hear this, you're within a mile of my location...*"

"It's coming from your duffel bag," Carmen said, squeezing her fists with excitement.

Cautiously, Xandra unzipped the bag and pulled out her radio. She clicked on the microphone. "Hello? Who is this?"

The line was quiet for a moment. Then, "I'm Brendan Chogan. Who's this?"

30

"You don't have any milk, do you?" Orion asked.

Brendan watched the fighter pilot with a sort of awe at the way he plowed through a box of Corn Chex. The pilot didn't seem to notice the crumbs that fell from his fingers onto the couch where he sat.

"No milk," Vailea said, with only the minimum hint of apology in her voice.

Brendan could tell his wife was overwhelmed to have so many people in the living room; not just Ireana and Annalore, but now two fighter pilots, a representative from the Department of Defense, and a civilian pilot and his daughter. Not to mention the three kids playing in the basement with their daughters.

He wrung his hands, feeling bad for saddling her with so many guests. But not too bad. They brought news of the outside world.

"Of course they don't have milk, you food-sponge. Try to keep some dignity." That was Kelly, perhaps the more senior of the two, though Brendan hadn't quite figured out their relationship.

Orion gawked back in a challenge, but when Kelly didn't flinch he muttered, "Well, I'd eat dry cereal over rice and noodles any day—"

"Tell us about the war," Xandra interrupted. She'd been scanning frequencies on the shortwave radio, muttering to herself when the channels she sought weren't working. Her attention shifted to the Navy pilots, head tilted in a way that reminded Brendan of a bird. "I have the necessary clearance, if you prefer to speak in private."

"There's no need," Kelly said. "I don't have any information— classified or otherwise—to tell."

In a few sentences, she described the crash of her plane in the North Pacific and the journey onboard the Japanese container ship. But when she got to the part about seeing the invasion on the coast, Ireana let out a groan.

"We saw the armada, too," Ireana said. "We watched it land near Tillamook. That's what sent us here."

"You saw the battle?" Kelly asked.

"There wasn't any battle," Annalore joined in. "Just soldiers taking the beaches and shelling the town. The only military we saw were the ones that came from the ocean."

"Russians and Chinese," Kelly said.

"Really?" Xandra leaned forward. "Are you sure?"

"Absolutely," Orion said, Corn Chex spraying as he spoke. "We must've seen dozens of ships in the fog. But those were the only two ensigns among them."

"Not to mention the *Alexander Nevsky*," Kelly added.

He put down the cereal. "Moonshot, we've been over this."

"The *Nevsky*?" Xandra asked. "You mean the Russian OK-650B nuclear reactor submarine?"

"You know your subs, lady." Kelly nodded at the other woman's recall. "Yeah, we saw the *Nevsky* here in Portland. In the river, just hours ago."

Brendan thought he saw Xandra's interest growing, almost to the point of excitement. Not that he understood why. The prospect of a foreign nuclear submarine in the city dried up his mouth like gym chalk.

"Seriously, Moonshot," Orion said, "you shouldn't be spreading that story." He spread his hands toward Xandra. "Truth is, we don't know exactly what sub it was."

"I know what I saw," Kelly growled. "She's moored right by the amusement park."

Brendan nearly fell off his chair. "Oaks Amusement Park?" he said, trying to tamp down the lump in his throat. Nestled on the bank of the Willamette River, it wasn't more than three miles south. "That's an hour's walk from here." Russian troops were practically in their neighborhood!

He knew they should've gotten away sooner. Maybe there was still time.

"Really?" Xandra's face lit up. "An hour away?"

"I assume you have a plan," Carmen said.

Xandra ignored her and squared off toward Kelly. No longer did Xandra seem like a bird with a cocked head, but a raptor ready to sink its talons into flesh. "I'd like you to show me the submarine."

"Impossible." Orion wiped a dripping nose on the sleeve of his flight suit, then stuffed his arm back in the cereal box.

At the same time, Kelly said, "Why would anyone want to get closer to the Russian military than absolutely necessary? Do you want to get a bullet between the ears?"

Xandra didn't seem to recognize the sarcasm. "I have no intention of confronting troops of any kind. But I need to get onboard that submarine."

Brendan had had just about enough of this craziness. They were wasting time better spent packing up and rolling out in the opposite direction from these Russian soldiers.

"What if I told you there is a way to fight back?" Xandra said.

Orion stood from the couch, spilling Corn Chex from his lap. "I'd do anything." He balled a fist.

"You're right, Carmen, I do have a plan," Xandra said.

Orion almost danced with excitement. "What is it? I want in."

"Not you," Xandra said to Orion. "I need a fighter." Her eyes slowly consumed Brendan, examining the whole of him. "You," she said. "Can you swim?"

31

"This is a bad idea," Brendan muttered to himself.

The Cessna flew through the night, crowded with four passengers, a pilot, and a dog. Lorenzo and Carmen sat in front, Xandra and Kelly took the rear seats, and Brendan squatted next to Lykos on the floor. He was uncomfortable and aware of the space his body took up, but he didn't complain. It was about to get much worse.

"The bad idea was bringing that dog," Xandra said, tapping furiously on the milspec laptop. "Animals are inherently unpredictable. It should have stayed."

Brendan ignored her. He hadn't made any modifications to Xandra's risky plan, except for his adamance that Lykos come along. If they were going to risk their lives, he needed someone he could count on.

"Make sure your life jackets are secure," Kelly said.

Brendan had found two adult life jackets and two child-sized ones in his neighbor's garage. He wore the biggest one, though it wouldn't cinch. Xandra wore the other adult life jacket, while Kelly was content to just hold onto one of the child-sized ones.

"And remember," Kelly said, "when you hit the cold water, fight the urge to gasp for air. You'll aspirate river water."

They flew low, cloaked in almost complete blackness. Outside, smoke obscured the starlight so that there were only two sources of light. The first came from the instrument panel in front of Lorenzo. The second, and the brighter of the two, came from the computer on Xandra's lap where she scrolled, typed, and occasionally slammed her hand over the keyboard.

"How long until you've made all the changes to the code?" Carmen asked. "We're going to be there in just a couple of minutes."

"Don't rush me," Xandra snapped. "A few more lines should do it."

The cabin felt tight. Too tight. That iron taste of the quarry lake had returned, and Brendan couldn't flush it no matter how hard he swallowed. He closed his eyes and breathed deeply, wondering, for the hundredth time, if he really should have volunteered for this enterprise, especially over Vailea's objections and his own reservations. Over the frightened hugs of goodbye from his daughters. Over his own fear.

No, he reminded himself. *This is the only way.* This would protect his family. If Xandra's idea worked, it could stop the enemy. He opened his eyes.

"Could you explain the plan to me again, Lieutenant?" Brendan asked Kelly. "Just to make sure I've got it?"

"It's simple," Xandra interrupted, fingers pattering over her laptop. "It's standard Russian naval infantry procedure to form a perimeter around their submarine. But their defenses will only be for land attacks. They won't have anti-air capabilities for targeting a low-flying plane."

Brendan nodded. "I understand that part. But won't they hear us coming?"

"Certainly," Xandra said. "But Lorenzo is going to put us over the river and we'll jump. They'll hear the plane, and they'll watch it fly away. Meanwhile, we'll be quick and quiet, and you'll be back with your family before sunrise."

Brendan could picture dozens of ways this could fall apart on them, but all he said was, "Go on."

"You're the muscle," Xandra said. "Lieutenant Seong is coming because she knows the most about submarines—boarding them and their controls—"

"I don't really know much," Kelly said.

Xandra ignored her. "And I'll upload the code when we're aboard. I only had time to build a couple viruses. The first is similar to the one that took out the *Gerald R. Ford*."

Uploading code, that was the crux of this whole scheme. Xandra had created a virus on her laptop. A series of viruses in a packet. That was as much as Brendan understood. She'd put it on a thumb drive, that, once uploaded into the servers of the Russian submarine, would transmit to other ships. From there the packet of viruses would spread to naval facilities in Russia, and finally throughout the enemy's infrastructure.

Though Brendan had his doubts, he figured this was their best shot. If it worked, his wife and daughters might have a chance. Maybe the invasion would end. Maybe they'd grow up in a world with running water and working thermostats. Maybe they'd think about him sometimes. Because, despite Xandra's assurances, he doubted any of them would survive.

"What about the second virus?" Kelly asked.

"That targets—"

"Almost there," Lorenzo interrupted, turning the plane around. "Get ready."

* * *

"Bringing her around," Lorenzo said as he came about into the wind and pointed them north. They were flying toward the downtown fires now, back the direction they'd come from. It wouldn't be long until they were over the amusement park.

"You'll let me know when to jump, right?" Kelly said.

"Sure," Lorenzo said. "Are you all certain you want to do this?" He had grave misgivings. The flight plan was as simple as it was unwise. He would bring the plane low and slow over the stretch of the Willamette that bordered the amusement park, and the two women, the man, and his dog would jump out. As simple as that.

Simple. Also, maybe, suicidal.

"It's the only way," Brendan said.

Kelly tied her hair back in a ponytail and put her arms through the little life jacket. "Just tell me when to jump."

Lorenzo grimaced. "Good luck." They were going to need it.

There was a lot they hadn't planned for, like how they'd get onboard the submarine, or what they'd do when, inevitably, they ran into armed soldiers. Or how they'd get away after the deed was done. But Lorenzo felt glad enough to do his part. And even gladder to be done with this affair. After the would-be heroes jumped into the river, the Cessna would still have enough fuel for him and Carmen to find a safe spot to wait out the war.

"You're a very brave dog," Carmen said, unbuckling her seatbelt and running her fingers through the German Shepherd's soft undercoat. "You're all so brave."

"Put your seatbelt back on," he told his daughter.

She ignored him. All Lorenzo could do was frown at the disobedience and keep flying, bringing the Cessna below the tree line.

They were getting close.

"Open the cabin door," Lorenzo called back to Kelly. She would be the first out, since she was the strongest swimmer. They'd go one by one as the plane approached the shore, with Xandra jumping last.

Up ahead the silhouette of a Ferris wheel materialized. They would be there in less than a minute, even though Lorenzo was flying at just under forty knots, as slow as he could to stay airborne.

"Tell me when," Kelly shouted, pushing the door ajar. Wind rushed into the cabin, screeching in Lorenzo's ears.

"Twenty seconds," he called back.

They were traveling at thirty-five miles per hour, the minimum to keep from stalling. The window for deployment would be short.

"Now?" Kelly yelled.

"Ten more seconds."

"Does everyone have their emergency blankets?" Xandra asked, putting the thumb drive into a plastic zip bag.

"Check," Brendan said.

"Tell me when," Kelly said again. She'd scooted up to the door, sitting now on the edge with feet dangling into the open sky.

"Almost." Lorenzo bit his lip and sent up a prayer. "Now," he said.

As soon as Lorenzo spoke the word, Kelly jumped. Arms tucked in tight around the life jacket, she disappeared out the door without a word. Brendan went after her, only a second later. Then the German Shepherd after his master. And last, Xandra fell into the smoky night.

Lorenzo couldn't hear the four of them hit the water over the rush of air, nor could he see them. But he had done what he could. God protect them.

"Close the door," Lorenzo called back.

His daughter didn't reply. "Close the door, Carmen!" he shouted, louder.

"I'm going, too."

The words spun Lorenzo around so that he almost fell out of his seat. His eyes bulged when he saw Carmen standing, wearing a child-sized life jacket and holding onto both sides of the open door. The wind sent her long black hair flapping in every direction as she leaned out over the water.

"No!" he shouted.

"I love you, Pop. But you can't always protect me."

To his horror, his thirteen-year-old daughter—his only living relative, his soul, and his life—jumped out into the midnight blackness. Into the very shallowest part of the river below.

And he was left alone in a plane that seconds earlier had been full.

* * *

"Can I get anyone a drink?" Vailea rose from the couch. "We don't have much water left, but there's some beer."

Though it was late, none of them could sleep. She doubted she would until Brendan came back. *He will come back.*

"I won't say no to a brewski." Orion leaned back, throwing his bare feet onto the ottoman. "Craft beer if you have it."

"Anyone else?"

When Ireana and Annalore declined, Vailea marched through the kitchen and out to the back porch. The wind wailed when she opened the door, hurrying her toward the cooler she'd stocked with provisions.

"Whew, that's *some* breeze," Orion said when Vailea returned with the beer. "Is it always so cold in November?"

180

"Usually," Vailea said, handing him a lager. "Where are you from?"

"Phoenix. And Kelly's from some little shithole—excuse me." He grimaced at the five kids, all asleep near the fire. "Kelly's from a little town in Georgia. Can't remember the name."

Vailea smiled at the sisters, hoping to make everyone as comfortable as she could. "How about you?"

"Los Angeles," Annalore said. "Born and raised."

"We're not used to the cold, either," Ireana said, tugging her borrowed coat more closely around her shoulders.

Vailea grinned. "That makes four of us."

"Thank you for the fire." Annalore rubbed her hands together. "This is the warmest we've been in nearly a week." Her eyelids drooped, but she blinked away the sleep.

Embarrassed by the thanks, Vailea changed the subject. "What do you do, back in LA?" It felt strange to ask about their jobs, almost like she should be asking in the past tense. It was a foolish thought, and she shook it away. Of course they'd go back to their old jobs when this was over. Soon, hopefully.

"I teach lexical theory at Cal State," Annalore said. "Functional grammar, that sort of thing."

Orion yawned. "Sorry." He covered his mouth.

Annalore continued. "I don't really love it, though."

"You don't?" Ireana said. "That's news to me."

"I'd swap departments if they'd let me. Next term, I was hoping to teach a course in the Department of Modern Languages."

Ireana waved her hand toward her sister. "She speaks four of them."

Orion stretched, loudly.

Annalore pursed her lips at him. "What about you, Orion. You're a naval officer?"

He beamed as the topic changed to himself. "Yup, I'm the weapons systems officer on a Super Hornet. That's a carrier-based multirole fighter. Got about a hundred hours in, so still pretty new at it."

"Any family back home?" Vailea asked.

"Mom and dad in Phoenix. I'm an only child. How about you?"

"All my family is here." She tried not to think about her husband, who was probably just starting the most dangerous part of Xandra's reckless plan. "How about you ladies?"

"I've got a husband back in LA," Annalore said. "Taggart. His friends call him Tag."

"As for me," Ireana said, "it's just Jeremiah."

"No husband?" Orion took his feet off the ottoman and leaned closer.

"Not for years."

"Hmmm," he said. "Do you drink wine? Vailea, do we have any Chardonnay? A Merlot, even?"

Ireana made a choking sound, goggling around the room for help. Her eyes landed on Vailea. "What do you do?"

"I work for a private engineering firm here in town. We build walls. That's all we do—all I do." She laughed, trying to make light of the situation. "I haven't heard from them since this all began. They owe me a paycheck!"

Ireana grinned. It was the first time Vailea had seen her smile, and it transformed her face. One moment, she was haggard and beaten down, the next she glowed. Years tumbled off her like layers of dirty clothes.

Orion seemed to notice, too. "Where are we on that wine?"

Before Vailea could reply, her ear caught a noise outside, close. In the backyard. It sounded like something—someone—had fallen.

They must have all heard it, because everyone stopped talking and swung toward the kitchen. Kiri stirred in her sleep. The fire crackled. No one breathed.

"Wake the children," Vailea whispered to Annalore. Then to Orion, "Smother the fire."

"What is it?" Ireana asked.

Vailea reached toward the gun on the mantel, then pulled away, lamenting her waste of bullets. Instead, she grabbed Brendan's baseball bat from against the wall. "There's someone outside. Quickly. Get upstairs."

32

From forty feet up, Brendan dropped from the plane. He couldn't gauge the distance, couldn't even see the black water approaching. All he could do was hold his breath and close his eyes, knowing the icy river was somewhere below.

He fell into the open air, wind coming from all directions. Time stretched. He wished he could claw back into the plane.

The water slapped his body like every punch he'd ever taken at once, fists of ice. Cold ripped across his exposed skin, flaying and burning. He struggled to escape, not knowing up from down. The current pulled him under the surface, where it was darker even than above.

He flipped in the gyre, end over end, air escaping from his nose and mouth.

Just as quickly as it had brought him down, his life jacket lifted him back to the surface, gasping, lungs compressed as if mashed into his spine. He couldn't breathe. Every gasp left him unsatisfied. More air, his brain screamed. More oxygen.

His ears rang. Whether it was from the fall or the cold, he didn't know. The splash of the others barely registered as they struggled in the water, not far away. Closest among them, came paddling, soft strokes, air through a dog's nostrils.

The river flowed faster than Brendan had expected. He hadn't counted on just how cold it would be. Or how rapidly it would sweep him away from the shoreline and the submarine.

Another minute and I'll be too far north to reach the bank. He corrected himself. *Another minute and I'll be dead.*

Forcing his muscles to obey, he took a stroke toward where he thought the bank must be. Another stroke. And another. The lifejacket got in his way. And each stroke became more difficult than the last as his muscles cramped and froze.

As he swam he could hear his college boxing coach yelling at him to get up. Brendan cast his arms about and forced himself forward. It wasn't so different from pushing himself off the canvas after a punch between the eyes. "Get up," the river screamed in the voice of his old trainer. "Get up and fight!"

Frigid water stiffened his body. He paddled slower, too slow to keep the water from lapping against his face and into his mouth.

Get off the gaddammed ropes, Chogan, he heard his coach say. *If you take the count you can kiss that scholarship goodbye.* Sputtering, Brendan swam harder.

His head ached, as if all the warmth from his brain had fled toward his core. He could no longer hear Lykos, Kelly, or Xandra. Everything seemed so far away, even his own body in the river.

The water no longer felt so frosty. It tingled instead, an edge of warmth. And for the first time in six days, he thought seriously about letting go.

His knee smashed into a rock. The searing pain brought him back to reality. His foot scraped against something—gravel, sharp stones.

With the last of his energy, he forced himself onto the bank, first splashing, then one foot in front of the other, and finally sprawled onto the cold mud. Lykos padded toward him, shaking off the water, droplets flying.

A shiver wracked him. Gasping for air, cheeks pressed into the mud, he tried to concentrate. It was like the last minute in the last round of a match, when the body started to flag and the only thing that kept it going was training and discipline. Except it had been years since he'd been in any kind of fighting shape. Still, he crawled farther up the bank.

He pulled the emergency blanket from his pocket and worked it in his numb, shaking fingers, opening it slowly. It took longer than he wanted to wrap the blanket over his shoulders, and warmth took longer still.

Before he could congratulate himself, a mechanical sound rebounded from up the bank. At first, he thought it might be Xandra and Kelly. But that wasn't it. *Crank. Chut chut chut. Whiiii.* The whirring sounds of a generator.

A beam of white light split the night. It shone along the riverbank and came to a stop right where he and Lykos stood.

Brendan froze. He covered his eyes with his elbow and squinted into the spotlight. He could see nothing. But at least he could hear. Men farther up the riverbank. Soldiers. The shuffle of boots and clatter of guns, maybe twenty yards away. Raspy breathing and the click of safety catches. Ammunition loaded into magazines.

For a few seconds, no one spoke. And then came a command from a bullhorn.

"Hands in the air, Amerikanski," the soldier said from above, accent thick. More click of guns, and boots running to join the group by the spotlight. "Give yourself up now, or be shot dead."

* * *

In the darkest hour of the night, Sierra skulked through the neighborhood. There wasn't any hurry. No one would be outside—no one who could challenge her or the two men at her flank. To challenge her would mean death, as it should be.

Sierra's boots carved a path through the leaves, crunching and cold. Happiness was unswept leaves. Leaves that fell and rotted, with no street sweeper ever coming again. Happiness was when the few people remaining here huddled in their homes, too afraid to set foot outside—day or night—to see the beauty of fallen leaves and burning buildings and war and a victory for the strong.

"You go too slow," one of the men said at her side, prodding her along.

She smiled at him in the darkness. "There's no hurry. Enjoy this. Enjoy the hunt as much as the kill."

He curled his upper lip, but said nothing else, as his training had no doubt instilled. Yuri was a soldier, after all. Russian naval infantry. He and Zakhar were the only two men Gavriil would lend her for this expedition.

185

But two would be sufficient.

Especially when they came armed with Bullpup assault rifles that could shoot eleven rounds per second.

She grabbed Zakhar by the shoulder. "That's the house." Boards covered the windows and door. But boards would never keep her out. "Let's go around the back, boys."

The men prowled invisibly in the night. Both wore black fatigues and black knit caps. They glided beside her, noiselessly, edging around the house.

"Light," she said.

Zakhar flicked on a flashlight and pointed the beam toward their feet. He continued cautiously, eyes sweeping the side yard for signs of a sentry or trap. But there were neither, and they arrived at the gate at the back of the house.

Yuri chuckled silently and said something to Zakhar. Then to Sierra, "They have fire burning. Smoke in chimney. No guard." He laughed again, low and mirthless. "Will be easy."

"Don't forget the man and his dog. They're dangerous." Hadn't she already warned these simpletons not to get too confident? She remembered, all too clearly, how the dog had dispatched of Evgeny. How she'd fled, ignominiously, back through the open window. "Just don't get cocky, okay?"

"Da," was all he said. And then they were professionals again, moving easily through the darkness. Nothing separated them from the back door but a short fence and small, frosty patch of grass.

Sierra lifted the latch of the back gate. Locked. At least the fools had the sense to secure their back fence. Not that it would save them.

"Yuri, give me a boost." She was going to have to risk her dress after all.

Up and over the fence she went, mercifully without issue. She even managed to keep her hem from the ridge so that it didn't tear. But on the way down she lost her balance, only slightly, and landed heavily. The scattering of rocks beneath her feet seemed to echo in the night.

And inside the house, voices rose, muffled but alarmed.

"They have heard you," Zakhar said, alighting nimbly beside her. She resented his silence now.

"You are loud," Yuri said, falling onto the grass with only the soft crunch of hoarfrost beneath his boots. "Surprise is gone. We leave."

"No," she said, forcing herself to keep her voice low. "We're not going anywhere except inside that house as agreed."

"They have, you said, one of the guns. We go now, maybe we are shot."

"A moment ago you were telling me how easy this was going to be. Now you're ready to run home?"

"Da. Like said Zakhar: they have heard you."

Sierra wasn't going back to the base. And they weren't either. "Gavriil ordered you to come with me. Ordered it! Now get to it!" Crouched low, she sidled up to the wall, just below the window.

Carefully, she edged higher, eyes just above the lip of the window well, just high enough to see inside. Shadows fled, silhouettes, scurrying to safety in the darkness. She lifted her SIG Sauer and pressed the barrel against the pane.

Then she fired.

Glass, like shrapnel, detonated forward. She fired again and again, laughing. Recoil with each shot, gun growing warmer in her hand. She couldn't stop. She fired until the clip was spent and she slumped backward, exhausted. Her pulse, slowed. Her eyes dilated.

"You are fool," Yuri said.

Zakhar came up behind him and said much the same thing. But she didn't care.

"I think I hit one of them." She couldn't repress her laughter. "Let's go see."

* * *

You can't always protect me.

His daughter's words echoed in Lorenzo's ears as he flew without thinking, without knowing where he was or where he was going. He couldn't process it. His little girl, gone.

He'd known Xandra's plan was crazy. That had been her choice.

Brendan had gone to save his family. Kelly had gone because she was a pilot and a fighter. They all had a duty.

But Carmen? She hadn't needed to do this. This wasn't her fight. And Lorenzo had allowed her to fall from a moving plane—his plane—to face a watery grave.

The urge to drink welled up in him, suddenly, the strongest time in years. He could almost smell it—a glass overflowing with Fernet.

He shook the compulsion away and circled the plane around. He needed to get back to Carmen. To help her. Though he wasn't sure how. He just knew he needed to do something. What wouldn't he sacrifice for his little girl?

Not that he had much left to give.

When the Cessna completed its yaw, Lorenzo scanned the horizon. Ahead, fire seemed to consume the city, flames still distant enough that they didn't pose a threat, though smoke poured into the heavens. In an hour or two there would be too much smoke to safely navigate.

None of that mattered. In an hour, he and Carmen would be flying safely away, or else … he didn't finish the thought. *I'll find her. This can all be fixed.* He just needed to think.

Lorenzo wanted to redline it back to the section of the Willamette where Carmen had jumped. To get there as quickly as he could. But instead, he slowed to a minimum controllable airspeed. Any slower and he wouldn't get sufficient lift to control the aircraft. If he flew too fast, he couldn't spot her and he certainly couldn't help her.

"But what can I do?" he wondered aloud. There wasn't anything in the cabin to throw down to her. No lifejackets. Nothing that would float.

Ahead, the Ferris wheel loomed through the leaf-bare trees and encroaching smoke. He was moving too fast. The river below was so black he couldn't distinguish water from shore, much less see his daughter.

Then, in a flash, blackness gave way to light. Hundreds of feet up the bank, a spotlight flipped on. The beam, though not pointed at him, glared brightly.

But it wasn't the brightness that took his breath away and sent chills through his body. It was the target of the spotlight. His heart shriveled and sunk into his stomach. "Carmen?" he murmured, focusing on the shape beneath the beam. "Is that you?"

At the edge of the river, a figure had just emerged from the water. The figure stood still, frozen in place, too far away to see clearly.

His mind raced. Was that Carmen, caught like a butterfly in a net, too scared to escape?

He needed to know for sure. What then? He had no idea.

All around the spotlight, forms and shadows started to appear. Soldiers, by the discipline of their formation. Dozens, congregating around the light, homed in on the figure that Lorenzo felt more and more certain must be his daughter.

His vision blurred. Gripping the yoke with strained knuckles, the hand of fear reached down his throat and clasped his heart. The fear only a father could feel when faced with the loss of a child.

Crack-crack-crack.

The sound jolted him back to reality. Gunshots.

Then came a blinding light, so bright he almost let go of the yoke. It was the spotlight, pointed on him now. The soldiers below refocused their attention to Lorenzo and his plane. And now they were shooting.

Crack-crack-crack-crack. More gunshots, louder with every passing second as he closed the gap between them.

Carmen was down there. Lorenzo felt suddenly sure that was her. And if they caught her ... there was no telling what those invaders would do.

Her words still echoed in his ears. *I love you, Pop. But you can't always protect me.*

"I *can* protect you," he answered, suddenly confident.

Now he understood. The hand of fear surrendered his heart and passed from his body the way it had come. He knew. He would protect her one last time.

Crack-crack-CRACK-crack-crack.

A bullet smacked into the thick windshield of the airplane, a second spider web of shattered glass. He didn't care. Nothing they did now could stop him.

Lorenzo directed the nose of his plane toward the spotlight, pointing straight at the soldiers on the ridge. He couldn't see them anymore, but he didn't need to see. The plane's three-hundred horsepower engine roared. The propeller whirred. Air whistled past the wings and fixed landing gear. He could smell the diesel fumes, the polyurethane foam in his seat, the bile in his mouth—the residue of fear that had now departed.

I love you, Pop. But you can't always protect me. He heard the words once more, picturing his daughter as she said them, black hair whipping in the wind.

"I love you, too, Carmen."

Lorenzo was still smiling when he directed his airplane into the group of fifty Russian naval infantry soldiers clustered around the spotlight. He could imagine the fear that would be crawling across their faces when they realized, too late, what he intended. Some continued to shoot. Some began to scatter. But, oh yes, it was too late for them.

The last thing he felt was the weight of his Cessna as it tore into the crowd, throwing bodies into the air and crushing them under the speeding fuselage.

33

Gunshots broke through the window amid a shatter of screams. Ireana spun. Behind her, the children burst out in fright. Her sister threw her hands over her head, yelling obscenities. Vailea shouted directions that Ireana couldn't make out. She heard her own voice, though, as loud as anyone else.

Beside her, Orion fell heavily to the floor.

Already the children were scampering up the stairs, with Vailea and Annalore behind, urging them faster. The patter of feet and the hiss of the fire were now the only sounds. The gunshots had stopped. The screaming, too.

"I'm shot." Orion rolled on the ground, shrieking. Blood pulsed from his leg. "Oh, god, I'm shot. I'm gonna die."

Smoke and steam filled the living room from the doused fire as Ireana knelt beside him. She put her hands on his shoulder. "Hold still. And hush. I'm here, hush."

He screamed, louder if anything.

She slapped him. "Shut up."

He stopped and stared at her.

"Quiet," she said, more kindly this time. "We've got to hide."

That was the first order of business. More important than staunching the bleeding, more important than stabilizing the patient. They needed to get somewhere safe.

Orion flopped onto his stomach, writhing.

"Into the closet. Hurry." Grabbing under his arm, she half-pushed, half-dragged him, blood wiping across the floor. Once inside, she closed the door, shutting out the light.

"I'm gonna die," he said again in a sob.

"Hush. No, you aren't going to die." She pulled a shirt from a hanger and improvised a tourniquet. Not arterial, thank God. "No one bleeds to death from an extremity wound. Not under my care, anyway."

His sobbing quieted somewhat.

Ireana applied pressure with a second shirt, wishing for a trauma kit. "How do you feel?" she whispered in his ear. "Dizzy? Nauseated?"

"None of those. But it hurts ... oh, momma, it hurts like hell."

His breathing had slowed, and his heart rate seemed normal. "Any pain, besides your leg?"

"Isn't that enough?"

She rolled her eyes. Difficult patients were everywhere. "You aren't in shock, and there's no internal bleeding. You're going to be fine."

As she said the words, the back door creaked open. A man coughed. Boots crunched on the ground. She held her breath. Orion shifted under the pressure of her hands.

"Watch out for the dog." A woman's voice. In the kitchen.

Tears stung Ireana's eyes—whether from the smoke or the fear, she didn't know. Her hands on Orion's leg shook, and she suppressed a moan. They were coming closer.

"Go upstairs, Yuri," the woman's voice said. "Zakhar and I will sweep this level."

More boots clomped on the fir floors, the only sounds besides Orion's stifled breathing and the drumbeat of her heart in her ears. A door groaned as it opened. Ireana peeked through closet slats, the beam of a flashlight slicing through the living room.

"We're going to die," whispered Orion.

He was right. She knew it now: they were going to die. But that didn't matter. Her death was unimportant. Heavy footfalls echoed off the stairs. Headed up. Toward Jeremiah.

* * *

Xandra sloshed up the bank, one hand groping for a root or fallen tree, the other pressed against the pocket that held her thumb drive. It wasn't much warmer on the bank than in the river. Both were cold. Painfully so. Much worse than expected.

I was lucky. She'd only been in the frigid waters for forty-three seconds, by her count. Well, not lucky. She didn't believe in luck, exactly. Chance could explain her situation. Chance, the objective reality of random outcomes in the real world. Luck, on the other hand, was a consequence of the subjective value one might place on random outcomes. So it had been *chance* that caused her to land in a spot in the river that was deep enough to keep her from hitting the rocks of the riverbed, but close enough that she'd been swept to the bank almost immediately.

But chance wouldn't save her from hypothermia.

"Better get that Mylar blanket around yourself."

Xandra squinted at Kelly, striding toward her on the bank. The pilot shivered, wrapped in her own reflective silver blanket, but managed a confident wink regardless. That Kelly had gotten to shore first impressed her, given the sequence of their jumps.

"Did you see Brendan?" Xandra asked, teeth chattering. She unfastened her life jacket and let it fall. The emergency blanket fought her shaking hands as she unwrapped it.

"Nope. But if he's a good swimmer, he'll be south of us. If he's a bad swimmer he'll be north, taken by the current."

She couldn't waste time worrying about where Brendan had come ashore—or if he'd made it at all. There was the mission to consider. "We'll head to the submarine," Xandra said throwing the emergency blanket over her shoulders. "Brendan will know to meet us there."

"North, then," Kelly said, leading the way up the bank.

They proceeded along the edge of the water, not speaking, ice crunching underfoot. Here, the riverbank narrowed, black water on one side, dark vegetation on the other. In the distance, a front of smoke partially covered the sky, below which stood the enormous silhouette of a Ferris wheel.

The submarine would be just to the west of that landmark. Lorenzo had put them close.

Up ahead, the scrape of a foot. The crack of cold limbs and chattering teeth. Kelly held up a fist, signaling them to stop.

"Xandra? Kelly? Is th-that you?" A girl's voice in the night.

Kelly stared. "Who's there," she whispered.

"It's Carmen," the shivering voice said.

"Carmen?" Xandra couldn't believe it. What was she doing here? And how? She must have jumped from the plane. "Oh, you foolish girl, what have you done?"

Kelly, though, didn't seem angry at all, as Xandra would have expected given the girl was further imperiling their missions merely by her presence. Instead, the fighter pilot scowled at Xandra, though she couldn't guess what she could possibly have done to deserve that.

"Here," Kelly said, wrapping her emergency blanket around Carmen. "Put this on. My flight suit is keeping me warm anyway."

They stood for a moment, the winds flapping at their blankets, all of them cold. Every second they lost weighed on Xandra. They needed to continue. "We're going to keep moving," she whispered. "Explain to me on the way why on earth you decided to join us. Your father must be quite alarmed."

Sodden shoes shuffling through the bank, they walked quickly and quietly north. Xandra's eyes, meanwhile, had begun to adjust somewhat to the darkness.

Shrubs grew to their right—*Malus fusca* and Pacific Ninebark. To their right, the river ran, wind chopping at the surface. Far ahead, above the leafless trees of a little river island, downtown still burned, its fire too distant to add much light.

Suddenly, the quiet evaporated. The crank of a generator echoed across the otherwise silent riverbank.

Kelly froze. Carmen grabbed at Xandra's arm until she shook the girl off.

Where was it coming from? They stopped, holding their breath. Not more than fifty meters away, a searchlight popped on, painfully bright even pointed elsewhere.

Shouting erupted from the far side of the amusement park. The shouts of soldiers.

"What's happening?" Carmen whispered.

"Shhh," Kelly said. "I don't know."

It seemed clear enough to Xandra what had happened, though. The soldiers had seen something—someone. Brendan, most likely. And, doubtless, the man had not only been found, but also captured, which might mean an end to the mission. The element of surprise was gone now. Along with the best hope for a counter attack.

Then another noise broke through the others, louder still. An engine above.

"It's a plane," Kelly said.

Carmen looked up. "Pop."

Xandra recognized it then, the aircraft engine over the water, growing louder. "He's flying this way."

Tat-tat-tatt-tatt. A gun discharged. Then another. The soldiers were firing into the sky.

Xandra stiffened as the shouts grew louder, the gunfire more frequent. Of all the noises, the Cessna roared loudest, almost on top of them. Outlined against the smoke and the stars, the plane flew low, nearly touching the riverbank, tracked by the searchlight.

Then the crash. Xandra's breath caught when the Cessna converged with the earth. So close, so loud, followed by a fireball. The riverbank to the north lit up, a fire-burst as tall as the trees, accompanied by a titanic explosion.

Xandra covered her ears against the blast and squinted at the fire, a thousand torches illuminating the carnival rides and pavilions. Carmen's face became a mask of fear.

The noises from the soldiers and the crack of their gunfire had suddenly gone silent.

"Oh, Pop!" Carmen howled. And before Xandra or Kelly could say anything, the girl bolted toward the site of destruction.

* * *

Back to the wall, just inside the doorway to Kiri's room, Vailea shook uncontrollably. The baseball bat rattled in her hands. Her heartbeat migrated from her chest to her throat. Darkness enfolded everything.

"We can do this," Annalore whispered, a silhouette on the far side of the doorway. "Be strong."

Vailea barely heard her.

Hahana and Kiri hid under the bed beside the boys. Some of the children cried, quietly.

Vailea barely heard them, either.

Only one thing existed in her world. The darkness.

In the night. In the alley, in the mud, in the streets without streetlamps. In the ocean, past the coral reef where the water was deepest. These were the birthplaces of her fear.

Heavy footsteps echoed up the stairwell.

The blackness of the room pulsed and spun.

Now came fear. Like a hand on the nape of her neck, like hot breath in her ear, she felt the stranger. Worse than it had ever been. The darkness had swallowed the city. It would swallow the children.

Footfalls grew louder, nearer. Someone was coming up the stairs, moving deliberately. Someone heavy and strong. A man.

"Be ready," Annalore whispered, just in the range of hearing.

Vailea felt the weight of the bat in her hands, arms mushy, like breadfruit left too long in the sun. She couldn't swing it. She could barely lift it, and this was the only weapon they had.

The man reached the top of the stairs. His flashlight swept the darkness back, just a little. Not enough. A rifle raised, held just above the flashlight, pointing toward the open door to her daughter's room.

The man stepped inside.

Vailea, shaking at the edge of the door, waited for him to cross the threshold into the room where she and Annalore hid, knowing she didn't have the strength or the will to swing the bat. All she could see were the shadows slithering across the walls, driven by the flashlight. All she could hear was her heartbeat above the frightened cries of her children.

The man strode toward the door.

"*Za toboy! Ostirizhno!*" The cry, like a warning, came from Annalore. She screamed it quickly, almost frantic.

The man at the doorway spun, the beam of his flashlight cutting an arc through the black passageway. Turning, hunting for some unseen danger at his flank.

"Now!" Annalore said.

Like a stone lifted from her chest by a great wave, Vailea felt a pressure leave her. The stranger was there, but he fell back. And in that moment, she awoke. There wasn't just a stranger in the darkness, alone. There was a woman, as strong as the fear. Stronger.

The bat came up in her hands and she swung. It connected. The man fell under the force of her strike. A gun clattered on the ground. She swung again.

The stranger in her mind lay next to the stranger on the floor of her daughter's room. Maybe dead. Maybe breathing. Knocked, perhaps, into unconsciousness or into hell.

"What … what did you say to him?"

Annalore smiled weakly. "I told him to watch out behind him. Must have believed me for a second." Her smile intensified. "We have a flashlight now."

"And a gun." The stubby, black rifle would have to be enough. Her daughters' lives depended on it. "One gun against however many left below."

34

Brendan climbed toward the wreck of the airplane. A minute of scrambling up the bank and over a short fence, and he'd gone as far as he could. Fuel burned across a length of at least a hundred feet. Within that mass of shrapnel and fire laid more bodies than Brendan could count. Armed men, their weapons splayed where they fell.

The fire burned too hot to get any closer. Over the pavement of a walkway. Over grass and corpses. Black smoke churned upward into a black sky, fuel spread in all directions.

The fuselage of the Cessna burned hottest of all. Its charred cockpit had collapsed inward upon impact, and now fire charged through every side, paint peeling, alloys melting. The airplane's wings had torn free and lay far from the cockpit. The tail had scattered. Everything was broken, burning.

"They died to save us," Brendan said to Lykos, standing steadfast beside him. "Why? Why did they do it?" He imagined Lorenzo, steering the plane into the crowd of soldiers. He pictured Carmen beside her father, black hair like a flag, screaming in the last instant as Lorenzo pointed the Cessna into its final descent. "How could he?"

The fire held no answer. Just death and emptiness.

Lykos swung his black muzzle away from the flames. Someone was coming. More soldiers, maybe.

Brendan spun, ready to fight or die—whatever he had to do to survive.

"Pop." A girl's voice.

The flames cast shadows across Carmen's face, eyes sparkling with tears. "Oh, Pop," she said again.

Brendan should have been surprised to see her there. She was supposed to be on that plane. She'd been there when he'd jumped off just minutes ago. But here she stood, alive, as near to the wreckage as heat would allow.

"Don't get any closer." It was a stupid thing to say. Not the first words a child should hear with her father's corpse cremating in front of her. "He seemed like a good person," Brendan added, wishing it didn't sound so inadequate.

"He was." Her voice barely quavered despite the tears that flowed down her face. "And a good father."

The crunch of shoes from the riverbank heralded other arrivals. Kelly came first, with Xandra behind. Their shadows pressed and retreated in the firelight as their faces took it all in.

"He's dead," Carmen said focused deep into the undulating inferno.

"Why did he do it?" Kelly grasped Brendan's arm.

"To save me," he said.

"I want to see him." Carmen lurched closer to the fire. A second step. A third. Slowly, forearms on her face, as if to shield herself from the heat.

"There's nothing left," Kelly said. A strand of hair came loose from her ponytail and thrashed in the wind.

Carmen kept edging forward. "I want to see him!" she shouted, firmly this time.

"Are you out of your mind?" Xandra hissed. "More soldiers will come any minute."

Carmen stretched out toward the fire.

"We have to go," Xandra said.

"Her father died," Brendan said. "Give her a minute to grieve."

"He was a great father." Carmen bent down and picked something up off the ground. Brendan couldn't see what it was at first—something hot no doubt, by the way she juggled it between her hands.

"I'm sure he was." Xandra coughed. Every shift in the wind sent smoke swirling toward them or away.

"He really loved me."

Brendan could see what she'd picked up, now: the better part of a propeller. Long and sharp. An odd souvenir, but he understood. She'd want something, anything to remember him by.

"I know he loved you." Kelly took her hand. "Anyone could see that. And he was proud of you. But Xandra's right. We have to go. You'll have time to mourn." She led Carmen away from the fire.

Brendan thought of his own daughters. How they might cry when news of this night reached them. How they'd hear it from Vailea, their father wasn't ever coming home. How he'd left them for good.

Flames illuminated the path, making it easy to find their way back to the river. Walking slowly, they followed the water north. It wouldn't be long before more Russians came. Before another searchlight touched down on them; before more guns opened fire from the bluff.

The river, now much more visible, shimmered in the remaining firelight. Long shadows from the oak trees fell across the beach. The night was quiet, peaceful, except for the distant crackling.

Xandra pointed across the water to where a floating dock jutted into the middle of the river. "Do you see that?" At the end of the dock bobbed a shape Brendan had seen many times in books or on the Internet, but never in real life.

"Is that a submarine?" Carmen sniffled.

"Not just a submarine," Kelly said. "A ballistic missile submarine. Nuclear powered. That's the *Alexander Nevsky.*"

* * *

From upstairs came the wooden crack of objects knocking into each other. A muted thud. Then a fall.

"Yuri?" Sierra called.

No response.

"Zakhar, did you hear that?"

He nodded and shrugged. "Combat. Yuri will not lose."

She didn't want to miss out on the killing. "Let's go up."

He hushed her with a finger to his lips, scanning the floorboards with his flashlight.

Sierra stood in mute rage. The insubordination of it! Gavriil had commanded these two men to follow *her*. To help *her*. Not to shut her up or keep her from the fight.

"Do you see?" he asked, in his halting accent. "On floor?"

She didn't see. "Upstairs!" she said again, trying to regain control.

"Blood," he said.

And then she saw it. Droplets, faint in the darkness and oversaturated by the beam of his flashlight. But, yes, blood all the same. A trail.

All thoughts of Yuki forgotten, Sierra scanned the ground. "There." She pointed.

The speckles of blood grew thicker, becoming a smear that led out of the dining room, past the couches and fire of the living room, and into a hallway. The trail ended at a closet.

Sierra reached out to open it.

"*Ya otkroyu dver. Pereyekhat.*" Zakhar shoved her aside, roughly. "We must breach."

Before Sierra could comment on his rudeness, he lifted his knee to his chest and kicked in the door with his heel. Splinters flew. A woman screamed. Zakhar sidestepped nimbly, assault rifle trained on the closet.

On the floor, a man and a woman huddled. They shook pitifully, hands pushing the broken door to keep it from falling over them. Blood covered the wall and the scattered clothes, making Sierra wonder which one she'd shot.

"Cute couple," Sierra said. "Sad it has to end like this."

* * *

Two-thirds submerged, the black-bodied submarine protruded from the river, maybe fifty feet from shore. Unlike the chop of the river waves, the bobbing of the floating dock, and the flickering of distant fires, the *Alexander Nevsky* floated transfixed. Dark and ominous. Almost as if it had been waiting for anyone foolish enough to enter.

Brendan spit on the ground, trying to rid his mouth of the dry taste of iron. It didn't help.

He knew he shouldn't be afraid of the submarine itself. The threat came from people inside. But still, he couldn't shake the thought that this black-metal beast would eat them when they entered its maw.

"What are you waiting for?" Xandra shuffled toward the interconnected tubs of plastic that formed the dock. Carmen and Kelly ran ahead.

He wiped his mouth. "Coming—"

A crack resounded from the shore, cutting him off. A bullet whistled past. More shots and shouts from the ridge.

"Go on ahead," he said, trying to ignore the tightening of his chest, the pleating of his stomach. "I'll delay them." This is why he'd come. He needed to give Xandra time to upload her code. "I'm the muscle, after all."

Russian soldiers darted down the slope, yelling commands, unconcerned with the noise they made. At least they'd stopped shooting. Perhaps they didn't want an errant bullet to hit their own submarine.

"This way." Brendan motioned to Lykos, dashing for the cover of trees at the bank. He didn't need to tell the German Shepherd to hurry. Bounding, the animal reached the copse before he did.

Just in time.

The first of the soldiers broke free of the undergrowth, his long rifle held in both hands, black fatigues and hat obscuring his shape against the dark beach. A second soldier and then a third appeared. Moving quickly, in a line, rushing toward the floating dock.

Brendan didn't wait.

There were only three of them. Three armed, trained soldiers. He wouldn't survive this encounter, but at least he could stop them.

From his place of concealment in the trees he jumped forward, at the backs of the soldiers. As quickly as he ever had. And though he struck fast, Lykos was faster.

The lupine eyes of the German Shepherd made yellow streaks in the night as he closed the space between himself and the middle soldier. The dog's jaws clamped onto the elbow of his prey. Teeth tore through cloth and sinew. The soldier cried out, a high-pitched scream that dominated all other sounds on the riverbank.

Brendan didn't hesitate. Before the rearmost soldier could react to the Lykos' attack on his compatriot, Brendan was on him. The soldier didn't have time to turn, only to crumple as Brendan's fist pounded into the back of his head.

Years ago, Brendan's fists, properly wrapped, could break a concrete slab. And on this night they still had force, maybe as much force as they'd ever had. Enough to kill a man.

In front, the soldier did not just collapse. Instead, his skull caved in like the cockpit of Lorenzo's plane. A disgusting, horrifying spectacle.

Brendan had known what his fists could do in the ring, and he knew what they could do to a man. And yet he'd done it anyway, to an opponent, back turned.

Brendan watched the corpse of the soldier fall forward, and saw the foremost man spin, rifle in his hands. This was it. The moment when the match ends and the last bell rings.

Lykos stood on the back of the middle Russian soldier. A howl rose, not from the dog but from the man on his belly in the icy mud, arm nearly severed from body, crying out in what could only be pain and fear and surprise.

Blood pooled onto the beach. Black blood that covered the muzzle of the German Shepherd. It pulsated from the soldier on the ground, lifeblood flowing as quickly as the Willamette.

In these seconds, Brendan's senses captured everything around him. The unwashed men; the reek of onions and milk. The stale fishiness of river water. Salt from sweat that dripped off his brow. The smell of hot guns and smoke filling the night.

These were the last smells he would ever know.

"This is for my father," Carmen said, shattering the silence.

Brendan blinked, trance broken. From the floating dock, he saw the girl running toward them, the propeller she'd salvaged held over her head. The long, sharp piece of metal hadn't been a souvenir of her father at all. It was a weapon.

The Russian soldier twisted, gun directed toward this new threat. But before he could fire, Carmen launched the propeller into the air. It spun mercilessly toward the naval infantryman. And, with the *thunk* of a cleaver into a pumpkin, the airfoil-shaped blade buried itself in the Russian's chest.

The soldier ogled the wound, then back at the girl, surprise his death mask. Last words gurgled unintelligibly in his throat as he collapsed.

Brendan stammered. "I ... thank you," he managed at last. A thirteen-year-old had saved his life.

The scene around them wasn't what he'd have wanted a young girl to witness. The dead men, strewn on the strand, their blood and brains splattered across his clothes. But Carmen had beheld worse today, and this latest hell didn't seem to touch her.

"That was for you, Pop." She glanced up at Brendan, almost—he thought—as if she hadn't seen him until just now. "Xandra sent me to get you. She needs your help."

Brendan tried not to growl. "I'm sure Xandra knows I was a little busy." He picked up one of the guns from the dead men. "We might need this." He brandished the weapon. "But no more killing."

"No more killing," Carmen agreed.

The walk across the short stretch of beach and onto the floating dock took only a minute. But at the end of it, he was surprised to see Xandra and Kelly still on the dock. He thought they'd have long since gone inside the submarine. Instead, Kelly was kneeling over Xandra, who lay prone against the tubs that rose and fell with the current.

Immediately, he saw why. Xandra had been shot.

The wound didn't appear fatal, and the fighter pilot was doing her best to apply a tourniquet over a leg that pulsed with blood. "Field dressing was never my thing," Kelly said, seemingly unperturbed. "This one isn't bad, though. She'll live."

"Never mind that," Xandra said, clearly more annoyed than anything. "I need you two to pay attention."

Kelly yanked the tourniquet tight. "We're listening."

"Finish the job. Upload the code."

Brendan had no intention of leaving this woman on the dock to be captured. "You can do it. If you can stand, come with us."

Xandra exhaled sharply and shook her head. "It shouldn't be difficult to upload. Carmen is going to help me get out of here. If I stay, I'll jeopardize everything."

"I don't—" Brendan started.

"Take this." Xandra held out a zip bag. "The code is ready to install. All you need to do is plug the thumb drive into the combat systems server. Kelly knows where it is. Starboard side of the control room. There should be a port."

"Should be?" Brendan found himself less and less confident with this plan.

"Yes. Lieutenant Seong can help you. All the systems are fiber-optics server-based, super-computer levels of processing. There's sure to be a port. Now go. We'll try to lead any other soldiers away from you."

Brendan kneaded the broken cartilage in his nose, furiously. This was madness. Everything about tonight was madness. "Take Lykos with you," he said, finally. "You'll need the protection."

Xandra smiled. He doubted this woman smiled very often. "Thank you. Admiral Kalb would be grateful." Whatever that meant.

Brendan grabbed the thumb drive and motioned Lykos to go with Carmen.

He and Kelly began the short walk down the dock, toward the submarine.

35

"**C**ome on down and I won't kill them."

Vailea shuddered at the top of the stairs. Not from fear of the dark now—she wasn't afraid anymore—but from the woman's husky voice, taunting them. The same woman who'd threatened her on her lawn. Who'd broken into the basement. Who'd attacked their home with fire.

"They have my sister," Annalore said, pleading.

"We can't go down there. I know this woman. She's not going to just let us leave."

Kiri poked out from under the bed. "Mom, what's going to happen?"

"I wish Daddy was here," Hahana said.

Vailea put her finger over her lips. "Hush, girls. Stay where you are."

A muffled conversation continued below and then the woman called out again. "This one says her name is Ireana. She says not to hurt her babies. Why not come down? I give you my word I won't harm the children. I never hurt children."

"What do you think?" Annalore asked.

Vailea shined the flashlight at her. Annalore gripped the baseball bat tight, held out in front like a sword. "I think we stay here." Vailea brandished the rifle. "They might not risk coming up. And we've got to protect the kids."

"She says she won't hurt them."

"And you believe that?"

The bat shook in Annalore's hands. "I don't know."

"We stay here. I'm not giving them my girls. I'm not surrendering any of us."

Annalore seemed to draw courage from that. "So what do we do?"

"Last chance," the woman said from the bottom of the stairwell.

Vailea ignored her. "We make a stand."

The woman said something low and indiscernible. Floorboards creaked.

"Here they come," Annalore said.

* * *

The conning tower of the *Alexander Nevsky* jutted above the more-than-five-hundred-foot-long hull, with an antenna sticking up still higher. Beside the antenna, wind stirred a dark banner. Spray stung Brendan's face as he climbed the ladder affixed to the side of the sail structure.

Kelly met him at the top of the conning tower. He handed her the rifle of the dead naval infantryman then pulled himself to the edge of the hatch.

"When we go through, expect a sentry, a helmsman, or both," she whispered, just audible over the wind.

"Okay. But no more killing." The vision of the skull he'd crushed by his own hand was too fresh. He couldn't do it again.

She crossed her arms. "This is war."

Brendan thrust his jaw forward. "We don't kill," he said again. "Not unless we're defending ourselves."

They stared at each other for a moment in the darkness. The wind whipped at her black hair, framed by the night and the obsidian submarine. Spume soaked them both. But he didn't budge, and neither did she.

Finally, she bit her cheek and nodded. "Fine. No killing. Most submariners aren't armed anyway." She crouched over the hatch and rotated the wheel. It made a metallic rasp, despite her slow, measured cranking. "But when we get inside, I give the commands."

"You're the boss."

The hatch opened, and she slipped inside, moving quickly down the ladder.

Brendan followed, one foot then another, easing himself into the abyss. Restricted by the tight space, he gasped, trying to keep quiet. He held steady on the rungs, clutching, palms clammy on the steel. He squeezed his eyes shut, listening to the rhythmic thump-thump of his ventricles. Gradually, his heartbeat relaxed and his breathing moderated.

He cracked one eye open. The dim light of the conning tower revealed an orange-painted frame above metal grates. Kelly stood on the grate, a finger to her lips, rifle directed at the man in front of her.

Some "muscle" he was. While he'd been panicking at the tight space, she'd gotten the drop on a guard.

The submariner at the wrong end of her gun wore the same uniform as the other naval infantrymen—black hat, black clothing. Hands above his head, he stood unmoving, except for his eyes, which darted to the left and right.

"Shhh," Kelly said, waving her weapon at his throat. "Don't make a sound."

Brendan realized the precariousness of their situation. Even if Kelly wanted to, she couldn't fire without alerting the rest of the crew to their presence. She couldn't let the sailor go. If he escaped out of the hatch he'd bring reinforcements. And if he went below he'd alert the crew and spoil the mission.

"Let me," Brendan said, springing to action. He roped his arm around the submariner and held him in a bear hug. The man struggled for several seconds, even as Brendan asserted ever more force on his body.

Finally, the breath went out of him and Brendan laid him on the grate, choked out and unconscious, but not dead. "He'll make it."

The edges of Kelly's mouth curled up in what was almost a smile. "Nice work, big guy," she whispered. "Remind me never to hug it out with you."

Brendan sleeved sweat from his brow. "Better than—"

Kelly put a finger to her lips and stepped over the collapsed submariner. "This way."

Moving as quietly as he could, he followed her down another ladder, then a small flight of stairs, and through a watertight hatch that wouldn't have seemed out of place in a bank vault. The deeper they journeyed into the interior, the slower they went, expecting another sailor to jump out at them. But they made it to the control room without seeing a soul.

"This is it." Kelly pointed her gun forward. "Follow me and do what I say."

Before he could nod, she threw herself through the doorway. Brendan ambled after her, his heart jumping rope.

The command and control room was filled with men.

"*Chto ty zdes delayesh?*" one of them said. Sailors gawked at Kelly and Brendan as if processing how a sopping wet man and woman had suddenly appeared in their midst. Perhaps trying to understand why the woman was pointing a gun at them.

The room was much bigger than he'd expected, though cramped with equipment. On both sides, men swiveled in white chairs, a double monitor stacked vertically in front of each. Desks and controls filled the center. Officers shot up from the charts and screens. Overhead, fluorescent bulbs flooded the space with yellow light.

Kelly swung her rifle across the room. "Everyone stay where you are."

They froze.

Among the dozens of men, only two had a sidearm. Perhaps no one had expected an enemy to penetrate this far. A chill took Brendan, sliding down his spine. Perhaps they'd crushed every other resistance.

"Who here speaks English?" Kelly said, a stony stare that dared any of the men to reach for their pistols.

No one responded.

"Fine," she said. "Slowly, I want you to stand up, hands in the air, and move aft. Anyone who doesn't do exactly that is going to take a thirty-nine-millimeter to the face."

Again, no one responded. No one budged.

A white-haired man at the center of the room put his palms up and treaded forward. Short and muscular, his blue eyes regarded Kelly placidly, though he spoke loudly for the crew. "*Vykhodite iz komnaty. My vernemsya.*"

One by one, the sailors filed out the door at the back of the room.

A different door than the one Kelly and Brendan had entered through.

The white-haired leader left last. When they were all gone, Kelly ran to the door and slammed it shut. "Get me something to jam this with!"

Brendan ransacked the closest desk. There was nothing. Every piece of equipment was bolted down, and there wasn't anything bigger than a pen.

"Never mind then." Kelly pulled the magazine from her rifle and stuck it in her pocket. With a grunt, she jammed the weapon into the wheel. After testing to make sure it wouldn't open, she nodded in approval. "They'll get a welding torch on this any minute. Assholes and elbows, Chogan! Let's get to work." As she spoke, the fluorescent lights went out and red bulbs flashed. Then the honk-honk of a horn boomed over the speakers. "General alarm," Kelly muttered. "We don't have much time."

Brendan pulled the thumb drive from his pocket. "We need a port," he shouted over the cacophony. "Anything we can plug this into."

"I'll take 'combat-systems.'" Kelly rushed to the starboard side computers.

That left Brendan to scour what he could only assume were the sonar stations—blue screens with vertical lines dripping down like dribbles of green paint. He ran his hand over the stations, leaning in close, hunting for a docking point.

"Goddammit," Kelly yelled from across the room. "Nothing over here. On a *Virginia*-class sub there would be dozens."

From the doorway, the hum of a motor revved, followed by the hiss of a halogen torch cutting into the metal.

"Goddammit," she said again.

Brendan kept searching, but there wasn't a port of any kind along this wall. Time was running out. And it appeared Xandra had been wrong about the location of a thumb drive port.

"There's nothing here," Kelly said. "We're finished."

* * *

Vailea's chest rose and fell. The night was all around, but she wasn't afraid of it now. She wasn't afraid for herself, only her children.

"They're coming up," Annalore whispered, choking up on the bat. She lingered at the other end of the doorway, back against the wall like Vailea. Between them, the first man who had come up lay sprawled, halfway inside Kiri's bedroom.

"I'm ready." Vailea pushed up her sleeves and whispered to the kids. "Stay under the bed."

The stairs creaked. The short, black rifle felt sticky with sweat in Vailea's palms. Smoke whirled at the rim of her nostrils, acrid.

Time to fight or die. But she knew it wasn't her night to die. Or her children's. Not tonight.

"Come on out," the woman said, climbing the stairs. "We've got your friends. A pretty pair. Come on out and no one else will be hurt."

"Don't listen," Ireana said from below. "Get the kids out. Through the window—"

A slapping sound and a cry cut Ireana short.

"Last chance," the woman said.

Annalore shook her head, all the while her body visibly trembling. Whether fear or rage, it wasn't clear to Vailea.

Stairs creaked some more, closer and closer, then stopped as the intruders reached the top. The beam of the flashlight fell on the Russian beneath the door jam. A man cursed in a language Vailea didn't know.

"You'll wish you hadn't done that," the woman said from the other side of the wall. She pushed Orion near the door. A hostage. A shield.

Vailea readied her rifle.

Ireana came through, in a headlock. A man's arm wrapped around her neck, his gun pointed over her shoulder. She let out a long, strangled moan.

Annalore swung.

Baseball bat held high, she took a half-step from her hiding spot at the edge of the doorway and struck with all her force.

But she missed. The swing went wide and crashed into the side of the door.

The man sidestepped, pushing Ireana in front of him and angling his rifle around for a clear shot. His finger tugged at the trigger. But not before Ireana shrieked and reached out toward her attacker.

The gun fired.

But Ireana's hand smacked it away just enough that the shot missed. Bullets tore across the room, spraying the far wall. Ireana and Orion, both screaming now, fell forward, away from the man and woman who'd held them.

Annalore struck once more.

The bat connected soundly across the man's black knit cap. The crunch of wood-on-bone resounded. The man cried out and fell, landing near the other one on the floor.

The children screamed.

Vailea watched, horrified, as the woman's flashlight arced through the room and settled on the children—her girls—hiding beneath the bed.

In that split second, Vailea went from dread to rage. She hated this woman. She hated her tight dress and her blonde hair. She hated the blood on her hem and the bloodless smile on her face. This woman had tormented them from the beginning. And she had to die.

The blonde woman raised her gun at the same time as her flashlight, swinging it across the room.

This woman—the one who'd invaded her home so many times now—would not shoot her daughters in cold blood. Not while Vailea still had breath to draw.

Would the woman have shot her children? Vailea would never know. She pulled the trigger, firing until the magazine emptied and the woman's yellow dress changed to crimson.

36

"We've got to go," Kelly shouted from across the command and control room. The general alarm blared, unceasing. Red lights flashed. "They're going to break through that door any second."

Brendan scoured the sonar stations, the bulkhead, the ceiling, telephones, displays, and dozens of instruments for which he had no name. There had to be a port somewhere. He hadn't come this far, hadn't killed a man with his bare hands, just to run back in failure.

"Mr. Chogan," Kelly said again with a tone that was meant to be obeyed. "Back up the hatch. Now!"

"One more—" An object in the middle of the room made him stop.

Soldered unnaturally to the top of a table, almost as an afterthought, sat an unusual piece of equipment that resembled a twenty-year-old vacuum tube monitor and keyboard, encased in a modern metal frame. The computer had a USB port.

"Kelly. Take a look at this."

"No time," she said, rushing over to him. But when she saw the computer, she paused. "I recognize this metal. It's a nano-laminated, layered alloy." She ran her hand over the machine. "And this. We have one like it on the Jerry, a microwave-based wireless wide-area network."

"What's it do?" Brendan asked loudly, over the sound of the alarm and the squeal of the welding torch biting through the door.

"Intrafleet communication device."

"What's that mean?" Brendan inserted the thumb drive into the port.

"For when you want to talk securely to other ships that aren't in your fleet. Like other countries."

Brendan flicked on the Intrafleet computer. Its keyboard resembled every one he'd ever used, without any of the Cyrillic letters dotted across the rest of the room.

"English is probably the common language between our enemies," Kelly said. "The Russians don't speak Chinese. The North Koreans don't speak Persian. But every ship has English speakers."

The machine whirred on. As it started up, foreign characters appeared on the screen. "Is that Chinese?" he asked.

"Korean," Kelly said. "Built by the North Koreans. I'm guessing so they could communicate with the Russian and Chinese fleets."

After the startup screen, the language changed to English.

LOADING

The computer began to run an executable file.
Then it stopped.

ENTER PASSWORD

☐ ☐ ☐ ☐ ☐ ☐

"Come on, Brendan. We've got to go. It's password protected."

"I can do this. Just give me a minute."

At the far bulkhead, the torch against the door went silent. Metal crashed against metal. And again, rhythmic. The submariners were hammering on the door. And it was slipping slowly forward.

"No. We've got to go. They'll be in here in seconds."

They couldn't give up now. Not when they were so close. "All we have to do is think of a six-letter password. How hard can that be?"

He gave it a try.

The Intrafleet communication device beeped.

ACCESS DENIED
2 ATTEMPTS REMAINING

☐ ☐ ☐ ☐ ☐ ☐

The banging grew louder. Brendan glanced over his shoulder at the door. It bulged like a cork in a Champagne bottle.

"Now, Chogan!" Kelly screamed in his ear, over the wail of the alarm.

His hands on the keyboard shook under the red light. "Another few seconds. Just hold on."

He tried again.

N E V S K Y

The device beeped, louder this time.

ACCESS DENIED
1 ATTEMPT REMAINING

☐ ☐ ☐ ☐ ☐ ☐

Sounds intensified in the closed space. The clanging of a hammer on the door, the blast of the general alarm, the beat of his heart in his chest.

"They'll be inside in seconds. Please, we have to go right now."

"I can do this."

He closed his eyes, like he used to before a fight. Calm washed over him. The noises of the sailors and the door and the alarm faded away. Kelly's pleas fell away, too.

Each thought came singularly, contained. He could do this.

So much had changed in the past six days. So much pain and death. Suffering for his family. Suffering for his country.

He could picture it—that moment when everything went awry. It felt as if he were there again, sitting in that job interview, answering questions he didn't understand, belittled by the manager. What was his name? Milo? Brendan felt no anger at the man—Milo could be dead for all he knew. But Brendan could hear his voice, dripping with condescension, even now. "Mr. Chogan, I'm afraid I have some bad news for you."

It had seemed like the most important thing in the world at the time, finding a job. Not anymore. That had been a small problem. Nothing like trying to keep his family alive. Nothing like jumping from a plane into an icy river or storming a hostile submarine.

Brendan smiled at the simplicity of it, hearing that he hadn't gotten the job. Smiled at the arrogance from Milo and the rest of the developers. Smiled at that first email he'd seen—the first hint that something was wrong, the one that had gone to every inbox in the country, all at once.

What had it said? He remembered.

```
No force in the world can check   the   advance
of   our   army   and   people.   We   rush   forward
like   the   blizzards   of   Mount   Paektu.   Final
victory undoubtedly belongs to us.
```

Brendan opened his eyes. That was the answer. It was his last chance.
"You said this machine was built by the North Koreans, right?"
"Yes. But come on. We have to go."
He typed in a password; his third and final attempt.

| P | A | E | K | T | U |

The Intrafleet computer hummed.

ACCESS GRANTED

The files began to transfer. He'd done it.

Kelly patted him on the shoulder. "Leave the thumb drive, big guy. We've got to get out of here."

The metal door clanged to the deck as it surged free, and Russian submariners pouring into the control room. But they were too late. With Kelly beside him, Brendan sprinted to the conning tower, up the hatch, and out into the darkness. He didn't stop until he was home.

37

"Sir, the intruders have fled to the beach. They've escaped, sir."
Gavriil glowered at the petty officer and stormed into
his violated command and control room. The red lights had
stopped flashing and the alarm had stopped honking. But the urgency of
the situation was, by no means, lessened.

How could this have happened? How could two Americans—soldiers
probably—have penetrated all the way into his submarine? Why hadn't
the stationed naval infantrymen prevented the incursion? And what
would the admiralty in Saint Petersburg say when they read his report?

He expressed none of this, though, to the saluting petty officer.
Reputation demanded he maintain composure. "Very good, Mr.
Kuznetsov," was all he said.

A yeoman approached, holding a thumb drive. "Captain, we found
this, plugged into the Intrafleet comms unit." Across the room, other
yeomen scoured the space for explosives. So far, the thumb drive seemed
to be the only article left behind by the Americans.

"Give it to the electronics technician," Gavriil said. "Perhaps it will
tell us more about these trespassers."

"Yes, sir. And what of the comms unit?"

"What of it?"

"The Americans might have tampered with it, sir. Perhaps we should
inform the fleet that the encryptions may be compromised."

"Yes," Gavriil said. "Inform the admiral." It seemed unlikely that
the Americans had been successful in their attempts to access the unit
before his men had chased them off. He changed the subject. "Give me
an update on the status of enemy movements."

"Sir," the petty officer said, "reports indicate thousands of US Army troops near Tillamook. But our initial battles have been victories."

So, the American military had finally come to the invasion site. He wasn't surprised. If anything, Gavriil was amazed it had taken them so long. The US Army base was two hundred miles from Tillamook. Perhaps it had taken nearly a day to pinpoint the location of the armada, and, marching at thirty miles per day, another five to reach the landing spot. "Are the American troops in Portland yet?"

"We don't know, sir. Except, of course, for the two we chased away. If that's a sign of a larger counter attack, we don't know."

"Still, better to be cautious," Gavriil said.

On the other end of the control room, the starboard side, combat system operators typed commands to open the outer doors of the vertical launch system. All it would take was an order from the officer of the watch to send Viyuga cruise missiles toward any target on land, sea or air. But launching missiles wouldn't save them from any real threat. Here, on the surface, the *Alexander Nevsky* was at its most vulnerable.

"Take us down, Mr. Orlov. Let's dive as deep as we can in the river," Gavriil ordered his executive officer.

"The other men, sir? On the beach? Are we leaving them?"

"They have their orders, Mr. Orlov, and so do you. Now unless you want to spend your retirement in a gulag, you will follow those orders."

"Taking us down, sir," Orlov said, repeating Gavriil's command. He seemed to be sweating. Nodding to his skipper, Orlov passed on the order. "Bring her down to six meters." That was about as deep as they'd be able to go in the river.

"Six meters, aye, sir," the skipper replied.

At the bow, ballast tanks flooded with water. The submarine began to submerge.

"She won't go much deeper than the cigarette deck, Captain," Orlov said, referring to the top deck of the *Nevsky*. "Just enough to be invisible to the naked eye. But an easy target from the sky."

"Understood, Mr. Orlov." Gavriil still felt like strangling the man for his earlier insubordination, but instead he continued as mildly as possible.

"When she levels off, bring her to the center of the river. We're going to have to move quickly, and I want to get as deep as we can."

"Aye, aye, sir." Orlov rolled toward the helmsman. "Helm, left full rudder, bring her to course one-one-zero."

The submarine came about with satisfying quietness. With the submarine rigged for silent running, only the most advanced systems would be able to detect their presence. Now that they were underway, Gavriil began to relax.

His satisfaction was premature.

At the far end of the control room a commotion arose, starting with a sonar technician whose screen went suddenly blank. The other sonar screens blacked out. Next, on the starboard side, the combat system screens shut down. Men turned to their officers.

"What's happening?" Gavriil said. "Mr. Orlov, get an engineer up here."

The executive officer approached Gavriil, face wan, lips bloodless. Microphone in hand, he blinked rapidly. "Sir, the radio has malfunctioned. No channels working, sir."

"Impossible. Get the—" But before he could finish his thought, the lights above went out. Not just the fluorescent lights, but the red bulbs, too.

It was unthinkable. The *Alexander Nevsky* had lost power.

Gavriil stood, barely breathing, in total darkness, as his submarine sank, in painful slowness, coming to rest on the muddy bottom of the Willamette River.

38

Ashes blew into the wind and out over the river. Carmen, standing alone ahead of Brendan and the others, took another handful and scattered them into the air. Cinders of her father shimmered against the midday sun. She took another handful, then another.

The city still burned. But the same wind that took Lorenzo's ashes also blew the smoke away from them, into the hills. It was a fitting pyre, in Brendan's mind, for a man who'd died in flame, though he didn't say so. There was nothing he could say. Nothing any of them could say. This was Carmen's loss alone.

Brendan's mind wandered back to the events of last night. The frantic escape from the submarine. The miles of running in the darkness, afraid of the soldiers who might come after them. The joyful reunion with Vailea, shattered when he'd learned what had happened in his absence. The pain in her eyes when she told him how she and Annalore had killed the intruders. And then Vailea watching him and Kelly unceremoniously dragging the three corpses downstairs, to be tossed into the river in the morning.

It had been there, at the riverside, that Carmen had pleaded with him to go back for Lorenzo's ashes. He could never have refused her, not after what Lorenzo had done for him. Not after what she had done, too. Father and daughter had both saved his life.

"Are you okay?" Vailea nudged against him, pulling him back to the here and now. Hahana and Kiri peered up from where they shivered in his lee, hiding from the wind, arms entangled in Lykos' fur.

"I'm good," he said, not sure if it was true. "We're safe. That's what matters."

"For now," she said.

The rest of his new friends huddled on the esplanade in a line. Orion leaned on Kelly, leg bandaged, biting his fingernails. Xandra limped next to Ireana who glanced occasionally at her handiwork to make sure the stitches stayed in. Annalore and the three boys waited, too, faces as grim as when they'd first come to Brendan's home.

"Don't cry for a soul set free," Carmen said, tears running rivulets down her soot-covered face. She lifted a handful of ashes into the air. "Your place, Pop, was always above the clouds."

Residue from the crash covered her from her hair to her shoes, sticking to her sweat-streaked skin. Cinders clung to the snot at her lip. Soot smeared her brow. And she shook with the cold. But her words were clear and her hand was steady as she lifted the ashes into the wind, one fistful at a time until the last of it had drifted west. Flakes caught the light like snow, glittering, framed by the blackened city beyond.

"Thank you," Carmen said at last. She wiped a tear with the back of her wrist, which served only to smudge her cheek with soot. "He would have liked that."

"He would have," Kelly said. "That was beautiful."

Brendan transferred his weight between feet. The others, too, shifted restlessly.

"Where do we go from here?" Orion asked, spitting out a fingernail.

No one answered. Brendan stared into the distance where blackened buildings still glowed red with fire, smoke pluming.

Kelly shivered. "The war isn't over."

"No," Xandra said. "It isn't."

"We have children to worry about," Ireana said. "War or no war, we need to find someplace safe."

"Is anywhere safe?" Annalore said. The sisters shared a glance that could have meant anything.

Vailea pulled herself free from under Brendan's arm. "You're all welcome at my house for as long as you need."

"We won't be safe at your home," Xandra said. "Your home is in the middle of a war zone. This city has fallen."

"When this all started," Vailea said, "the radio told us the attacks spanned from coast to coast.

Xandra nodded. "Every town, every city has fallen."

"There's got to be someplace we can go," Orion said.

"No matter what we decide," Brendan said, "I think we should stick together." Out over the river, his breath floated away.

They stared at him, measuring his words. Xandra cocked her head. Carmen sniffed and ran a blackened hand over her nose. Orion coughed and winced slightly at the pain.

"We stick together," Brendan said, a little louder. "In this new world, we'll need all the friends we can get."

A *tip-tap* pattered off the esplanade. For the first time in a week, it began to rain.

39

Han-yong measured tea into a strainer and placed it into the teapot. Small, white hairs covered the leaves, a fur that bestowed both splendor and delicacy. To some of his fellow officers the processed tea leaves evoked orchids, but only to the politically-connected ones who'd grown up fat and rich in Pyongyang. Han-yong was from Chongjin. And there were no orchids in Chongjin.

He loved the tea, though not because of its beauty. And not for the white hairs, either—if he was being honest, that part revolted him. And not for the taste. He preferred the instant coffee his father used to bring home when he was a child. No, he simply enjoyed the process of making it. And even more, the shape of the leaves, like mountain peaks, that reminded him of home.

While the tea steeped, Han-yong scrolled through the data logs on his computer. First, he checked in on activity in the United States, South Korea, and Japan. Those were the targets he cared most about. Let others gawk at the collapse in Western Europe, Israel, and more. Han-yong didn't care if those countries thrived or fell apart. He knew who the true enemy was.

As expected, there was nothing to report. He jotted a quick note on a pad of paper:

```
USA - no activity
Japan - no activity
South Korea - no activity
```

In truth, there were hardly any logs to review. The three nations had been reduced to a pre-industrial state, without any sort of verifiable communications. Everything that had been connected to the Internet had been destroyed. Everything that had been manufactured in China to have a backdoor—engines, generators, and more—had been destroyed. Every light was out. Every building was cold. And every one of the Imperialists, invaders, and puppets was suffering, just as they deserved.

Best of all, the Imperialist's nuclear reactors would still be overheating. In a matter of days, the reactor cores would have boiled off enough water that the fuel would begin to melt through the containment vessels and barriers.

And then the real destruction would begin.

He laughed out loud. There wasn't even any point in hacking into the Chinese satellites anymore. The view from the sky hadn't changed in days. Enemy lands were in ruin. Great cities had burnt to husks, darkened, ravaged by riot. And all without a single North Korean boot on the ground.

Han-yong's chest puffed with pride. He'd done his part. The interconnect logic bombs he'd built had worked perfectly, crippling the American power grid. Project *Sonnimne* had worked as well as he could have dreamed. Better.

Han-yong removed the strainer and poured himself a cup of tea. It tasted like victory.

He hadn't grasped the scope of the conflict at first, even after listening to the daily reports from his team. He had only come to understand the whole of the cyber war by reading the log files, uncovering where the different attacks were coming from and where they were going. And what he'd learned amazed him. The scale of it. This was bigger than Unit 101. The attacks had required international coordination.

Who could have guessed that Unit 61398 of the Chinese Army would have been able to open the floodgates on every dam in the United States? Or overflow the sewers in Tokyo and Seoul? Or cut off the water supply in every city of its choosing?

Who would have guessed that the botnets of Russian signals intelligence would be able to tear down international banking? Or that its agency of Government Communications and Information would be able to override the critical systems of target satellites?

Who would have guessed that Iran's Cyber Defense Command would be able to put its boot on the throat of worldwide Internet communications and broadcasting? That every server, every computer and every Internet-enabled device, submitted to its complete and merciless control?

He took another sip of tea and listened to the noises of a television from another room down the hall. The marching tune made him smile. There would be another parade in Pyongyang today, just as there had been every day for a week. A victory parade. He hummed along with the music.

Bloodstains on the hills of Jangbaik-san
Bloodstains in the meanders of the Aprok-san
Today on the laurels of our Korea
Bloodstains shine resplendent

Almost no one sat at their desks this morning. They'd been working without rest for a week, and the senior command had finally given them a reprieve for a few hours. But Han-yong didn't need a break. He enjoyed sipping his tea and checking the logs without interruption.

He scrolled through the data, scanning records for the power grid in North Korea. As expected, it was fine. He hadn't checked on it for a few days, because there really wasn't much of a need. There would be no counterattack against North Korea's infrastructure. Where would such an attack come from? The Imperialists were scratching in the dirt right now, not redirecting malware.

Next, he checked the Chinese power grid. Fifteen minutes of sleuthing revealed nothing of consequence. Finally, on a whim, he moved on to the Chinese ships off the West Coast of the Imperialist state of Oregon. Not that he expected to see much, of course. All their data was encrypted. But it would be fun to spy. Maybe he could even see how far into their networks he could penetrate. After all, China might not always be an ally. And the Russians might cross the Tumen River the day the cyber war was won.

He took a sip of tea and found it cold. He sipped anyway, too transfixed by the code to care. Instead of the firewall he expected to obstruct his path, he slid right past into the onboard computer of the first Chinese warship he attempted to penetrate. It was a Type 055 destroyer, and it was wide open.

He kept going, deeper into the code. There was something here. Some reason that the gates to this city had been flung wide, allowing anyone with a little technical proficiency to saunter in.

Then he saw it. Just twelve lines of code, but they made his teeth freeze. He knew that code. After all, he'd been the one to write it.

"Junior Lieutenant Pak!"

The call from his commanding officer bolted Han-yong up from his chair, hand raised in a salute. He almost fell down he was so surprised, caught like a child with his hands in the kettle.

"You don't need to salute. Sit down. Relax. Celebrate." The senior lieutenant wobbled forward while Han-yong gaped. The man was drunk.

"We've been up all night." A glass of brown liquid sloshed over the senior lieutenant's hand. "Come celebrate. We're going to watch the parade on TV. The war is won."

"Sir, there's something I want to talk to you about." Han-yong's words came out breathless. His heart pounded in his chest like a pickaxe in a labor camp.

"You amaze me, Junior Lieutenant Pak. You never stop working. But you should, just for the day."

"Sir, it's these data logs. I think one of our viruses has jumped protocol." He halted, afraid to say more. Should he mention it was his code? That it seemed to have breached an allied ship?

"Raise your glass, Junior Lieutenant," the commanding officer said. Had he heard a single word Han-yong had just said? He pointed to the cold tea on the desk. "Raise your glass to the Supreme Leader and all his accomplishments."

"Sir—"

"Do it!"

Han-yong obeyed. And together they toasted the Workers' Party, and project *Sonnimne*, and death to the Imperialists. And when they finished, Han-yong pointed to his computer. "Sir, I believe a worm we created has spread. Perhaps from Imperialist infrastructure to Chinese ships. Look at the data, sir."

"Drink your wretched tea, you fusspot. If the viruses we built had spread we wouldn't be celebrating, now would we?"

Han-yong ignored the circuitous logic and pressed forward. "Sir, we should explore the possibility that the viruses we created may have entered our own networks. If they could worm into one unintended location, they might go further."

The senior lieutenant kicked the chair where Han-yong had been seated. "Would you, for once, just shut up and enjoy ..."

The lights flickered.

"... yourself," the senior lieutenant finished. He didn't seem to have noticed the lights.

They flickered again.

And went out.

The senior lieutenant cursed. Han-yong ignored him, hoping in those first few seconds that the lights would come back on.

They didn't.

"It's happening, sir," Han-yong said. "The virus ... it spread into our network." He didn't know why he was so sure, but he knew. The code had slipped its orbit and come crashing down into a place it had never been meant to go. His code. Maybe others' as well.

The implications of it hit him, and he pulled his cell phone from his pocket. It was dead. He stared at it in the darkness. He hit the power button over and over while the senior lieutenant issued commands that Han-yong, for the first time in his life, ignored entirely. The lights had gone out. His phone was dead. And he knew with perfect clarity that the Internet would be down, too. And soon Chinese satellites would be falling from the sky.

He stumbled to the window. But there was nothing to see there.

The street was dark. The city was dark. He tried to process what was happening. To think. And so when the tea cup slipped from his fingers, he didn't notice, or even care, that it tumbled to the carpet and spilled all over the floor of the darkened room.

Acknowledgments

I owe many thanks to my publisher and editor, Kate Foster, who took a chance on me and brought the best out in this book. Thanks, too, to the rest the talented team at Lakewater Press, especially Jodi Gallegos who plucked my manuscript out of the heap, and was instrumental in crafting a vision for the third act, among other edits.

Many writers influenced my work. Most prominent among them is counter-terrorism czar, Richard A. Clarke, whose book *Cyber War*, provided my first in-depth exposure to the threat. Also, thanks to James Howard Kunstler, whose personal correspondence, musings, and book *The Long Emergency* helped me realize the frailty of global systems.

Thanks to my brother and parents, Jon, Dave, and Dara, for acting as beta readers. And to my children, Vivian and Charlie, who have been among the most excited about this project, and who will be happy to see their names in a book.

Finally, and most importantly, I thank my wife, Tehra Peace, who edited multiple drafts and asked the toughest questions. The book would never have come together without her. She's a gifted writer. I'm lucky to have her in my life.

Thank you all.

About the Author

S am has worked as a wildland firefighter, journalist, and owner of a mid-sized marketing agency. Though he's lived in France and Spain, his heart belongs to Portland, Oregon, where he lives with his wife, Tehra, two wonderful children, and a messy cat that keeps them from owning anything nice.

To keep up to date with Sam's author news, visit his website www.cyberwarbooks.com

CPSIA information can be obtained
at www.ICGtesting.com
Printed in the USA
LVOW08s1535130318
569702LV00002B/419/P